DISORDER

Cover and book design by Alex Dimeff
Cover photograph: Bert Kaufmann, "Goodbye to winter . . . for the time being": https://flic.kr/p/dQp8SY

Library of Congress Cataloging-in-Publication Data

Names: Crider, Amy, author.
Title: Disorder : a novel / Amy Crider.
Description: New Orleans, Louisiana : University of New Orleans Press, [2021]
Identifiers: LCCN 2021028527 | ISBN 9781608012206 (paperback ; acid-free paper)
Subjects: LCGFT: Psychological fiction.
Classification: LCC PS3603.R525 D57 2021 | DDC 813/.6--dc23
LC record available at https://lccn.loc.gov/2021028527

Printed in the United States of America on acid-free paper.

UNIVERSITY OF NEW ORLEANS PRESS
2000 Lakeshore Drive
New Orleans, Louisiana 70148
unopress.org

DISORDER

A NOVEL

AMY CRIDER

UNIVERSITY OF NEW ORLEANS PRESS

CHAPTER ONE

I am not an unreliable narrator. How reliable is anyone? We all see through our narrow windows.

Madness bonds the world together, sticks people to their beliefs and to their fellow lunatics. Some of us are labeled. Marked. To you it is a hard line separating us, separating the crazy people from yourself, from your friends and family. You live in a cocoon, a soft nest that gives you ease, the silky, feathered belief that at least you and yours are sane. Not like those people. Not like me.

Sometimes I'd like to slap you. Look around. Listen.

You're at your cousin's wedding. You find yourself chatting with someone who seems like a nice, normal woman. A reliable narrator. Her hair is freshly cut, her eyebrows well groomed. You're chatting about a recent mix-up, an amusing anecdote about a misunderstanding you had where autocorrect made you sound like an axe murderer. This woman, laughing over her champagne glass says, "Mercury is in retrograde. That's why. It causes miscommunication, lost keys, lost cell phones. Don't worry, it comes out of retrograde on the eighteenth." And she means it.

Do you glance around and slowly back away? Does the hair on your arm prick a bit to be face to face with utter madness? That you're talking to a woman who believes a rock forty-eight million miles away caused her to lose her keys? No. You laugh and say, "Well, I'm a Taurus."

Nearby, your Uncle Ned is holding forth. The uncle with the three strands of combover glued to his forehead with gel and sweat. He's always jolly, good for a laugh. He and the cousins seem to be in the middle of an interesting conversation. You sidle over, hoping for a good punchline. He gulps his champagne in two swallows and declares that climate change is a Chinese hoax.

Do the cousins' eyes dart to each other? Do they anxiously whisper about his dosage of Zyprexa or Seroquel? No. They nod vaguely and ask him about the trade war.

Then Uncle Ned mentions that this morning he stumbled and almost hit his head on a pipe, but just missed it. He credits God for saving him from hitting his head, and everyone agrees, believing a loving God allows children to be gassed in Syria but cares enough to spare Uncle Ned's red, bald forehead from a boo-boo.

The next day, you're walking through a park, and ahead of you a small running child trips and falls on his face. Rather than hold and comfort the crying boy, his father grabs him by the arm and proceeds to scream at him in a rage. Do you haul this man off to the psych ward, where he belongs? No, you walk by.

And you still think the world is sane? Now you're thinking, *Wendy, you're being rather defensive; I didn't expect this screed.* (And if I'm so unreliable, would I know what you're thinking?)

Please, don't mistake my passion for snark. It's just today, I feel irked by this whole issue. It's been a long time. For years I didn't have the confidence to defend myself. But it's been long enough now, and I'm old enough not to take any more BS from anyone. That's the crux of it.

This story goes back six years. It starts the night I was looking in the mirror at the Hellmanns' party. I know, I know, I'm not supposed to start a story with the cliché of looking in a mirror. But that's really what happened. I was exhausted and splashed some water on my face. And in the mirror, I looked unfamiliar. There was such a frightened look in my eyes, like I was a refugee, my eyes wide open, far apart like a prey animal's, guarding from the dangers of night. Voices echoed from the party in the living room, laughter among friends I didn't feel part of. A weird sensation crept over me that I was there to be sacrificed. I tried to dismiss it and tell myself I hadn't slept, not to mention I'd had a concussion earlier that day.

I tried to change my expression, but the haunted look in my eyes remained.

When I dried my face, I was brought back to reality by streaks of mascara on the pristine white towel. I'd forgotten I'd put on a little makeup before leaving the house. Feeling like an idiot, I rinsed it off as best I could. This was a home with nice things, thick white towels and modern African art, and along with those streaks of mascara came the sensation that I didn't belong in a grown-up house.

Someone tapped on the bathroom door. I opened it to a classmate I didn't know well, named Carolyn. "Do you have a tampon?" she whispered, her eyes nervously big behind her glasses.

"Sure." I quickly found my purse on the bed. "Here you go."

"You're a life saver."

Before it all broke down, that was who I was: the girl who always had a tampon. I had a handle on things. My self-image was one of incompetence and childishness—that was why I was seeing a therapist. Not because of my disorder, but because I never felt like an adult. But I really was an adult. I was thirty. I just didn't have any confidence, and that made me a girl. Maybe I should call this *The Winter Girl*, or *The Girl Under the Snow*, or *Bipolar Girl*, since this sort of title is so popular. But in that moment, I was the girl who had a tampon.

I headed to the dining table for a plastic cup of wine. Squinting, I tried to determine if I had double vision, wondering if maybe my head hitting the windshield was more serious than I'd thought. But it wasn't that bad.

Dr. Hellmann put a few more bottles of wine on the dining table. "Reinforcements," he quipped, smiling. He set them next to a tray of gourmet cupcakes, and I wondered where the Hellmanns could have gotten them. They must have driven all the way to Hamilton for them.

"Thanks," I said. "It's so nice of you to do this."

He shrugged a shoulder. "There has to be some reward for this grunt work."

I laughed. "Enriching the lives of young people with the best of world literature is grunt work?"

He winked. "You'll find out, soon enough."

I sometimes overheard freshmen cooing over their handsome English professor, but as I looked up at him, I thought that even though he was handsome, I didn't find him attractive, and I wondered at that difference. He was well built in a soft cabled sweater, his graying hair weaving around strong bones, but he didn't do it for me. Hellmann was the poetry guru of the department, putting our school on the map in certain circles, the place to come if you couldn't afford a prestigious school. There was talk of finally creating an MFA program, which he would head, though it seemed this talk had been going on for a long time.

His remark—that I would find out soon teaching was grunt work—gave me a pang of anxiety. "You got my note, didn't you? Is it okay?"

He gave me a strained smile. "You don't have to write me a note, just talk to me." My throat went dry. He continued, "We would have given you the grant in any event. You're an excellent student, don't worry about it."

Relief sweetened the sip of wine. "Thank you."

He nodded absently and went off to mingle.

I wanted to find a friendly, reassuring face. Though this was my third semester, I didn't know anyone well, didn't really have a friend. I glanced around. I was envious of this great room with its sleek sofas and trim Roman shades, custom-made. The lamps matched, and cast the right amount of light, unlike my own dark living room with its corduroy Salvation Army rejects. It hits me now how materialistic I was, more interested in these furnishings than the people, but I was poor, and poverty does that.

My glance traveled across the sofa to a corner where a lone man stood, a stranger who looked familiar. He was staring at me, and I didn't know why, wondering if I imagined it. When you're self-conscious, it's all about you, so I figured I was being egotistical to think he was looking at me. He was probably staring at the nude statue on the table. When I looked back at him, he quickly looked away and studied the charcoal drawing of a skeleton beside him.

Across the room a group was laughing at some anecdote by Dr. Kind. I joined them. "And that was how I bicycled around Greece. Next time I'll tell you about the volcano. I thought we were all going to die!" The group erupted in laughter. It was strange to imagine prim, bow tied Dr. Kind bicycling around Greece, much less around a volcano.

Dr. Kind turned to me, his tongue darting to dab some wine off his gray mustache. "Wendy! I want to talk to you. Our little journal, you know that awful rag we put out every semester."

I giggled. "It's perfectly fine."

"No, not this last one. I didn't like it at all. That Diana . . ." He shook his head.

"What's wrong with Diana?"

He twitched his gray mustache. "No sense of humor."

"She's hilarious!" Later, when I talked with people about Diana, it was odd that I seemed to be the only one who knew how funny she was. Her sarcasm even now is something I treasure, something I still emulate.

Dr. Kind shook his head. "Did you read that volume? There was something so dismal about the whole thing. She's a terrible editor. Dr. Hellmann agrees with me." He spread his arms. "I want you to edit this spring issue. You're the one who's hilarious. I saw your story in *The Iowa Review*. You would have just the right touch."

I felt myself beaming. "You want me to edit it, really?"

"Well, you aren't teaching this semester. You have the time. Actually, I want you to co-edit it. I know just the right person. I have a feeling you'd make a great team. Here he is now." He put his hands on my shoulders and forced me around. And there he was, after five years, wearing the same plaid flannel shirt he always wore. The man who had been staring at me. The man I should have recognized in a flash, and who clearly recognized me, but who avoided saying hello. My best friend, lost like a favorite mitten years ago. "Scott, do you know Wendy?"

Scott's face was blank. "Yes, we've met."

"Good, I want you two to edit the spring issue of the journal. What do you think? I'd consider it a great favor."

Why had I failed to recognize him? What was different?

"Sure," Scott said. "We can do that."

My throat was too dry to speak.

"Great!" Kind's hands were still on my shoulders, squeezing down. "I know you'll do us proud." He gave a final squeeze and walked away.

"Hi," I finally said.

"Hi." His face was still blank.

Then I realized he looked different because he wasn't wearing glasses. His dark eyes looked so naked and vulnerable with their long lashes. And there was a touch of gray at his temples. Gray! Had it been so long?

"How long have you been going here?" I asked.

He shrugged. "Just since the fall. I graduate this term. Accelerated program. Haven't actually been on campus much, spent some time studying windmills in Denmark. But I can't stay away from literature for very long."

"You were always a Renaissance man."

Not even that brought a smile. Unable to read him, I wished he would smile, even if he didn't mean it. But he would never do that, never do or say something he didn't mean. It could be painful, but it was also something I could trust. I'd lost him the winter that my bipolar symptoms began, when I'd lost my job, my brother, and my few friends. Scott was the last to go and the most wrenching. *If I can win back your friendship, it will mean I'm really well. Everything will be behind me.*

"How about you?" he asked.

"Since last year. This is my last semester of classes, next year I just write a thesis."

"What on?"

"I'm not sure. What are you taking in the department?"

He nodded toward Dr. Kind. "Kind's class. Circles of Hell: Dante and Milton."

"I'm taking his Gothic Literature. We're just missing each other."

The music from the iPod speaker changed from Michael Bublé to a woman playing a lonely piano riff. Her voice rose in a worn, melancholy plea. Something about not too late.

"Who is that singing?"

"Norah Jones."

Not Too Late. The song echoed across the room, across the years, a cascade of time collapsing like a quantum wave function, the collapse of probabilities until this inevitable moment. I looked away to hide my wet eyes.

"Scott!" another student nearby called out. "You have to settle an argument."

"Excuse me." He turned and walked away to the group, his face animated as he greeted them, as they welcomed him.

How do you join a conversation at a party? They seemed to turn their backs to me, enjoying a shared joke. It still strikes me how alone I was, that after a year I didn't really have a friend. As the young women laughed, they tossed their long, lovely hair that glinted in the light. They had perfect makeup; their sweaters weren't baggy and pilled like mine. Feeling lonely, my head pounding, I thought I'd get some fresh air. I passed Mrs. Hellmann unloading a bag of more wine bottles in the kitchen and slipped out the back door.

The moon was behind a bank of clouds, making the sky a milky white, the black trees below as if sketched in charcoal, soft and unreal. I wasn't familiar with the Hellmanns' backyard and tried to orient myself. There was a flagstone patio bordered by a low stone wall, and a bulk of something that made a vibrating noise. A hot tub. The sound made me unsteady—it was so weird that they had a hot tub in the backwoods, backward dairy farming country of upstate New York.

A black cat ran up to me, and I bent to pet it as it rubbed itself against my leg, purring. Out of the darkness, a man's voice said something like, "You're not alone." I caught my breath. It was so much what I wanted to hear just then. I strained to look and realized there were two figures sitting on the wall beyond the patio, their backs to me.

A match flickered and one of the figures turned slightly. A face. A life. My housemate Diana was briefly illuminated, her elfin face glowing a moment. I was sure it was her, though people doubted it later. Did I imagine it, because I wanted to see her? We'd had a fight recently, and I hadn't seen her since, because we'd both left for Christmas break. I almost called out, wanting to hug her, wanting to make up, glad to take the blame. What if I had? What if I had called out at that moment, brought her inside, asked her to recite poetry and regale us with her humor? Because Dr. Kind was wrong, Diana was hilarious, I certainly knew that. In that moment of seeing her face lit up in the dark, all seemed possible: understanding, friendship, a future. I felt all that in the fraction of a moment. Then it went dark again. I felt she and whoever she was with wanted to be alone, and I didn't call, didn't bring her inside. Didn't save her.

Instead, I picked up the cat and went back into the kitchen, where Mrs. Hellmann was opening a bottle of wine. "Is it okay to bring him in?" I said, holding up the purring cat. His fur was warm against my cheek.

She rolled her eyes. "That's not ours. It's the neighbor's. Could you please put him back outside?"

Embarrassed, I went out the door and set the cat down. "Sorry, you have to go." I nudged him away. The two figures were gone.

I went back in, determined to leave. The coats were piled on the bed in a guest room. As I struggled with the zipper, Carolyn entered, stumbling against the bed. The headband on her red and black striped hair was falling off.

"I'm glad to see you," she said, slurring slightly.

"What's the matter?"

"I can't drink California wine. It gets me drunk. And some weird guy I don't know is offering me a ride home."

"Let me take you."

"I can tell you're someone a person can defen—depend on. I don't feel well. I'm starting to wonder if the guy put something in my drink."

"Let's go." I helped Carolyn into her thin jacket and wrapped my scarf around her neck.

"I'm not from here. It's cold here, isn't it?" she said.

"Yes."

I briefly thanked Dr. Hellmann, explaining I had a headache, my arm around Carolyn. He gave me a look that acknowledged Carolyn's condition and gave my shoulder a grateful pat.

As we came out the front door, the night suddenly exploded in snow. Thick, friable clumps the size of quarters pelted us as we slipped our way across the road to my car. I kept Carolyn upright and buckled her in. She was already half asleep.

When I turned the wheel, the back-right tire slid down into the drainage ditch. "Great," I muttered, determined not to go back in to ask for help. I started rocking the car forward and back, revving it gently. A knock on the window startled me. I rolled it down.

"Stuck?" Scott asked. He hugged himself against the cold. "I heard the familiar sound of revving."

"I think I got it."

"Do you want me to push?"

"No, you'd be standing in the ditch. Why does New York have drainage ditches everywhere?"

"That's why we don't have mud season, like Vermont."

"Right. Stand back. I almost had it."

He took a few steps back and I rocked some more, gaining traction, until the car lurched forward onto the street.

Scott came back to the window. "Good job. Are you okay? I thought you only just got here."

"I hit my head earlier today. Have a headache now."

"You never get headaches!" We shared a brief laugh. It was something I had said to him in the past, long ago, so often it was a joke between us. This was the moment I'd been waiting for, a moment of friendship. Scott had such a nice laugh, soft and helpless. "Send me an email about this journal thing we're supposed to do."

"What's your email address?"

"The same."

I felt a pang. The address I'd sent so many messages to, ending in the terrible argument, when he ended things saying we couldn't communicate anymore. Was he thinking of that? But there was no anger in his face now. There was possibility. In the dark he looked young again, like the old Scott I knew so long ago.

"Thanks. Good night. See you soon." I tried to see if he was waving as I drove off, but the snow was too thick in the air. I turned to Carolyn. "Where do you live?"

Carolyn mumbled an address on the opposite side of town. Not that anything was far away in this town, but it began to snow harder, streaking in the headlights, blowing across the dark hills, and I looked forward to getting out of this storm. When we arrived, I was glad to see plenty of lights on. I left the swooning Carolyn with two responsible-seeming roommates before heading up the hill home.

That was me, in the beginning, rescuing a fellow student. That was my potential before things fell apart, before I kept stumbling over dead bodies and found that becoming the unreliable one only meant that there was no one I could trust.

CHAPTER TWO

The house was so quiet as I made coffee the next morning. Something felt wrong. Diana and I had both just returned from break, and I arrived home the day before only in time to get ready for the Hellmanns' party, so I still hadn't spoken to her yet, not since before Christmas.

I went to Diana's bedroom door with the morbid feeling I would find her dead in her bed. The latch never worked, and the door swung open to a room white as snow: white walls, white comforter, white trim. Diana wasn't there, her suitcase still packed by the bed as if she had set it down upon returning home to open later. An easel with a painting stood before the window.

It was a portrait, but the face had been covered in gray and yellow smears. Only its white teeth showed, predatory and long. Gray hair waved around the obscured face. I didn't like looking at it. The creak of the old wooden floor echoed in the empty house as I turned away.

In my own room, gathering my notebooks, I looked at the small watercolor painting of a red rose, about four inches square, on the desk. I picked it up and sat on the bed. On the back was scrawled, "A rose for Wendy." This was Diana's apology for our stupid argument. I propped the painting against the lamp on the nightstand. I wanted to leave a note for her, but there wasn't time; I had to shower and go.

I avoided the bathroom mirror. I knew what I looked like, my blonde hair thin with no particular style, my body twenty pounds heavier since I'd been put on lithium three years earlier. I did like my dark hazel eyes, at least, but I went around without makeup, didn't moisturize or use mousse. I wore drab, lumpy clothes.

Diana's toiletries on the counter were lovely and grown-up. She had moisturizer soft as meringue, eye serum with secret ingredients, a mousse labeled "bodifying foam." There was no hair stuck in her brush. Her toiletries were from her home of Chicago, probably bought at a nice department store, the kind with thousand-dollar handbags where they spritz you with perfume as you pass. The kind of place that didn't exist for at least fifty miles around North Carthage, New York.

As I drove to campus, I wondered what it would be like to live in a city like Chicago. I couldn't imagine it as I passed the white fields fringed with hemlock trees. Campus was nearby at the top of the hill.

My first class of the semester was Women's Greek Mythology, with Dr. Hellmann. I tried to focus. The uneven little desk rocked each time I moved, startling me every time as if I'd be pitched over. Meanwhile the heating pipes whined like a distant alarm.

Dr. Hellmann passed out the syllabus and read the introduction to us: "In ancient Greece, women were a problem."

We began with Persephone, and women and death. At one point I tried to bring up Demeter's grief and the topic of motherhood, but somehow the point didn't land. I usually didn't say much in my classes, because I often felt that somehow there was a disconnect between my observations and the direction of the class. It made me feel slightly invisible. Dr. Hellmann's meandering asides, sliding from ancient rituals to riffs on postmodernism, which seemed to enthrall my classmates, didn't help. So after one or two comments, I fell silent. It was a popular class, about thirteen of us, so there were plenty of other voices.

I started to ruminate about where Diana could be. It was odd she hadn't come home the night before. How soon was it time to worry about someone missing? I decided to ask Dr. Hellmann about it after class.

When I stopped him by the door, he sighed and put down his briefcase, barely looking at me as he glanced at his watch.

"My roommate is Diana Cerf. You know her, don't you?"

He paused and looked away. "Yes, of course I do. Fine poet."

"Did you see her at the party last night?"

"No, she wasn't there."

Dr. Kind came in, as his class was next. He stood close to us to enter the conversation. It's funny, looking back on it, I realize Dr. Kind wasn't particularly tall. Maybe not any taller than I was. But in those days, it felt like everyone towered over me.

I turned to Dr. Kind. "Did you see Diana Cerf at the party last night?"

His pale blue eyes seemed to smile. "You look worried," he said with an easy, authoritative manner.

At last someone had divined my feelings; my shoulders relaxed. "She didn't come home last night."

Dr. Kind exchanged a look with Dr. Hellmann and said, "Well, she was probably with a boyfriend. Who was she going out with? I forget his name."

"I thought I saw her outside on your back patio," I said.

Dr. Hellmann, who'd been gazing off around the classroom, snapped his attention back toward me. "That's odd. Why would she hang around and not come inside? You must be mistaken."

"Yes, of course you are," Dr. Kind agreed. He cocked his head sympathetically. "Don't be so worried. She's a strong young woman."

I took a breath, trying to be calm, but my anxiety rose. "Yes, she was the opposite of me."

Dr. Kind smiled, amused. "Don't say 'was.' You've killed her already, haven't you?"

I felt my face go red. "I, I guess I do always expect the worst."

Dr. Hellmann picked up the briefcase. "You are a worrywart. Come on, they have to start class."

"Would you please ask your wife if she saw her?"

The professors exchanged a look of bemusement, and I felt foolish. Hellmann turned his smile to include me. "I will. But you know Diana—she's probably dancing under a tree somewhere, chanting incantations." He left as Dr. Kind gave a little bark of a laugh.

The next class was Dr. Kind's Gothic Literature. A few students
left, a few more joined in. It was a smaller class, about nine students.
As we were getting started, a harried-looking young man paused in
the doorway.

"Advanced astrophysics?" Dr. Kind asked, winking at us.

Panic flashed across the student's face. "I'm looking for Gothic
Literature?"

"Yes, come in."

I laughed, a little loud. I think I was the only one.

Dr. Kind jumped up and made a circling motion with his arm.
"Come on, this isn't kindergarten. We're grown-up." At his direction
we moved our little desks into a circle. I liked his attitude; I appreciated that he treated us like adults.

The syllabus was precise, his talk timed to the minute. Our first
book would be *Frankenstein*, followed by *Jane Eyre*. "Ladies first,"
he said. We would also cover *The Turn of the Screw*, Poe, and some
contemporary men, among others. "It's a long list, but unlike the
drear of my colleagues, our work is *fun*." His lecture proved this; his
notes were snappy and sprinkled with humor.

After class, I couldn't wait. I decided to go to Dr. Hellmann's
house to ask his wife about Diana. I drove down into the town and
up another hill. Most of the country roads were something-Hill
Road, when they weren't Summit Road, Pinnacle Road, or Peak
Road. There was Snowdon Hill Road, Grange Hill Road, and Cooper Hill Road rising up from the main street through town, which
had the unlikely name Doctor McShane Boulevard. On the corner of McShane and Cooper Hill, there was a mailbox that said
McShane. The family still lived in North Carthage after probably a
hundred years, and I don't think they were still producing doctors.
The Hellmanns were on Cooper Hill Road, next to an old apple
orchard, their property a bite taken out of what had once been a
large farm.

I didn't know how long the Hellmanns had lived there. I thought
they'd been at the university a long time, but their house was new.
It was large and multilevel, hard to imagine how the rooms inside

related to the walls and windows. It was stucco, a poor choice, already showing fine cracks, a harsh surface at odds with the rural landscape. It belonged in California. Instead of gleaming in the sun, the gray skies made it look dirty. Along the foundation was a ring of splashed mud like the soiled hem of a white dress. A Japanese maple grew stunted by one corner, and the hemlock hedge should have been wrapped in burlap to protect it from the wind; the wind side was drying into rusty twigs.

I parked in the driveway and rang the bell. It seemed like a long wait in the cold air before the door opened. Jean Hellmann was a trim athletic woman with a neat gray bob. She was belting a camel hair coat over her black turtleneck, a blue silk scarf perfectly tucked into the coat. I felt conscious of her being neat and put together. Maybe it was the scarf, glowing in the monochromatic winter light.

"Oh, Wendy. Hello. I was about to leave. What can I do for you?" Her face looked slightly stressed at this unexpected visit.

I coughed. "I was wondering, this is probably stupid, but my roommate, Diana, well, it seems like she hasn't been home since the party."

Jean looked at her watch. "Diana? Which Diana?"

"Diana Cerf."

Jean ducked her head and lowered her eyes, suddenly looking tired. "I think I've probably met her. What about her?"

"She was at your party last night, and she hasn't come home."

"No, she wasn't at the party. I'm sorry, but I think I knew everyone there."

The wind picked up as we stood at the door. I was losing my nerve now, but tried again. "I saw her. When I went outside, I thought she was on the patio."

Behind me a car pulled up. Dr. Hellmann parked his SUV at the side of the road, because my car was in the middle of the driveway. He strode up to the door looking exasperated but indulgent.

"Well, hello again. You're blocking me," he said.

"I'm sorry."

"I said I would ask Jean when I got home."

"I don't think she was there," Jean said. "At least she never came inside, and it was so dark and cold out. I can't imagine why she would've been out there." She smiled with sympathy, as if sympathy were a solution. "Of course, you're worried. You should call some of her friends. I'm sure you'll find her."

Dr. Hellmann opened the door wider to go past Jean into the house, and Jean stepped out. "You're blocking me, too. Oh, you have a crack in your windshield."

"I hit a deer yesterday on my way home."

Jean stopped and looked more concerned. She was a biology teacher who taught premed. "On your way home from the party?"

"No, on my way home from Ohio, before the party. Guess I hit my head."

Jean looked at me, her eyes searching my forehead. "Wendy, you should go get an X-ray. You probably have a concussion. Take care of yourself."

At the time, I was touched. My family was not the type to worry or show concern, and her attitude brought warmth to my cheeks. Now, all these years later, I think she was also trying to dismiss me, as she came down the step, walking me to my car, but certainly hurrying me along my way.

Once home, I looked in Diana's room. Still the suitcase, the oil painting with its creepy, smeared-out face. It was one o'clock. I decided to try calling her cell. Though it seems crazy, I didn't have my own cell yet in 2007, and I called from the living room landline. In the empty house, the air swirling from drafts, a loud ringing made me jump. It was her cell in the bedroom, the mournful echo of my call, like a peacock scream.

That impotent scream of her cell made me feel certain that something was wrong. I went back out and drove over the county road outside of town to the sheriff's office.

CHAPTER THREE

I waited on the hard bench outside the sheriff's office door while the deputy spoke to his boss, a silhouette in the window of the door. Soft male voices echoed from within, hushing me, it seemed, like nurses in a hospital. My footprints, damp with snow, marred the glossy linoleum floor. Was I taking too much responsibility? But all my life, I rarely had taken any. It was time to act.

The deputy came out of the sheriff's office and sat next to me on the bench, which surprised me. In first grade the school psychologist sat beside me when I was crying on the bench in the hall outside my classroom, where I'd been sent for forgetting my math homework. The psychologist sat with me only a minute, but it was soothing; I don't even know now why I knew who he was. The deputy seemed to be taking the same care, to sit and be still with me, calming and inviting my trust. He was young, with his dark curly hair and big eyes like a lamb's. Perhaps that was why he was being so thoughtful: too young to be jaded.

"You think you saw your roommate last night?" he asked.

Hot in my down coat, I ran my fingers through my damp, messy hair. I had come in a hurry without a hat. "I think so, but I'm really not sure."

"At a party, you said? Where? Would anyone else have seen her?"

"At Professor Hellmann's house. It was an English Department party. I went outside and for a moment a match flickered on the patio, someone lighting a cigarette. I'm pretty sure it was Diana. But she didn't come home."

"When was the last time you saw her, before that?"

I tried to slow my anxious breath. "I just got home from Christmas yesterday. So it was before break. Her suitcase is here."

"Her suitcase is here. There's no sign she's packed anything and run away?"

"No, I don't think so."

He was sitting very close, talking quietly. The shoulders of our down coats touched. Again I felt he was being careful with me, even tender.

"And how sure are you that you saw her last night?"

"I'd say ninety percent."

He nodded, and with a note of closing the conversation, he shifted slightly away. "So it's been less than twenty-four hours. She could have spent the night with a boyfriend. What you need to do is ask around among her friends. She'll turn up."

I swallowed, words falling down my throat. He wasn't going to help me. Anyone else would insist, maybe demand. But I couldn't. I had that underwater feeling I sometimes had, something since childhood, a sensation I was being held under water so that I couldn't speak. And my throat was dry, so dry.

"How soon can I report her missing, then?"

He stood up. "Come back tomorrow morning if she doesn't come home tonight. But you'll find her. Don't worry. Ask around. Nine times out of ten, it's just a misunderstanding."

"And ten?" I forced myself to ask.

He smiled with a glance to the ceiling. "We don't get a lot of murders around here. Trust me. Here, take my card."

I studied it: Deputy Polozzi. Someone once said to me in high school, "Upstate, you're either Italian or Polish. And if you're not, you know it." I put the card in my purse. "Wasn't there someone who disappeared here five years ago? A young woman?"

His smile became a chuckle, sounding eerie in the empty hall. "So you're already looking for a serial killer. I don't think a serial killer waits five years to strike again."

"Like, when you hear hoofbeats, think horses, not zebras?" Long ago, someone had said that to me. Someone who was wrong.

"Something like that. Let me know either way. If she turns up later, let me know."

I rose and he walked out with me. In the nearly empty parking lot, the snow swirled around us, blowing up from the ground. It was overcast, and the pine wood behind the office was the darkest green. There were no other buildings close by on the country road. Here the authorities were, the fortress of solitude, hung with icicles, lonely, lonely.

"What was the name of the woman who disappeared?" I asked.

"Cassandra Sommers."

"Were you on that case?"

Polozzi shook his head. "No, it was already pretty cold when I started here." He opened the door of the rusty old Dodge for me, then paused. "Your windshield has a crack. You need to get that fixed right away. I'd hate to give you a ticket."

I nodded quickly. "I hit a deer yesterday. I will as soon as I can. Thank you." I got in, buckled the seat belt as he watched, and then pulled away.

The sheriff's department was on Route 20, a few miles outside of town. I drove west toward the house. The day before, I'd been driving east from Ohio. His pointing out the crack on my windshield reminded me. It had been such a strange and long drive: Driving and driving, the roar of a bad wheel bearing from underneath, a roar that stayed with me when I tried to sleep.

I'd hardly slept during the break, staying first with my mom and then with Dad. Sleep was always an issue. All the driving wasn't good, how the road stayed with me, how it continued to roll under me in bed, my thoughts like a radio that kept changing stations.

And the radio on the drive didn't help. On Route 90, the DJ had said, "Some bad news for a couple in Florida, getting a phone call from their nine-year-old daughter saying something about a man with a knife before it was cut off. In sports, the Pacers beat the Nicks 54 to 48." He glided from the nightmare to the sports news without a moment's hesitation.

As I drove I thought about how people say drivers are isolated in their metal boxes. I didn't feel isolated from the others, but rather connected, watching this driver signal to change lanes, the other drivers slow down, trying to go the right speed for merging traffic, all connected by an invisible thread.

Finally in the afternoon, I was off the thruway and heading south from Syracuse, the Midwest truly left behind. The landscape started rolling and the views grew wider. I had not been born here; my family had moved here when I was eleven, and when they went back to Ohio, I stayed to attend college, first in Utica and now here. I felt upstate New York was the last undiscovered territory. Land and houses were cheap. Decades of government neglect as the City siphoned off all aid and attention had left the area undeveloped. Hawks sat in trees by the country roads, snapping turtles stopped traffic by the reedy Unadilla. Once a wild mink crossed in front of me while I was walking; it stumbled on its semi-webbed feet, its back making an S-curve, chewing a mouse, and nothing about it was cuddly.

Hunters complained about the dangerous overpopulation of deer and shot each other in winter. Diners opened at six a.m. and closed at two o'clock in the afternoon. Farmers worried about the lack of mothers with babies to buy their milk, their debts rising higher. There was field corn, hay and cows, blue silos with silver domes, barns with faded red paint. Some of the old barns were full of antiques for sale, a crazy jumble of rust and oil paintings, where you could find a Venetian glass chandelier for a hundred dollars. In the more suburban areas houses were built to look quaint with mansard roofs, to emulate farmhouses, except the real farmhouses looked nothing like them. The farmhouses were white peeling to gray, with narrow rotting porches and aluminum storm doors tacked in front of the heavy wooden ones, thick paint encrusted over the trim.

There was no such thing as a straight road. The roads followed Mohawk and Oneida trails, followed deer paths, followed streams where great blue herons looked for frogs in spring. In the summer, cedar waxwings plucked huge black garden spiders from the center of webs spun between the hay stalks. Bluebirds nested in fence posts. Loggers brought home baby raccoons for their children to play with until the raccoons grew up and turned mean. Dogs were never tied up, cats were rarely fed. Rabid possums gnawed on roadkill.

In the winter, the streets were plowed and salted well. It was rare not to be able to get around, except that sometimes the thruway itself, the most modern thoroughfare, had to close because the wind heaved a wall of snow across it. But these days it didn't snow as often.

I was glad for the salt and the plow as the county road wound between the muddy fields. Newer houses appeared on the sloping ground the road sliced through as I entered tiny North Carthage with its unlikely state university. The kind of school that would take anyone.

During a fight with my brother the year before, Peter had insisted I leave, not go backwards, back to school. He wanted me to move to Indiana near family and get a job at a call center. How could he understand the heart-stopping beauty of these fields, of these hills that tumbled and sped like a wild reel?

As a shadow jumped through my headlight, I instinctively jammed on the brakes with a sickening thud as my head hit the windshield. When I woke, a man in camouflage was unbuckling my seat belt.

"You okay?" he'd asked. "Talk to me."

"Did I hit a deer?" My voice was thick in my mouth. I looked up at the man, whose face was grizzled and whose breath was beery. A truck was in the other lane, facing me.

"I saw it as I was coming up. It flipped in the air, flew. Broke its neck. We'll take it, if it's all the same to you. The hide will work."

I stumbled out of the car and he held me up. "Do you want us to run you to Saint Luke's?" His voice sounded far off. I took some quick breaths. By the side of the road, two men also in camo were tying up the deer, a big doe.

"Too bad you missed the buck. He got away, a ten pointer."

"Sorry." I bent forward to breathe, but that made my head pound.

"Let me run you over to Saint Luke's, get yourself X-rayed."

I stepped in front of my car to look at the damage. The hood was dented, and the windshield had a crack. Otherwise it seemed okay. "I think I'm all right. I'll be fine."

"I'll follow you home at least, how's that?"

It was getting dark and the truck's big headlights lit up the inside of the car as we drove to my house. That was only the day before. It already seemed long ago.

CHAPTER FOUR

One thing that will be less reliable about my story is that I will guess at other scenes, other points of view. You don't want to be in my head this whole time. Hell, I don't want to be in my own head all the time. So I'm turning this over to a glimpse of the Hellmanns after I left them.

Jean followed Dan back into the living room. He shrugged out of his wool coat, throwing his scarf on the back of a chair. Out the window, my car pulled away.

"Don't you have class?" he asked, reaching into the closet. The hangers tangled and he struggled with them, softly swearing.

She stared out the window, stiff, her class all but forgotten. "What if it's Cassandra Sommers all over again?"

"Don't be silly." He got his coat into the closet and snorted with exasperation. "I shouldn't have bothered to hang it up, I still have to move the car. She had a boyfriend, she's probably with him."

"Why do you say 'had'?"

He slapped the closet door and pulled his coat back out. "Not because she's dead. Because I don't know if he's still her boyfriend. It was on again, off again. They fought."

"Was Diana here last night?"

"No. I didn't see her."

She turned around. "When was the last time you saw her?"

He turned red. "I don't remember. Before break, at least." He picked up his keys. "You have class." He put his hands on her shoulders, forcing her to look him in the eyes. "This is not Cassandra again—"

"I feel like we only just got past it." She stared down at the floor, wanting to crumple onto the carpet, waves of cold across her back.

He put his arm around her. "You know that Wendy wrote me a little confessional note before break. She's bipolar."

"Really?" She leaned into him. The warmth oozed back into her hands. "Is she crazy?"

"Hard to say. Now, run along to class like a good girl." He gave her a little shake at the door as he let her go.

Jean tightened the belt of her coat against a sudden wind outside. When she opened her car door, she turned, expecting him to have followed her, wanting to see him again now, wanting to feel at peace, but he had disappeared inside.

CHAPTER FIVE

Home from the sheriff's office, I took my midday dose of lithium and had a quick lunch of Ramen noodles. When I opened my computer, there was an email from my mother: "I was digging around and found something you wrote in college. An opera comedy. Would you like me to send it to you? Might inspire more writing?" I'd forgotten about that, my project with Scott from the class where we'd met. His voice came back to me, the tenor lilt. "Sure, I'd like that, no rush," I wrote back. I wanted to send her a longer note, including the fact that Scott was back in my life, but I needed to buy my books, before my therapy appointment. To my surprise, she replied again quickly. I usually didn't hear from her often, as her work as a technical writer kept her busy. "How is that house working out? Can you write there?" She was sure getting an MA in English meant I was doing a lot of creative writing, but I was there to beef up my credentials for teaching high school. I'd hardly written a thing in months. Writing was my mother's dream. I had to get to my appointment, and I let the question hang.

As I stepped outside, I realized I hadn't told the deputy that Diana's car was still in the driveway, covered by a thick layer of snow. That was probably important. I opened her car, unlocked as was usual around here, to take out the snow brush. A small scrap of paper blew off the seat, just a drug store receipt. I crushed it into my pocket, and cleared off the snow.

I thought about the poetry reading I'd missed in November. Diana had come home and given me a full review, laughing, scathing towards our classmates. "The way they read, making every line end on a question mark. I felt like every reader was a teenager asking me out on a date. 'Please, date my poem; don't break my heart.' The girls in miniskirts and Doc Martins, and some Mr. Flannel Shirt trying to get my number. Hellmann and Kind were there, Mutt and Jeff." I smiled recalling it as I brushed off the snow. I wanted her car to be ready for her, thinking it good luck to assume she'd be back, any minute. Then I went to campus.

I usually walked with my head bowed, but I looked up now, glancing all around to see if Scott would walk by. Coats and hats glowed bright red and blue and green against the snowy day, like the first I had seen of color in a long time.

The bookstore was in the basement. I checked my backpack at the counter. Then I realized I needed the syllabus. The clerk gave me a puzzled squint when I asked for my pack, and I felt she thought I was stupid for having to come back for it. What would Scott say? That the clerk is busy with a thousand things, tired, will have forgotten me thirty seconds later. When I smiled at the clerk, she smiled back as if she understood. *See, people don't think you're stupid*, I told myself. *It's okay.*

Loud voices bounced off the black cavernous ceiling where lights glared at odd angles. I craned my neck to read the poster-board signs indicating subject matter, passing math and geology, but lingering at the history books for a few minutes, because I had always been torn between history and English. As I reached rows of psychology books, I recognized some that were on my therapist's shelves. When I got to English I found as many used versions of the books as I could, flipping through them to find ones that weren't highlighted. The big stack was heavy in my arms.

A large clock over the checkout said two-fifty. My appointment was for three o'clock. The lines snaked around the store. I considered just putting the books back and coming back later, but sometimes they got sold out. My heart pounded. The line inched forward. I peered ahead. In the gloomy black and concrete space, harsh light bounced off the mask-like faces. There was something about teeth and lips and wrinkled brows that reminded me of Diana's abstract painting. I swallowed and looked at the clock again. The minute hand seemed to change quickly, while the line and the faces moved in slow motion.

At three o'clock there were just two people ahead of me. *Please, please.* But there seemed to be some problem. Clerks were conferring, a customer gesturing impatiently. There was supposed to be a disk in the book, from what I could make out, but it was missing. A clerk hurried to the back of the store while the one at the register shouted the course number after him. Finally the disk was retrieved.

There was one more customer ahead of me. I bobbed up and down on my toes, *I'll make it, I'll make it.* Then the student's credit card was denied. He wanted to call the credit card company then and there. *Oh my God.* After some argument, the student produced a large wad of cash from his wallet. Change was counted out, all in slow motion, all gestures drifting through the air as if they were on the moon.

I dropped the heavy stack of books on the counter, my arms aching. The girl behind the counter didn't look at me. I got out my credit card and tapped the counter with it. The clerk whisked the books into two bags furiously, swiped my card, and thrust a pen and the receipt toward me without looking up. I made a quick squiggle for a signature and slid the receipt back. Her face was like a mask, her expression seemed to leap out with cartoon-like intensity, a hostile grimace as she thrust back my card.

I stumbled my way to the front counter for my backpack. It was 3:05. My throat hurt and sweat poured down my sides under my heavy coat as I struggled with the books, then swung the pack over one shoulder as I ran up the stairs to the Health Center.

I apologized for being late as soon as I stepped into my therapist's office. Ann waved it aside. "Only a few minutes." She smiled, welcoming. Ann wore no makeup on her young, narrow face. Red-rimmed glasses framed her gray eyes. Her short hair was brown streaked with blond, brushed standing up on the top of her head. She was usually in black and had a minimalist air. Her mild demeanor was in harmony with the soft snow pelting the window.

She sat with her chair turned away from her desk, over which was a case full of books, including ones I'd just seen at the bookstore, about dysfunctional families, adult children of alcoholics, role models—now that I think of it, families were the main topic of all her books.

I sunk back into the chair and relaxed, relieved it was okay, and felt the softness of the light in the dim blue office. By my side there was a small table with a box of tissues. I rubbed the worn arms of the chair where stuffing came out of a small hole.

"How are you?" she asked.

"I don't know."

"Tell me what's new. What did you do last night?"

I pulled at the stuffing in the hole. "I do dumb things."

"Like what?"

"My roommate didn't come home last night. It hasn't even been twenty-four hours, and I've already gone to the sheriff's office, like some kind of hysterical person."

Ann furrowed her brow, and opened her mouth in puzzlement. "What?"

"I know, I'm stupid."

"Your roommate hasn't come home? Do you know where she last was? This isn't stupid at all."

"No?"

She sighed, almost exasperated. "Does your roommate—what is her name?"

"Diana."

"Has she done this before? Does she have a boyfriend?"

"Last I knew, she was single. She would usually leave a note or something if she was going to be very late, like the night of the poetry reading."

Ann set aside her notepad. "Wendy, this is serious. What did the police say?"

"Just that it's too soon."

"Well it isn't. You aren't stupid to be concerned." There was a pause, and I knew my expression looked conflicted. She continued, "And the sheriff or whoever shouldn't be making you feel stupid."

"It's just that so many news stories exaggerate the number of people who are abducted. Like, children who disappear are usually taken by a non-custodial parent, not a stranger. So, it's like . . ." I trailed off.

"So you're buying into this idea that you're simply a hysterical woman. Instead of an intelligent, thoughtful person who knows her roommate well enough to know she wouldn't just run off and not tell you. Wendy." Ann's voice hardened. "Don't let these *men* give you this kind of crap. Trust yourself."

I nodded. She was right, and her validation felt good.

"And don't avoid anything. Don't avoid the situation."

I smiled weakly. "Because I always avoid everything?" This was a common theme in our sessions.

She didn't smile back. "This is serious. I hope you'll trust yourself and not let these men walk all over you."

"Okay. Are you . . . mad at me?"

"Why would I be mad at you?"

I wished she would just say "No." Of course my question was nonsensical, but her firm advice felt like an admonishment. I took a deep breath, fiddling with the stuffing in the hole. The radiator buzzed.

"So, you'll do what's necessary?" she asked. "Because I know you can handle this. I know you have what it takes to handle this situation."

"Thanks." That made me feel better. I waited for her to continue. I always let Ann guide our sessions.

Ann picked up her notebook. "Tell me about your role models. As a child. Your father drank, so he was no role model. You haven't said much about your mother. You saw them? How was Christmas?"

"I drove to my mom's first, then my dad's. Mom is alone, but Dad has a new wife with grandkids. It was weird. Mom knows I like marmalade, and diet soda. But it was almost the only food she had in the house. Dad had turkey, ham, all that."

Ann's look was confident. "With your mother, you felt indulged, but with your father, you felt taken care of."

That felt like a good insight, well put. But looking back on it, it seems understandable to me that having a big family around would mean my father would have a lot of groceries, unlike my mother who was alone. I'm not sure now if Ann's judgment was fair. But that was before I understood what Ann was really after.

"Did you see your brother? Peter?"

I shook my head. I was thinking of telling her about the fight we'd had, but Ann pursued the subject of adulthood instead. "Tell me about someone in your life that seems like a true, quintessential adult to you."

On the desk behind Ann, a water bottle glistened. I swallowed, wishing I could ask for a drink. "Maybe . . . Diana."

Ann nodded. "All right. What makes her seem more adult than you?"

"She's so strong. So . . . direct. It's hard to put into words. I'd like to be more like her."

"How old is she?"

"Twenty-four."

"And you're thirty. She's a few years younger than you. It sounds like this is about confidence. You need to find confidence in yourself. Did you get the grant?"

I swallowed. "I wormed my way out of teaching."

"We agreed. We decided a grant was appropriate for you until you feel stronger. You're a brilliant student, you've gotten published. Why must you turn it into something negative?"

I knew the thing to do was to tell her about the letter to Dr. Hellmann, the one I wrote begging for the grant, beyond the application, confessing I'd been struggling with bipolar disorder. I was ashamed of it and couldn't tell Ann, but I did want to find a way to get past note writing. "There's this thing. I'm afraid to talk to people sometimes. Most of the time. I end up writing a little note, and I usually end up annoying them."

"What would happen if you talked to them?"

They would trip me up. They would fold my words like origami, turn them inside-out until they hear something other than what I'm saying. I'd be misunderstood. "When I write, I'm in control."

"It makes sense that you're more comfortable writing. You're a writer. And that's how you feel in control. But the funny thing is, you still aren't in control, writing a note. You're probably even more likely to be misunderstood."

"It's hard to talk to people, sometimes."

"Why is that?"

People hypnotize me until I say what I know they want to hear. "I don't know. I'm shy. The thing about getting the grant is, I should be teaching."

Ann straightened her red-rimmed glasses. "Should? Why should you? It sounds like you wrote a letter to get out of it, and they understood. You took control. You didn't feel ready to teach, and they honored you with the grant. This all sounds positive."

But I wanted to be a teacher, and I shouldn't have been afraid of it. I scratched my scalp with both hands, feeling itchy all over. "I don't feel like an adult, getting out of it." I stopped fidgeting, leaned forward and tried to be still, to say this with emphasis. "I don't know how to feel like an adult. Could you tell me?"

Ann gave a little laugh. "I wish I could. We all feel that way, at times."

Stop normalizing my problems. This is serious to me. "But this . . . it really bothers me. It's the issue I want to deal with. That I'm not an adult."

Ann closed her mouth into a smile, cocking her head. "You are an adult. And when people honor you, like giving you a grant, it doesn't seem like you take it as a compliment. It doesn't give you the confidence it should."

"Maybe." She was right. When positive things happened, it didn't seem to make a dent in my lack of confidence. It was years before I really took that in.

"Believe me, this is normal. I have a homework assignment for you. Make a list of things that mean adulthood for you. Signs that would make you feel like an adult."

"Okay, thanks."

"I want you to think about your strengths. I want you to keep track of moments when you do feel like an adult."

It was a good idea. "I guess I dwell on the dumb things."

"Like what?"

"Last night, I was at this party at my professor's. I saw a cat outside, so I brought it in. And it wasn't their cat. I had brought in this total stranger's cat."

Ann cocked her head. Then she laughed. Then I laughed too, deeply. It was too ridiculous. "That's hilarious," she said.

"It is." It was a relief to laugh about it. "I just felt so childish."

"You didn't do any harm. It was just a silly mistake. And very funny. Now tell me something adult you've done recently. We covered that you're looking into Diana."

"I gave a classmate a ride home. She had too much wine."

"See! There you are."

I felt lighter. Though I already knew this was a competent thing to do, it helped to get this validation. "And Dr. Kind asked me to edit the literary journal."

"That's great!"

"Co-edit. Actually . . ."

Ann leaned in, her eyes glowing with interest.

"I was reunited with someone from a long time ago. His name is Scott. I was an undergraduate with him. Five years ago, we had this falling-out." Ann started writing while I spoke, gesturing for me to tell the whole story. "We were best friends. Really close. Never lovers, it wasn't like that. Like brother and sister, like twins. But I hurt him, in a way. It wasn't entirely my fault, but I should have . . . I don't know."

"What happened? I have a feeling it wasn't all your fault."

Feeling that it actually was more my fault than I'd ever admitted to myself, I turned toward the window. The snow was falling faster, blowing up and down. It was a long story, and I considered how to sum it up. "I had this good friend named Sophie. She was a poet, talented. But she started to have kind of a breakdown. She believed in reincarnation. And she started to think she was the reincarnation of Sylvia Plath. She went on about reincarnation and astrology and all that, quite a lot. Scott didn't believe in any of that stuff. Superstition, pseudoscience. All junk to him. By then we had graduated and were living in different cities. So we were emailing."

Ann tsk'd. "You know how email is."

"Right. I was worried about Sophie. But Scott . . . he could only argue against her delusions like it was an intellectual debate. He'd present arguments against the existence of reincarnation, and how astrology was illogical. I finally said that he was getting caught up in irrelevant trivialities. I mean, I was worried Sophie might kill herself, and he was arguing science."

"How did he react to your comment about trivialities?"

I stared at the snow. "He was furious. He . . ." I didn't want to tell her. "He just replied F-you, in all caps. He never swore. We had that in common. So he was really upset." I didn't tell Ann how it terrified me. It was as if I had opened a secret cellar door, where the pack of wild dogs were kept.

Ann's pen scratched the pad. Then she set it aside. "Wendy." I reluctantly turned toward her. "You aren't renewing your friendship with him?"

"I want to, very much."

"Why would you possibly want to be friends with this person?"

How could I respond? Scott was . . . he was my twin, he was my . . . "Scott was the best man I ever knew. His integrity. His honesty. His kindness. If I made him angry, I want to accept his anger. Maybe learn from it. There's no one else like Scott." I didn't usually open up like this, but as I spoke the feelings flowed out. "The way we could talk to each other. And it was email, right? You know how you can't really communicate that way. I should have called him. And at the time, I was doubting my own sanity, too. So I wasn't sure what the reality was. I was afraid and let it go, but now I have a chance for a new start. You don't know Scott. I would trust him with my life."

She sighed, looking like she was choosing her words carefully. "It sounds like you've really put him on a pedestal. That isn't healthy." I did feel Scott belonged on a pedestal. I couldn't feel otherwise. "He is someone I would avoid."

Avoid? I thought avoiding was my problem to overcome. I wanted to say this, but couldn't.

"It seems like you often put people on pedestals, like your roommate Diana."

"They have their lives together."

"So do you."

"But . . . It's different."

"Everyone feels that way at times."

I sighed. It just didn't help to hear that, even though now that's the kind of thing I'd say to someone in my place. What she was saying was true, but I couldn't hear it. I checked my watch.

"Keeping track?"

"I don't want the next person to have to wait."

Ann smiled. "For someone who doesn't feel like an adult, you take a lot of responsibility. That's the mark of an adult."

I considered that. It made me feel a little better.

She closed her notebook, ending the session. "I can't tell you what to do, but I would be very leery of trying to be friends with this man Scott. Don't sell yourself short. Trust your gut."

My gut, everything in me, told me that I could trust Scott more than anyone in the world.

As we stood by the door, she asked, "What happened to your friend Sophie?"

The question caught me off-guard, and I choked up. "She got mad at me for being so worried about her and stopped talking to me."

Ann's look of sympathy brought out my tears as she touched my arm. "I'm sorry."

She grabbed a tissue for me, and I left wiping my eyes, feeling a little foolish to be crying. As I drove home, I thought about things I could have talked about. I would like to have said more about the letters, about Scott, and about my brother. Somehow, we always seemed to get off-track.

CHAPTER SIX

Maybe this is what happened. I imagined it because I hoped it was something along these lines.

Scott entered his small, compact apartment. It was in a cheap location behind K-Mart, but his unit on the end was bordered by sheltering pines, and it was quiet. He checked his email, and there was already one from me, sent right after the party.

"Hi Scott, it's a long story, but I want to tell you right away. I have bipolar disorder. That's why I started to act so strange. It was all my fault, I take all the blame. I lost all my friends eventually (not that I ever had many), I had a big fight with my brother, and I lost my job. I don't mean to be self-pitying. I was on disability for a while. I came back to school a year ago to get the M.A., in the hopes that the degree will improve my awful resume. Anyway, I'm really sorry. I was often tempted to write to you, but you asked me not to contact you, so I wanted to respect that. Thanks for saying last night I could write again. That's everything. Just, everything was my fault and I'd be grateful for your forgiveness. Take care, Wendy."

He read over again. It was the last thing he expected. I had been eccentric at times, but never unstable, not mentally ill, not when he knew me.

He went to the kitchen and did something he never did, opened a beer in the middle of the afternoon. He took it to the computer, something else he never did. Holding the beer in his left hand, he drummed his right fingers beside the mouse, debating his reply. Sweating, he pulled at his collar. The top button popped off. As he bent to pick it up, he remembered my showing him how to sew on a button, creating a thread shank. Memories flooded him. The humor in literature class where we'd met back in Utica, the comic songs we wrote for the class project. My voice. That voice.

He struggled out of his shirt and threw it on the floor. Why was it so stifling all of a sudden? He nudged down the thermostat, then sat in front of the computer again in his T-shirt. His hand clicked the mouse, almost on its own, opening the folder called Old Mail. The only email in it was mine, a folder he hadn't opened in years. He clicked again, opening the first message, from twelve years ago.

"Hey Scott, it was great meeting with you. Do you like David Sedaris? I thought for something different, we could write a song for the project, since you play guitar. I love to sing. Let's think about it. Take care, Wendy. PS Can you teach me to play the guitar?"

His wrist moved, scrolling through years.

"It's so great to talk to you. We just get each other. You're like my twin brother. Oops, I'm rhyming. There's so much I haven't read yet. I've never read *Catcher in the Rye*. A teacher said I reminded her of Holden Caulfield, she said it with a bit of an apology, but I don't know what she meant. Anyway, see you Thursday. Take care, Wendy."

"Hi, I was thinking I'd like to write some story of letters exchanged between Dostoyevsky and Tolstoy. They compare beard grooming tips. Something like that. What do you think? Funny I always need your approval, because you're so wise. So I should just write it, right? See you tonight."

He scrolled to the last one.

"I don't know what to say. You are sometimes so dogmatic. I can't always talk to you. You go off on irrelevant tangents. I was trying to say something. I can't always speak. You respond with trivial things. Sometimes I worry about my sanity. It doesn't help when you get caught up in some intellectual discussion when I'm trying to talk about perception and feeling. I know you don't respond well about feelings, but I don't mean childish emotion. Lately my mind is racing, and I can't sleep. I feel like I don't know you. I wish I had words you would accept. You and I speak two different languages. I'm sorry. I don't want to argue."

Five years ago, all he had seen was "dogmatic," "trivial." "Sometimes I'm worried about my sanity." He had never noticed that sentence before. "Lately my mind is racing, and I can't sleep." That had gone over his head. At the time, he was glad he had dodged the bullet, glad we were only friends and had never been lovers. He swallowed down his beer in a few long gulps. Then with a sweep, he dragged the whole folder into the recycle bin, as if sweeping everything off his desk.

His cell phone rang. He was startled by the caller ID: Diana Cerf. When he picked up, he was doubly surprised it was me.

"Is that you Scott? This is still your cell?"

"Yes. I just got your email. I wasn't sure what to say."

"Oh right. I forgot. I'm calling about something else. You're the one person I felt I could call. It's about my roommate."

"Your roommate is Diana Cerf? That was the caller ID."

"Yes. I think she's missing. She hasn't been home."

"Have you called the police?"

"I went to the sheriff, but they said it was too soon. I'm not sure what to do right now."

"Find out how to reach her family. And I'll come right over."

Later I racked my brain trying to remember: did I give him the address, or did he already know where Diana lived?

CHAPTER SEVEN

We hung up. I found her address book in the end table. I remembered something Diana had said, that her Aunt Jackie was the family's voice of reason. There was an entry for an Aunt Jackie in Chicago. Taking a deep breath, I dialed the number. A woman answered.

"Hi, my name is Wendy Zemansky. I live with Diana."

"Oh, yes, I remember the name. Is something wrong?"

My heart beat faster. "I hate to tell you this, but I haven't seen Diana."

"In how long? She should have been there yesterday. Did she get there?" Her voice was brisk, not panicked.

"Yes. She got here, and I believe I saw her last night, outside a party in the dark. I don't think she's been home since."

"Have you contacted the police?"

"I'm about to." I decided to skip explaining the previous attempt.

"All right. I'll call her mother right now. I'll call you back."

As soon as we hung up, I dialed the deputy's number. He answered right away.

"Your roommate hasn't turned up yet?"

"No."

"I'll come over. What's the address?"

I told him. It was over with. Now I had acted, and it wasn't so hard, and I had done the adult thing. I went into the kitchen and set the phone on the table, knocking off a scrap of crumpled paper I had tossed out of my pocket. I opened it to look before throwing it away, not recognizing it, then remembering it had fallen out of Diana's car when I took out the snow brush. It was a drugstore receipt. Three initials jumped out. EPT. Early Pregnancy Test.

I ran to the bathroom and looked in the garbage. Nothing. Then to Diana's room. I scooped the things out of the waste basket: A rag with paint on it. A tissue. An empty bottle of lotion. I went outside to the garbage can at the end of the driveway. I didn't really want to paw through the mess of it, but I lifted the lid to look. A small bag that had come from the bathroom was on top and I checked it. Just tissues and an empty toothpaste tube. Something stuck between the kitchen bag and the perimeter of the can caught my eye. A small black book.

I pulled it out. It was the volume of poetry Diana had self-published in the fall. She'd had a dozen copies bound and given them away to friends. I took it inside and sat down with it, wondering why Diana would throw it in the garbage. As I leafed through it, a small lavender program slid out from between the pages, the program from Diana's reading. Someone had written on it, "Keep writing! Dan."

Something came back to me. On the day I was struggling to write the note to Dr. Hellmann, Diana had come into the kitchen and scolded me. "Commit nothing to writing," she'd said, jabbing out her cigarette with an air of finality. It seemed odd, a poet saying that.

There was a knock on the door, Scott stood outside, his collar turned up against the cold. "You need to salt, it's getting icy." He came inside and put his coat on the hook by the door.

"The sheriff's deputy is coming over," I told him.

"Good. Do you have a picture of your roommate you can give him?"

"Good idea. Let's look." I led him into Diana's bedroom. I knelt in front of the small white bookcase next to the desk and found a photo album.

I brought it to the bed, and we sat side by side. In most of the pictures, Diana was too young to be of use. In the very back was an artistic, black and white nude of Diana. Her heart-shaped face gleamed from under her long dark hair.

"I guess we can't use this, either," I said.

"The question is, who took it?" he asked.

"Why?"

Scott turned the page as if to protect her modesty. "Because it's likely a person who'd take that picture would know where she is."

The next page had a picture from the previous summer, Diana in a flowing sundress. "We can use this." I slid it out of the album.

We sat in silence for a few moments. Things had never been awkward between us in the old days. We were always comfortable with silence. I gazed up at him. "You look older," I said. He laughed. "Why are you laughing?"

"Because people usually say the opposite. You know: 'You haven't changed a bit.'"

I laughed. "I'm so rude."

He shook his head. "No, you're just Wendy."

I wasn't sure how to take that.

There was a knock on the door. Deputy Polozzi entered with a notepad, writing down Diana's name, age, and description. He took the photo, and I gave him Aunt Jackie's phone number.

"Do you know any of her friends? Boyfriend?" he asked.

I twisted my hands together. "No. But I think when I moved in, the reason she was looking for a roommate was because her ex-boyfriend had just moved out. We didn't talk a lot. We kind of left each other alone."

"Anything else? You might know more than you think. What was her mood like recently?"

I thought of our pre-break fight, for the first time hoping that would not remain our last conversation. "She seemed oversensitive lately. But she was trying to quit smoking. I also found this in her car." I gave him the drugstore receipt with the EPT on it.

Deputy Polozzi scratched his neck with the back of the pen, his face revealing nothing of what he might be thinking. Afterward I deeply regretted not examining the receipt before handing it over.

He slid the photo and receipt into his notepad. Then a look of surprise came over his face as he realized what I'd said. "Her car?"

"Yes, in the driveway." I rushed on quickly. "I think she must have taken her bicycle. It was dry earlier, everyone talking about global warming. It didn't snow until that storm last night. So I can only guess she thought she would beat the weather. The car was covered in snow."

He frowned as he scribbled notes on his pad. "This changes things."

My stomach fluttered, to have forgotten something so important. The phone rang. Deputy Polozzi waited while I answered.

Jackie's voice on the other end was calm but firm. "Do you know if she arrived there at all? What about her luggage?"

"Yes, her luggage is here. The sheriff's deputy is here. Maybe you should talk to him."

"Yes, please."

I gave the phone to the deputy and they spoke. When he hung up he said, "Her family's coming tomorrow. And we'll have a news conference as well. You can come."

"Do I have to say anything?"

"No, not at all."

The three of us were standing very close, and I hoped I could contribute more, when Scott said, "I'm sure Wendy has done all she can. We'll leave it to you."

The deputy clicked his pen closed. "We'll all stay in touch with each other. If you think of anything, let me know."

I shut the door behind the officer, and leaned against it. Scott sat at the kitchen table, looking thoughtful. I knew that problem-solving look. Bit by bit these expressions, the way he tapped his long fingers on the table, were bringing back the old Scott I knew.

"I want to find her," I said.

"Do you feel responsible?" He asked as if he thought I should not.

I pulled at the hem of my sweater, feeling warm. "If something was going on with her, I should have known about it. I feel something was going on, and I didn't catch it." Suddenly I straightened up and headed for Diana's laptop in the living room. "It didn't occur to me, I could check her email. She uses Outlook. I don't need a password to check it."

He followed me. "Maybe you shouldn't do that. The police do that kind of thing. Maybe they should take the laptop themselves."

I stood in front of the small silver computer, my hand reaching to open it, feeling suspended between his rational hesitation and my urge to do something. When I opened the laptop, I could hear the weight of Scott's disapproval coming from behind me.

There were two days' worth of new emails. The subject of one read, "Where did you go?" I opened it and read it aloud:

"Diana, I'm sorry you missed the studio today. Are you still looking into changing majors? I think you have a lot of promise as an artist, and I'm looking forward to having you in class. Please drop me a line if you have hesitations about it. Cheers, Professor Andrews."

Scott cleared his throat. "So she missed class. We knew that already."

"But she was changing majors? That's pretty sudden. Why would she do that? There was something going on with her."

He nodded. "It is surprising. Wasn't she considered one of the strongest writers in the department? She edited the journal."

"So you did know her?" I looked at him eagerly.

He leaned back, moving his fingers in the air, fidgeting. "No, but I knew of her. Everyone knew of her. And you, too."

"You knew I was here?" I caught my breath in surprise.

"I found out in November. Heard you got in *The Iowa Review*. That's pretty impressive."

"Thanks." I wondered who he'd heard it from.

He reached for the laptop to close it. "We should let the police handle it. Not fool with this."

I wanted to disagree, but let self-doubt win. "It's getting late. Let's have some dinner."

CHAPTER EIGHT

It was well past dinner time, and I made us banana omelets while we talked. Scott scrubbed the coffee pot, which had been on, stale all day, and started a fresh brew.

"Diana was a poet—"

"*Is* a poet," Scott said. "Stop being dramatic."

"Sorry." I stirred together cinnamon and sugar to sprinkle on the omelets. "Diana is a writer. She had that book of poetry made. I know painting is important to her, too. But she suddenly decided to change her major. She threw away her poetry book—I found it in the garbage. She kept telling me not to commit anything to writing. And she bought a pregnancy test recently. Something big was going on." I set the plates of food on the table as Scott poured the coffee.

"So she was in crisis. *Is* in crisis."

"Yes, crisis, that's the word. Maybe the professors know why she was leaving the department."

Scott gestured with his fork. "I think that you should leave it to the police to investigate. Don't try to be Nancy Drew."

I felt myself blush. "No, I won't. But it's something I want to find out."

"Why?"

I stared down at my plate. "I lived with her for five months. And I barely knew her. Why didn't we talk? Why didn't she confide in me? She didn't trust me."

"Hey, look at me." I looked up to his serious face. "Don't drive yourself crazy this way. She had her own friends, *has* her own friends, and you have yours. What I see you doing is finding a way

to blame yourself. You're faulting yourself because she didn't confide in you. Like it's something wrong with you. You always do that.
You're going to find a way to blame yourself for everything, even
if it turns out . . ."

I held his gaze. He was so rational, so calming. "You're right." I
took a comforting bite of the omelet. "Diana taught me this recipe."

"See? You weren't total strangers."

"No."

"It's good." He dug into the meal. We didn't speak for a few minutes. We always did eat in silence. Once years ago he'd joked, "Someone watching us eat would think we were angry with each other."

As we finished he said, "And I think, too, that maybe Diana liked
the fact that you weren't all over her. You respected her privacy.
You didn't pry. She probably appreciated that."

"Thanks. That could be true." We finished the omelets and I put
the dishes in the sink. "Thanks for cleaning the coffee pot. I left
it on this morning for Diana. It's hard to believe that was just this
morning." I took the pill bottle from the cupboard for my evening
dose of lithium.

"Is that your medication?"

"Yes."

He turned his chair around and straddled it backwards, clasping
his hands, and looked up at me with interest. "Everyone seems to
be bipolar these days. But I don't know a lot about it. Would you
tell me? Enlighten me."

I swallowed the pink capsule and leaned back against the counter. "Well, it's not exactly the same for everyone. Basically you have
manic episodes sometimes. Like for me, I'd say it was getting to be
twice a year."

"What happens? I've heard of mania, but people throw the word
around."

"Right. It lasts a couple of weeks. You don't sleep, you don't want
to eat. You lose weight, the only good thing." I laughed a little.

He shook his head, his eyes wide and attentive. He didn't want
me to joke it off.

I sighed. "Way back, years ago, my first symptom was terrible insomnia. When I was in college, once when I hadn't slept in a week, I crumpled to the floor and told my roommate I needed to see a doctor. She was a nursing student, and she said she thought my brain produced too much dopamine. It was a Sunday, and we didn't know how to get in to see a doctor, so she took me to the emergency room. I know it's silly to go to the emergency room for insomnia—"

"You hadn't slept in a week. I don't think it's that silly."

I smiled. "Thanks, but the doctor did. He was this young guy and he was pretty annoyed. I told him about my roommate's theory that my brain produced too much dopamine. He said, 'When you hear hoofbeats, think horses, not zebras.' That insomnia is caused by emotional problems and I should talk to a therapist. He sent me home with three Benadryls. Later I started to have manic episodes. That insomnia was my first early symptom. And it's basically a problem of—"

"Let me guess. The brain producing too much dopamine."

"Yup. My roommate was perfectly right."

He nodded. "So what is the mania like?"

I had never had to describe it before, and I struggled for the words. His interest was reassuring, neither judgmental nor dismissive. "Your mind just can't turn off. Racing thoughts overwhelm you, crazy ideas. Some people behave compulsively, talk and talk, or spend a lot of money or gamble, maybe break the law, like steal a car to drive across the country. It was a little different for me, though. I wasn't talkative. Just the opposite. I became withdrawn, stopped talking at all, but I couldn't stop writing. That was my manic activity. I filled some journals and wrote people crazy letters. Shameful letters." I recalled some, and tears came to my eyes. I bent over the sink and splashed some water on my face. Scott got up and put his arms around me. I swallowed back my tears. "That was most of it for me. But later on, I found that my episodes became increasingly paranoid. I had horrible paranoid delusions. Messianic too. I thought I was going to be sacrificed. I thought my family was going to come at me with knives and cut me apart. It was horrifying." I put my head against his chest, smelling the familiar scent of his green soap, for a moment aching at the memory of our old friendship. "There's this cliché that victims of bipolar disorder like to go off their meds because they enjoy being manic. Supposedly they miss it. But that was never the case for me. I hated it, and if it were to keep happening to me, I'd probably have to kill myself. I couldn't live with it."

I looked up at him. His face appeared startled, and I realized how serious this really was.

"What do you take for it?"

"Lithium carbonate. It's nothing heavy-duty. Lithium is a mood stabilizer, not an antipsychotic. They prescribe it for a lot of things now. I take it three times a day."

"That sounds like a lot."

"They like it spread out. And I have tests for the level of lithium in my blood a couple of times a year."

"And who's in charge of this?"

"I have a psychiatrist for the prescription. But I don't see him a lot. I have a quick medication check with him every three months. Ann is my regular therapist. She's great."

"How often do you see her?"

"On Mondays." I sighed and stretched my arms. I had been so tense, and now it felt good to explain everything to him.

"If it's a biochemical condition, what is the therapy for?"

"A lot of things. You might remember I grew up with an alcoholic father, so we talk a lot about my childhood, the dysfunctional family and all." We sat back down at the table. I took a sip of coffee and there was a pause, a silence filled with the seriousness of it all. I had never simply told anyone this whole story before, except for Ann, and even Ann didn't know everything. Scott's understanding meant the world to me. "I guess maybe I'd like to talk more about the impact of it, and the last few years, and less about the childhood stuff."

He raised his eyebrows. "Then why don't you?"

I shrugged, feeling strangely guilty. "It's up to Ann."

He set down his cup and cocked his head, giving me the frank, forceful look I remembered from years before. "You should be in charge of your sessions. It's up to you to decide."

I rubbed my face. "I don't know. Maybe."

He took our cups to the sink. I felt he was deciding what to say next. "So, you're okay now?" His voice sounded uncertain.

"Yes, I think so. As long as I have my meds." I glanced at the clock. "I guess it's getting late."

"Yeah, I guess it is." He took his coat from the hook. He hesitated by the door. "Do you think you should spend the night here?" he asked. I looked at him in surprise, wondering if he was offering to take me to his apartment. "Maybe you should go to a motel," he continued.

I thought about the creepy painting in Diana's room. I didn't like sleeping with it in the house. But I shook my head. "I should stay here."

He put on his coat. "Okay."

Since he had his coat on and there didn't seem to be more to say, I opened the door. "Thanks. Thanks for coming over. It means a lot to me."

"Sure."

I didn't know whether a hug was coming. He shoved his hands in his pockets, digging for his keys. It was not. "Good night."

"Good night."

I watched him get into his car and then shut the door. Then I went back to Diana's laptop. I knew Scott would disapprove, but maybe there was something I could find out. At least I wanted a sense of who Diana's friends were. Diana was organized, and her emails were in various folders. One was for the November poetry reading.

I clicked on a group email about the arrangements for the reading, hit reply all, and wrote:

"Hi, I'm Diana Cerf's roommate. I'm wondering if any of you have seen her in the past couple of days. Just kind of looking for her. Thanks, Wendy Zemansky."

When I went back to my room, I remembered Ann's homework assignment, to make a list of things that would make me feel like an adult. I got out a notepad and started to write:

"Gain and keep people's trust.
Be more proactive in life. (how?)
Don't try to control what people think of me.
Decide on thesis topic.
Get salt for driveway (take care of things better).
Find out more about Diana—be more helpful.
Take a risk rather than always being safe.
Try to stop writing notes."

Suddenly exhausted, I turned out the lights and went to bed, and dreamt of rescuing a child from the path of a speeding car.

CHAPTER NINE

I was awakened by the jarring ring of the phone at eight o'clock the next morning. In those days we still had landlines, and our number was in the book. The sheriff's department had released the missing persons bulletin to the AP overnight. From my wake-up call on, there were calls from the news networks, the cable outlets. (We didn't have cable because service didn't extend up our hill; these were channels I'd scarcely ever seen.) Then there was the Syracuse newspaper, the Binghamton newspaper, and two radio stations. I fielded the calls anxiously, stumbling over what to say, and gave them the number of the sheriff's department.

I was about to just turn off the ringer when there was another call. "It's Daniel Quinn."

"Daniel who?"

"You know me. I'm in your Gothic literature class."

I made the connection to the program I'd found in Diana's book. "Keep writing! Dan," it said. This must be Dan. "Right, right."

"I just heard. I'm the grad liaison to the department. You didn't report this to us. I'm surprised."

I was puzzled. "I did talk to both Dr. Hellmann and Dr. Kind." I tried not to feel I'd done something wrong.

"I see. Let's just keep each other informed. I'd like to help any way I can."

"Okay, thanks."

I couldn't take any more and turned off the ringer. I needed to shower. In the little gray stall, I thought that, however isolated in the country I was, the world outside my window the previous day was big and expansive, and now my world was the size of this thirty-six-inch shower stall.

When I came out the light was blinking on the phone. I took a deep breath, and listened to the message.

"It's Mark," a strange voice said. "I'll come over later." I had no idea who Mark was. His voice sounded tight, tensed. I wondered what to do. My first instinct was just to avoid. Avoid everything. And I didn't want to bother anyone—Scott, Deputy Polozzi—to be a burden, as women so often feel. I decided to get out my books and just get to my schoolwork until the press conference that night.

Hellmann's assignments were light, and I couldn't help suspecting that was part of his popularity as a teacher. The first assignment for Kind was a literature review. Though class had only met once, I already had some thoughts about the paper proposal. I'd been thinking about the role of mental illness in Gothic literature. There was *Jane Eyre*, *The Turn of the Screw*, "The Yellow Wallpaper," and of course Edgar Allen Poe. It seemed a ripe subject for research, and I buried myself in books and online sources.

After a few hours, my Internet went out. I sighed. This wasn't unusual; our DSL was glitchy. I got up, feeling cold, and turned up the thermostat. I was wondering why it was still so cold when I tried to turn on the stove and found there was no gas. Great. I didn't know the exact name of the gas company. I didn't know where Diana kept the bills; there was nothing around the telephone or in the drawer of the end table. I felt panicky and like a child. Taking three deep breaths, I tried to relax and think of Scott and how calm he would be. This helped—and I realized the solution. I called the landlord.

"Hi, Mr. Kulik, it's Wendy. We ran out of gas and I was wondering if you know the name of the gas company, maybe their phone number?"

"Out of gas! I'll call them right away. You okay? How long you been out?" He was an old man, genial but much put upon. I hated to bother him.

"Just today. I'm okay. Oh, oh." I realized I had to tell him about Diana. "Diana is kind of missing."

"Kind of missing? What the hell does that mean?"

I explained it all.

"You're doing the right things," he said. "Do you want to stay here at my house for a bit?"

I warmed at his kindness. "No, thanks, thank you so much. That's nice of you. I'm okay."

"Well, you take care. I'm sure Diana will turn up. I'll call the gas company right now."

I hung up and went back to my little wall of books. The phone rang, and I was happy, thinking it must be Scott this time. I even answered, "Scott?"

"It's Mark," a strained voice said.

My whole body sagged in disappointment. "I'm sorry. You sound like I should know you, but I don't."

"I was Diana's boyfriend until the end of summer. You emailed me in the middle of the night." I'd forgotten the email, to the poetry reading group. "I'd like to come over. What is the sheriff doing?"

"There's a press conference at seven o'clock."

"Okay, I'll be there before then."

"Do you know the address?"

He made an impatient noise. "I lived there." He hung up.

Now I had this to be nervous about, meeting the boyfriend she'd probably had a bad break up with. As the kitchen grew dark, I wondered when the gas would be delivered. Outside the window a powerful-sounding car pulled up, and I hoped it was the gas company's truck, but it was the deputy. I let him in, and we stood in the kitchen.

"I just wanted to touch base," he said. "Diana's family arrived and is staying at the motel. They'll be at the press conference tonight."

"The press has been calling me all day."

He nodded. "You can refer them to us. Have you heard from anyone?"

We remained standing. He did not seem like a sitting-down kind of person. "Today—" I stopped. I couldn't possibly incriminate this total stranger.

"Yes?"

"Well, I talked to her former boyfriend today."

"What's his name?"

I felt myself blush. "Mark something. I don't know his last name. I'm sure she hasn't seen him in months—she never mentioned him. He's coming over here now."

Deputy Polozzi raised his eyebrows and cocked his head. "That's convenient."

I felt hot and dizzy, feeling I had set a trap for this man now.

It wasn't long before Mark showed up, a tall, thin young man with a shock of red hair. His eyes glowed with contained fury, his mouth turned into a hard line. There was something weirdly beautiful to his angry, ruthless face.

"I'm Mark." He stepped inside and was immediately faced by the deputy. He swung around and faced me with blazing eyes. "You called the police on me?"

"No!"

"Excuse me," the deputy said. "What is your full name?"

"Mark Leone. Are you going to read me my rights?"

The deputy gave Mark a steady, calming look. "We don't know if there's been a crime. We just want to talk to everyone who knows Diana. We just want to find her."

Mark exhaled and his shoulders dropped. He lowered his head, his glare pushing me down into the chair in the corner.

"I came here to find out what's going on, because I don't know anything," Mark said.

"When was the last time you saw her?"

I watched them, thinking they were two young men, who understood each other in that unspoken, gender-specific way, and that Mark was never going to make allowances for me the way the deputy was for him.

"It must have been November, at a poetry reading. It was the first time I'd seen her since we broke up. I wanted to see her read. I took her out afterward, but we got into a big fight. She stormed out."

Deputy Polozzi nodded, frowning. "Will you come with me and make a statement?"

Mark glanced around the room. I thought he probably wanted to look around the house for clues, that that was why he had come. He shrugged. "All right."

The two men left. I watched them through the window. The deputy had Mark ride with him in his vehicle. After they left, I realized Mark's car was blocking mine.

I called Scott's cell phone and got his voicemail. "It's Wendy. Please come over when you get this, my car's blocked in, it's a long story."

I paced around, feeling like a rat in a maze, or a leopard at the zoo. *Everything is connected, roads and telephones. You can go anywhere, communicate with anyone wherever you are, and I'm trapped here and there's no one I can call. I might as well be in a prairie cabin a hundred years ago. The only technology I have that works is the clock telling me my life is ticking away.*

I was hungry but there was still no gas. I thought about putting something in the microwave, but the only thing in the freezer was Diana's vegetarian lasagna, and I hesitated about eating Diana's food. It seemed like bad luck.

There was a knock on the door, and Scott opened it and leaned in. "Hello? Did you just try to call me?"

I ran and swung the door open wide for him. "It's been a crazy day, and I'm out of gas."

"Out of gas? I can go to the station and fill a can for you."

"No, I mean the house is out of gas."

He was about to take off his coat, then realizing how cold it was, he left it on. "Did you call the gas company?"

"They should be here soon."

"How long ago did you call?"

"I called the landlord, I think it was around 2:00."

He rolled his eyes. "They're taking that long? Did you tell them you were completely out?"

"Well, I'm sure they realize that. I don't know their number, actually, that's why I called the landlord."

"You should call him again."

"They know. I don't want to bother him again."

"Why don't you assert yourself? It's their mistake!"

I held up my hands in a gesture that meant, "Calm down," then rapidly patted his shoulder. "It's okay, it's okay," I said in desperation. I had so rarely seen him angry.

"I'm not upset with you, don't do that. That's annoying." He turned away from me, and I stepped back, cowed. "I just think you worry too much that you're going to upset people. They made a mistake, you're suffering for it, and it's up to them to fix it."

"Okay. It's—" I stopped myself.

"I'm not upset with you."

I swallowed and rubbed my eyes. "I don't know how to act."

From outside came the sound of a big truck, then clanking and banging noises as they filled the tank. "They're here," I said. Scott and I stood in silence until an abrupt knock startled me. The gas man was at the door.

"Got to light your pilots," he said. "Sorry about this, you were scheduled for yesterday, thought we could put it off one day. Guess we couldn't. Your tank is a small one, you might want to consider getting a second tank."

He went to the stove and lit the pilots. "Gas hot water heater?" he asked.

"I don't know. It's in the basement. There's a dryer too."

He nimbly trotted down the cellar steps, as if eager to make up for their mistake. He was back upstairs quickly. "You're all set. Have a good night now." He banged the door shut.

"I'm sorry," I said.

"Stop being sorry." Scott took my hand. "I just don't like it when you act like I'm upset, when I'm not. You overreact."

"Okay. I'm sorry."

He shook my hand firmly. "You don't have to be sorry all the time. Just stop it."

"Okay." He let go of my hand. I took a deep breath and composed myself. "Anyway, this man, Mark, was Diana's boyfriend. He was just here and left with the deputy and now his car is blocking mine."

"I'll take you to the press conference."

I tried to discern if this was an imposition. But his manner was that he had a duty to perform and was willing to do it. He was being responsible, no more, no less.

"So this guy Mark just came over?" he asked in the car. "I'm glad the police were here."

"There was nothing to be scared of," I said.

"Just don't be reckless. Don't become his new best friend. It's not your responsibility."

*   *   *

The press conference was in something like a classroom down a hall from the sheriff's office. Drawn blinds were broken and missing slats. Rust stained the acoustic ceiling. I was aware of cameras and microphones, some good-looking men in tailored suits from cable networks, and older sloppily dressed reporters from local papers. Bright lights shone onto a desk at the front where the sheriff was talking to a woman and a young man, Diana's relatives. The sheriff turned away to check the microphones.

Deputy Polozzi came over to Scott and me and introduced us to Diana's relatives. Her Aunt Jackie was about fifty, with blond hair pulled into a braid, her gray pantsuit subtly expensive looking, with smooth, unwrinkled fabric. Diana's brother Greg was in his early twenties, with thick brown hair and big dark brown eyes, tilted up a bit at the corners. I stared at him. I saw that these were Diana's eyes, but soft, without her piercing intensity.

I had to think about how to meet strangers, and held out my hand in a limp handshake. Jackie's handshake was brisk and firm.

"I'm not sure what I'm doing here," I said.

"Thanks for coming," Aunt Jackie said with a crisp nod.

The sheriff did all the talking, his manner calm, almost casual. He stated the facts that Diana hadn't been seen in two days, that evidence indicated she was last home the day before yesterday. He didn't mention the party or the receipt. He announced a hotline number people could call and said search parties would start combing the woods and fields the next day at sunrise. The heavy snow would be a hindrance. Then he introduced Jackie, who made a brief appeal for information.

The reporters focused their questions on whether this could be related to the Cassandra Sommers case. After the sheriff deflected those, they asked if this could be a runaway bride case, or whether there were any suspects for foul play. The sheriff was terse in his replies. I watched Mark the whole time. I saw that Greg was staring at Mark, too.

Afterward, Mark went straight to me. "My car's at your place. Can I have a lift?"

I nodded, then looked at Scott.

"Sure," Scott said, neither cold nor friendly.

"We'll follow you back to the house," Greg said.

I assented with a sinking feeling. I did not want to have all these people over, to have to talk to them. In the car, I turned around to Mark, who was slumped in the back. "I honestly didn't call the police over you. It was a coincidence."

His eyes still glowed with anger, anger not necessarily at me, but over the situation. "That's fine," he said.

I longed to ask if the police had brought up Diana's pregnancy to him, but I couldn't bring myself to ask. We rode in silence.

Aunt Jackie and Greg parked at the side of the road, and Scott pulled up beside Mark's car. "I'll be back another time," Mark said as he hurried out. But Greg rushed up to him.

"So she was having your kid," Greg shouted.

"Leave it alone, Greg," Aunt Jackie called out as she carefully trod the icy driveway in her heels.

"They told me she bought an EPT," Mark replied. "Which could just as well have been negative. If she's pregnant, it isn't by me. I haven't been with her since last summer. Now leave me the hell alone." Mark strode to his car, but Greg ran after him and grabbed his arm. "Don't be a jerk!" Mark exclaimed.

Scott hurried up to them. "Let him go. It's up to the sheriff."

Greg swung around to Scott while Mark got in his car. "The sheriff of East Buttfuck, New York? This hillbilly shithole? Barney Fife isn't going to find her. This is where people disappear."

Mark jumped into his car and sped away with a squeal of the engine that pierced the night.

"Let's go inside," Jackie said with exasperation.

Greg thrust his hands in his pockets and shuffled his feet, but didn't move forward. "What was she keeping secret, that she couldn't tell us?" He turned to me. "And he did see her since last summer. She said so in an email. She didn't talk to you?"

I wrung my hands to resist patting his shoulder, remembering what Scott had said about overreacting. "No. She was very private."

"Private," he said with a sneer.

"I feel guilty she didn't talk to me, too."

"I don't feel guilty, I'm angry!"

My mind raced to recover. Counseling training had been part of my teacher education. The important thing was to reflect, to summarize the person's feelings back to them. "You have every right to be angry and frustrated."

He squeezed his eyes shut for a moment.

"It's a frustrating situation and we're all feeling desperate. But this is only the beginning and we have a long road ahead of us. We have to be strong, for Diana. We have to keep a united front and help each other through this."

That calmed him. He took a deep breath and patted his pockets. "I left my phone at the motel. Let's go back in case someone calls."

"Good idea," Jackie said. We walked back to their car. "If you think of anything, please call us," she said, and they left. I took a deep breath; it felt like my first breath all evening.

Once inside, we were blasted with heat. "I forgot, I kept putting up the thermostat when I ran out of gas." I turned it down.

Scott loosened his coat. "Are you okay? I think you helped defuse that situation."

"I felt pretty helpless."

He took my hands in his. "We all do, that's normal."

"Thanks." I took off my coat, but he kept his on.

"Well, good night," he said.

I looked at him. I wanted to ask if we were friends again, if the past was over, if things could be the same as they had been before. He seemed to wait a moment. Then he gave my hand a squeeze.

"Lock the door behind me."

I closed the door as he left, and locked it for the first time.

CHAPTER TEN

During the night, the storm came like a pack of wolves. This was the winter I grew up with, fierce wind snarling at the windows, leaking in through every crack in the defense, the thin walls weak protection against the rage. The snow didn't fall, but lashed horizontally through the air, leaping, howling.

I lay awake. Winter had begun. As I tossed and turned, I came to one thing again and again—what was the date or the time on the EPT receipt? I wanted to be sure when the last day was that Diana was home, wanted to know if I'd seen her at the party, or if that was impossible.

When morning came, the wind subsided. The landscape outside rolled in waves of white. I took my medication and drank some coffee, not hungry for breakfast. The phone rang in the stillness. *Please stop calling me.*

"Hello Wendy, it's Jean Hellmann."

I felt more awake at the unexpected call. "Oh, hi Mrs. Hellmann. Professor Hellmann."

"Wendy, the deputy asked us about Diana. I'd like to ask you to stop saying you saw her at our party. She wasn't there."

I felt myself blush in shame. "I'm sorry. I was sure I saw her. I wanted to be accurate—"

"Didn't you say you had an accident that day? That very day? You hit a deer?"

"Yes."

"So you had a concussion. You could have been confused. You did seem out of it at the party."

"Did I?"

"I'm sorry you were hurt. I hope you sought medical attention. But it isn't right to tell people she was there when she wasn't. I'd like to ask you to stop."

I trembled. "Okay, I will. I'm sorry, Professor Hellmann."

"It's okay. I suppose it's too late now anyway. Take care of yourself, Wendy."

"Okay, thanks."

"Goodbye."

I stared at the phone. I thought about what Ann said about children of alcoholics, how they hate to do the wrong thing. Maybe it wasn't so bad, maybe I made it bigger than it was. A loud knock on the door made me jump.

Mark stood outside with his hands shoved deep into his pockets. I imagined they were balled in fists. Tiredness softened the intensity of his look, but his eyes still shone with anger.

"Can I come in?" he asked. It was a quiet demand.

He entered, taking off his coat and tossing it on the back of a kitchen chair. He wore tight black leather gloves that he didn't take off. They were the sort of gloves you wore to strangle someone.

"I'd like to see her room." Another demand, not loud but firm.

In the shadowy room Diana's paintings glowed. Mark slowly turned, taking them in.

"Have you seen these before?" I asked.

His mouth was a hard line. "I already told you I hadn't seen her. I suppose you're trying to trap me into admitting I've been here—"

"No, I—"

"Forget it." He waved his gloved hand and walked up to each painting. "She changed a lot since then. These aren't her. She wasn't bitter like this." He approached a sunny one, a field of abstract flowers. "This one I did see, early on. This is her. It's the only one I recognize."

I kept glancing at the creepy one on the easel, the gray smeared face with its long teeth.

"Did you know she was changing her major?" I asked.

He chuckled coldly. "Still trying to trap me. No, I didn't talk to her. You don't have to tell me. I can see by this something was going on. I don't know what. Do you?" He suddenly wheeled around and glared at me.

"No. I'm sorry."

He shook his head and turned to the portrait. "This sure looks like a killer. She nailed it." He stepped back, then suddenly walked out of the room. I followed.

"Have you even checked the basement?" he asked.

"What?"

He gave a strange, hostile smile. "She's been missing three days. Has anyone looked in the basement?"

"No." My breath felt icy cold in my lungs.

Without another word he headed for the basement door in the kitchen. The rough stairs creaked and strained underfoot, dangerously slanted. The single bare light bulb threw shadows across the rubble walls, their ancient white paint peeling and crackled. Chips of white paint sifted on the edges of the floor like snow. A smell of must rose from the damp concrete and dusty black pipes crisscrossed overhead, tentacles coming out of the boiler in the center. The landlord's shelves lined one wall with old paint cans and tools. A washing machine and dryer marked off the one clean corner, the wall painted yellow by Diana to keep back the decay.

There wasn't much to the space, and Mark circled the boiler, his eyes darting. In the last corner, deep in shadow, was an old chest freezer, unplugged. I wanted to block it from him, dreaded the thought of opening it. He went up to it, placing his gloved hand around the edge. It opened with a groan and a horrible stench filled the basement. I felt faint and put my hand over my mouth. *Please don't let it be her.*

He closed it again, coughing.

"What was it?" I gasped.

Mark wiped the sweat from his forehead. "The head of a deer. Hunted and forgotten a long time ago."

I fought to keep my head clear. "We don't know she's been murdered. She could have run away. She could be on a beach in California right now."

In the darkness a thin stream of light highlighted his tense jaw. He stared past me. "She's under the snow somewhere." His voice suddenly weak, plaintive.

We climbed back upstairs. In the kitchen, Mark rinsed his dusty gloves at the sink. We stood silently for a minute.

"She was going to have an art show," I said. "She was finishing those paintings for it."

"At the Spring Street Gallery?" he asked.

"Yes."

"She would never just abandon something like that. That's how I know she didn't run away." He clenched his gloved hands.

"Whatever happened, let's have the show. We can arrange it." I wanted so much to win him over.

He took a deep breath and his eyes grew soft. "We'll still have it. I'll get in touch with the gallery. It will be something. Thank you." He took off a glove and wiped his eyes, then walked to the door. When he faced me, he looked as if he was coming to himself. "Well, thanks for letting me in. We're going to find her. We're going to resolve this. No matter what."

It was nice that he said 'we.' "Yes, we will. Take care of yourself."

He nodded and went out into the bright snow-lit driveway and left. I closed the door, my heart beating fast. I hadn't actually looked into the freezer to see the deer head. Maybe I should. Would it make sense for him to have lied about it? I was right there and could have seen if it were anything different.

I crept down the stairs, slipping a little with each slanted step. All was still, as it was before, silent. My neck pulsed. I bent toward the freezer and slowly lifted the lid, choking as the suffocating stench rose again. The doe's eyes were open, glossy even in death, the tip of its grayed tongue sticking out the side of its mouth. For a moment, I was hypnotized by it. Then I slammed the lid down and ran stumbling up the steps.

CHAPTER ELEVEN

I emailed my mother that night and told her Diana was missing, and the next morning she replied:

"Wow! You see, cities are much safer than the country, in reality. Do you think you should get a gun? Or at least it's time you got a cell phone. I can send you the money. I've also heard a dog is a good idea. You could use a dog. A greyhound would be lovely. I can see you walking an elegant greyhound, with a pretty jeweled collar, like a drawing by Erté. Think it over. Let me know how much you need for a cell phone."

She was right, it was time I got one.

The gun idea was jarring, however. The mother of my childhood was disparaging of the NRA, but no longer. I wrote back, "I'll look into the phone, thanks," and hurried to school.

The first thing I noticed on my way to class were the flyers posted around campus, with Diana's picture and the word MISSING in large letters. Where had they come from? I was at the heart of it, had been the first one even to notice Diana had disappeared, and now all kinds of wheels were in motion that I wasn't even aware of.

I sat at the little desk. When Dr. Hellmann came in, he set down his heavy-looking briefcase, and immediately came over to me. Again I thought he was so handsome, like an older male model in his gray sweater and cords, yet oddly unappealing.

He looked chagrined. "I'm sorry about the other day. I really didn't think she was missing."

"That's okay."

"I've asked around for her all I could. No one has seen her. I spoke with the police."

"I'm sure the authorities will figure it out," I said.

His grim face seemed to ask, *Why would they this time? They never found Cassandra.*

During class at first, he seemed distracted and tense, and by the end he only seemed tired. The class was divided between those who were subdued and depressed at Diana's disappearance, and those who were chatty and excited that something had happened in our tiny corner of the world.

As the classes changed over from Hellmann's to Kind's, Dr. Kind came to the doorway and walked lightly up to him asking how he was. Kind's face was full of tender sympathy, squeezing Hellmann's elbow as he left, *as if Hellmann's the one this is happening to,* I thought.

When the Gothic literature class had settled in, Dr. Kind said, "I'm sure we're all upset and worried about Diana, and we'll do our best. I was out this morning with one of the search parties. But still, we do have to get on."

The students who had been excited and chatty got quiet, suddenly embarrassed by their attitude. "We also owe a little debt to Miss Zemansky here, for having the presence of mind to report Diana's absence so quickly." He gestured to me, and I reddened. The other students looked at me with surprise.

Dr. Kind conducted the class with his usual efficient, scholarly air, and afterwards a small knot of students surrounded me and asked about my part in the mystery. I floated out of the room in their midst. Some were acquainted with Diana, having seen her at the last reading in November, when she had made such an impression on the crowd.

We went to the cafeteria together and settled at a table by the window with trays of dry French fries, giant pizza slices, and subs with lettuce and onion spilling out of them. The group listened intently while I read to them from Diana's book, which I had brought with me.

"Jealousy, the dark heart of love that isn't love, but need,
A love that never comes to seed."

The group oohed. The girl from the party, Carolyn, asked "Do you think this is a clue?" Her eyes loomed inquisitively from behind her glasses.

Daniel Quinn rubbed his hands together with a flourish. "Of course. Maybe you should even share this book with the sheriff. Who knows what it might reveal? Are there any names in this book?"

I flipped through it. "I don't think so. No."

"Who was jealous?" he asked.

"You shouldn't read into it, Sherlock," said Carolyn. The group laughed.

"Scott told me not to be Nancy Drew," I said.

Daniel picked up the book. "Who doesn't love Nancy Drew? Besides, you want to feel useful. What's that note?" he asked, pointing out the lavender program.

"Looks like the program from the reading," Carolyn said.

I nodded and slid it out. "I was thinking of contacting the people on it, or giving it to the deputy."

"That's an idea. I wasn't there that night, but I heard about it," Daniel said.

I started. His note was right there on the program—"Keep writing! Dan." He seemed like a nice guy, eager to solve the mystery apparently out of intellectual curiosity. Why would he lie now? Was he trying to distract us, throw us off? Maybe that was too paranoid, like something out of a TV show.

"I think Professor Hellmann might have some insight about this poetry," Daniel continued. "You should bring this to him."

I coughed and took a big swallow of diet soda. "Well, I don't know if I should get into it with him. I don't have a lot of credibility there, anyway."

"What do you mean?"

I put the program back into the book. "Well, I thought I saw Diana that night, outside at the Hellmann's party. But maybe I was confused. I hit my head that afternoon." But I felt that perhaps the real reason Jean Hellmann had called me, doubting my story wasn't because of the concussion, but because the Hellmanns knew I was bipolar. Ever since Jean had called, I anxiously wondered if maybe they considered me a little crazy.

Daniel asked, "Did anyone else see her? I was at the party, and I don't remember her there."

"Did you see her?" I asked Carolyn.

She shook her head.

Scott entered the cafeteria and I waved. He crossed through the crowd of tables and joined us.

"You missed having lunch with us," I said, flushed with excitement.

"I'll get some coffee." He took off his coat and playfully wrapped his scarf around my neck.

"Let me get it!" I bounced up and bounded for the coffee before he could reply. It came back to me, how he took it, with a lot of milk and no sugar. When I got back, they were discussing the literary journal.

"Should we dedicate it to Diana, or, is that morbid?" Carolyn asked.

Daniel stroked his goatee. "I don't think so."

Scott was quiet, looking uncomfortable as he stirred his coffee.

"One o'clock," Carolyn said, looking at her watch. "More lectures await." The little group got up, leaving me alone with Scott.

He picked up Diana's book. "She was a great writer, too. I remember now, I was at the reading in November. It's been a while, so I didn't think about it." As he looked through it, I tried to read his face.

"Now you're saying 'was.'"

He answered with a pained squint. "Right. Sorry." He abruptly got up and put his coffee cup in the bin with a slow, tired gait. When he came back we sat in silence for several long moments. He looked embarrassed. "I was probably a jerk last night. There's something about the way you put yourself down. Somehow it triggers me."

It hadn't occurred to me that it was *his* problem. "When you get upset, I assume it's my fault. That I did something wrong."

"I know, that's what makes it so hard. I want to get the point across that you need a bigger ego, but I have the opposite effect. I can't seem to find a way out of this contradiction."

"We'll find a way."

He smiled in gratitude.

There was another pause, and then I ventured, "We never talked about that fight." He nodded, leaning forward, his face open and encouraging. "I know I was wrong. I understand I triggered you. That's the word, I know now."

He gestured to stop me. "Don't blame yourself. I overreacted. But I was baffled. I didn't understand what was going on."

Feeling assertive, I found the words for the first time. "I was worried about my friend's sanity. Sophie was my best friend. She was having delusions. You were arguing about the validity of her delusion, about whether astrology and reincarnation are real. As if that was the point. And I was scared as hell for her sanity, whether she might actually be suicidal. She thought she was Sylvia Plath. You know? How could you not get that?"

His eyes opened wide. He snorted in self-disgust. "Wow. I was a jerk. What a jerk. I'm sorry."

"It's okay. I'm just glad you finally understand." Relief flooded over me.

"I do." He grabbed my hand and squeezed it. As we sat there, the years flowed away and we were back, back to when we were in that strange, wonderful time of being best friends, better than lovers.

"Can I ask you for a favor?" I asked.

"Absolutely."

"Can you come with me to buy a cell phone? I don't know anything about them."

He drove me to the nearest phone shop in Corning and picked out a Motorola RAZR for me. I opted for silver.

On the way back, I told him my mother had urged me to get the phone. "And she keeps harping on whether I'm writing."

"You were always ambivalent about it, even years ago," he said.

"Was I?"

"Never wanted to call yourself a writer."

As the trees flickered by, I remembered our talks, our writing together. "Do you call yourself a writer?" I asked.

"It's been a long time since I tried."

"Me too. Well, we have that journal to edit."

We started to talk over the journal and make plans. When he dropped me off, I took off the scarf he'd wrapped around my neck and put it back on him, and he bent down and kissed my forehead. Like the old days. It was something, I realized then, that had always made me feel too young, like a child. It was never romantic, just a quirky part of our friendship.

"You can call me," he said with a smile. "Put my number in your phone."

I got out and as I watched him drive away, I thought that in the old days, I'd never realized how handsome he was.

CHAPTER TWELVE

"So she really is missing now," I said to Ann.

There was a soft tap on the door. Ann looked annoyed as she rose and opened it. The secretary stood outside, whispering, "Laura wants to see you."

"I'm in session," Ann replied, raising her voice.

"She just wants to give you a letter. She won't give it to me. She says she just wants to hand it directly to you. Something urgent."

Ann turned back. "I'm sorry, Wendy, this will only be a moment."

Looking back on it, I wonder what was more urgent than my missing roommate. I stood up to stretch, and idly began scanning the titles on her shelves. Meyers-Briggs, Patty Duke's memoir, Erik Erikson. My gaze stopped at a plain black spine, a thin volume. Diana's book. I went cold.

"I wasn't gone so long that you need a book to read."

I jumped at her voice and hurried back to the chair. "Sorry."

Ann tossed an envelope on the desk. "Where were we?" She settled down and took up her pad.

"Diana."

She put the pad aside to give me her full attention, and straightened her red-rimmed glasses to focus on me. "How are you?"

"I don't know. It's hard to know what to think."

"To think, or to *feel?*" She gave me a small smile.

I hesitated. For a change I'd finally brought a water bottle with me and I drank some. Ann made a throat-clearing noise as if she thought I was avoiding answering. This made me want to say the right thing, to get her approval.

"I want to do something. To help in some way."

"To take responsibility?"

I nodded, leaning forward. Our knees were almost touching. "Right. I'm joining the search party tomorrow."

"Why do you feel responsible?"

"We lived together. I didn't know her as well as I should have."

"*Should.*" Ann shook her head. "I'd like you to pay attention to how often you feel that, that sense of 'should.'"

I nodded, but I felt confused. I glanced behind her to the books. "Did you know Diana?"

"No." The word hung in the air. What was her voice like? Phony. Diana's book was right behind her. I knew confidentiality would prevent her from admitting it, but her answer was so quick, so easy. She picked up her pad, propping it on her crossed knee, in front of her chest. "You're using the past tense. Are you assuming Diana is dead?"

"I think it's a pretty safe assumption."

"But it's an assumption. Tell me more about how you feel about her. Before, you said you admired her. She's an adult to you."

"That's right."

"Maternal, maybe?"

I considered it. "I don't know. I wouldn't say she's the maternal type. She's tough. Take no prisoners. And funny. Quick-witted. Sarcastic."

"Humor means a lot to you."

I nodded.

"Humor means a lot to your family?"

"Sure. Yes. That's true, my mother loves comedy. British comedy."

"So Diana and your mother are both comedy aficionados."

"Right." There was another pause. I felt obtuse, like Ann wanted me to go in some direction, but I wasn't sure what it was. "Scott and I met that way, too. We were in a humor in literature class together."

Ann stifled a yawn and jotted it down. "Let's stick to this subject a moment." I wasn't sure which subject. I looked at her, waiting for her to tell me what it was. She looked at me, puzzled by my puzzlement.

"Your mother?" she ventured.

"Oh. Okay. It's just . . ."

She raised her brows.

"Diana . . ."

She nodded. "What I'm wondering is how Diana's going missing might be stirring up deeper feelings for you. Old feelings, issues from the past."

"Oh. Of course. I see. Actually I've been having these bad dreams, about accidents, about my Uncle Johnny."

"Who is your Uncle Johnny?"

I shrugged. "Well, he didn't live to become my uncle. He was my mother's younger brother. He was killed in a car accident when he was three. My mother was nine."

"What happened?"

I drank some water and straightened up, feeling like maybe this was what I was supposed to be talking about. "He fell out of their car when they were driving home from a picnic. This was before car seats. The door swung open, faulty somehow. He was hit by a truck behind them. My grandmother once mentioned how nice and understanding the truck driver was. She used to talk about it sometimes, when I was really little. She would say, 'He fell out of a locked door. A locked door . . .' I guess . . . it kind of freaked me out. It was a scary story."

"It certainly is! And how did your mother feel?"

"We've never discussed it. I've never asked her about it."

Ann's pen quickly scratched the page. "You know, this is a big story, and you've never mentioned it before."

"I don't know that much about it. When I was a child and we went to church, Grandma would always tell us to pray for Uncle Johnny. That's everything I know about it."

Ann looked thoughtful. "You say your mother was nine?"

"Yes. I don't even know why I know that. I guess I know what year he died."

"Is your grandmother still alive?"

"No, she died last summer."

"What about your grandfather?"

"He died when I was two."

Ann nodded. "This must have affected your mother's family very deeply. Did your grandfather drink?"

"I don't think so." I shrugged. "That wouldn't line up with everything I do know about him. It seemed like he was very busy, going to school at night, leading church committees."

"But perhaps he was a secret drinker. Your mother married an alcoholic."

This seemed unlikely. "He got an MA at night school. I think my grandmother years later went back to school, because she wanted to get the same degree as him. My mom went to night school, too, for the sake of her job, but she tells me not to be a school junkie, like grandma was."

Ann looked puzzled. "Still . . . your mother's family was quite the overachieving sort, wasn't it? I'm getting a picture of it. I've never really had much of a picture of your family."

"My brother . . ." I felt ready to talk about the painful argument we'd had. How he thought it was ridiculous to go back to school.

But Ann didn't seem to hear. "Think of how much you need closure for. There's this whole death of your Uncle Johnny, which has been with you like a mysterious family myth all your life."

"Right . . ." I wasn't sure what to say. Ann seemed so interested in me now. Maybe this was important. I spent some time talking about my childhood, my mother's restrictive Catholic upbringing and her running off to elope. I wanted to talk about what felt like pressure from my mother to be a writer, but it was hard to stay on topic—on the topics that mattered to me.

Ann checked her watch. Our time was almost up. "I know you want to feel like an adult." I sat forward eagerly. It felt like this was the first time she got it. "So I have an assignment for you. To pay attention whenever you actually do something adult. Get out a paper calendar, do you have one, in your kitchen?" I nodded, excited.

"And every time you do something adult, draw a happy face on the date. You'll see. You're doing it all the time, you just don't see it."

"Thanks. That's a good idea." I left, looking forward to drawing happy faces.

CHAPTER THIRTEEN

Above the rolling farmland, the hills were crowned with trees, and between the fields were creeks fringed in woods: Deerkill Creek, Owlkill Creek, and others, "kill" being the old Dutch word for creek. The locals called them "cricks."

I joined the early morning search party along the kill that trickled behind my house. The black water bubbled under icy edges. The trees were mostly hemlock and ash, with a few beeches shining with copper bark. The snow under the trees wasn't deep as it was in the fields, and some greenery poked through here and there.

The search party consisted of men in camo, hunters who knew the woods well. Some of them carried rifles out of habit, and one old man had a walkie talkie to communicate with another party led by the sheriff. We fanned out on each side of the creek, deeper into the woods and down the hill. Curious chickadees followed us amid the branches.

A young man identified tracks for me: the five-toed raccoon, the rounded gray fox print—he knew gray from red—and the parallel streaks left by leaping rabbits. Deer tracks were plentiful.

"Bambi's safe today, I suppose," he said, admiring the size of one hoof print. I had noticed hunters liked to speak contemptuously of people's sentimental attitudes by referring to deer as Bambi. "Suppose you like that," he said.

"I guess so."

"You look into those big brown eyes and you don't care about the infernal nuisance. They kill people. And they're good meat."

He wasn't an old man at all, maybe twenty-five, blond curls spilling out from under his camo hat, but a life among farmers and hunters, working the land and learning from it, had made him the same as any seventy-year-old farmer.

"I know," I said, wondering how to change the subject.

A familiar man approached us, Deputy Polozzi in his brown uniform coat. "Good morning, Wendy. Hi, Bill." He focused on me. "Can I see you?"

"Sure." We stopped and let Bill go ahead.

"I'd like to take Diana's computer. We want to search her emails and files. The FBI is coming tomorrow."

"I tried looking at her email a little, but then I wasn't sure I should."

"You didn't delete anything?"

"No, of course not." I wondered if there was more I could do. "I've thought a lot about Diana's situation. It seems like she was in a crisis. I'd like to talk to people and find out about it. I could, as a friend. It would be different than being questioned by you."

He looked at me with his inquisitive eyes. "That could be helpful, or dangerous."

"But it could help? I could tell you anything I find out. I'd like to know, to satisfy my own questions. I feel like Diana herself was a mystery, apart from her disappearance, a mystery I'd like to solve."

The deputy took this in in silence for a few beats. "I don't think I can stop you. But I'd like you to tell me anything." I searched his face for a sign of trust. "You seem like someone a person would confide in," he said, answering my search.

I was pleased. He did trust me. "Are you getting a lot of calls?"

He grimaced. "A few. Mostly not local. Nothing substantial."

We started again, catching up with Bill. Walking over the uneven, snowy ground was tiring and I breathed hard. After a while we reached an old drystone wall, green-speckled brown rocks, no mortar, at least a hundred years old. Bill stopped and leaned against it to light a cigarette. A little further on, some of the rocks had fallen in a little pile. I stared at them.

Polozzi seemed to notice the intent of my look. "What is it?"

I shivered. "Something about those rocks. They don't seem to have just fallen there. It doesn't look right."

Polozzi followed my gaze. Bill took a drag of his cigarette and said, "You know what, little girl? I think so too."

"It might be worth it." Polozzi took out his radio and spoke. "Can you come over to the wall behind Koval's farm with the dog?"

The white-haired, potbellied sheriff soon arrived with a German shepherd. Giving it a quiet command, he let the dog off the leash. It pounced on the rocks, pawing and whining.

I helped them pull away the cold, gritty rocks to reveal the black earth underneath. Lichen flaked off in my hands, sifting on the ground. Then I stood back while Bill and an old man gently dug with shovels, taking small scoops at a time. There was a shoe. It was plastic rather than leather, not degraded at all, still bright blue. A brown, mottled, skeletal foot was inside it, and they began to carefully uncover the rest of the body.

"That body's been here too long to be Diana," Bill said, taking a hard puff of his cigarette.

Polozzi nodded. "I think we just found Cassandra Sommers."

CHAPTER FOURTEEN

I thought Jean Hellmann was so different from me, with her no-nonsense air and brisk walk. I didn't know yet the tremor in those legs, the knot in her taut stomach.

Jean arrived at the center of Caspar Hall's labyrinthine corridors and tried to orient herself. Her office and classroom as a biology professor were in Kennedy Hall, which was still referred to as the new science building. Kennedy was modern and streamlined, the rooms in a clear grid. Serpentine Caspar Hall always threw her and she didn't like coming here. Stairs ascended on two sides like an Escher print, capped by an old skylight dim with snow. Voices echoed down the stairs, but the ground floor seemed empty. It was Friday afternoon and she was glad it was deserted.

She passed a forlorn rubber plant starved for light. The shell of a public phone holder hung empty of its phone, but the old phone book still lay under it. Phone books were supposed to be thick, but this, white and yellow pages together, made less than an inch.

She took the hall to her left. This seemed familiar. There were pale rectangles on the lilac walls where paintings had once hung, black holes like little bird's eyes where the hooks had been, taken down for a repainting job that never materialized. Another twist and she was at the door of her husband's office. She turned the knob to find it wasn't locked. He was careless.

The weak light revealed a tangle of papers on the desk, a partly open file cabinet, stacks and shelves of books. She winced at the mess. The book would be hard to find. Papers were layered and sandwiched, writing with notes on slips dangling out of them, books marked with folders or even other books tucked inside them, all these papers and books mating in an orgy of the printed word.

Jean had thought the slim black book would stand out somehow. She stepped around his desk to the bookshelves and ran her hand along the volumes, skimming the titles, looking for one with no title on the black spine. Would he have just put it on the shelf? Would it be in a special place? After a few minutes she realized there was some order. Textbooks were together, then novels. Closer to his desk were poetry books, thinner than the others. They were in alphabetical order by author. Amazing, he wasn't as sloppy as it seemed, it was there—with the C's. She slid it out and tucked it under her arm.

"Hey Jean." A friendly voice broke the silence. She jumped and turned around. Tommy Kind was smiling at her. "I have a nice bottle of bourbon in the drawer. Care for a little drink? It's Friday."

Tommy's reassuring arm guided her to his nearby office. He tugged his bow tie loose, his gray mustache twitching above his smile. He got out two Dixie cups and poured them each a healthy shot.

"Cheers." They raised the little paper cups.

"So, one of them has been found," he mused. "I'm so sorry, I know Cassandra was your T.A."

She took a gentle sip, warmed by the golden drink. She still clutched the book in her other hand. "Yes. But I'm not surprised."

"He hit her, didn't he? What was his name. John Paul Flaherty. They're already looking for him."

She nodded. "We had an intervention, actually. Dan and I. Got her away from him. For all the good it did."

He refilled her cup. "Sometimes you just can't help people. It's fate sometimes, you know?" He shrugged. "Anyway, I'm glad you're here. I wanted to talk to you." He wiped a drop of the bourbon off his mustache. "It's about Dan. Earlier today he told me he was thinking of moving on."

"Moving on?" Jean covered her confusion by finishing her drink in a big gulp. Moving on without her?

Tommy poured another shot. "He's going to tell you tonight. Tired of the big fish in a small pond thing. Maybe go to some big city, where you could go to med school. I know you once thought about that. But for God's sake, he's tenured. He can't just give that up."

Jean closed her eyes. Yes, get away. Anywhere away from this little mud hole.

"So you have to talk him out of it."

Jean took another sip, feeling good and warm now. "Maybe it would be for the best."

He gave her a puzzled look. "You're not serious. Leaving now? Your daughter just started college. You need security. And you couldn't afford med school, realistically. He's *tenured*. So are you. Are you going to let her drive you away?"

"Her?" She wished she didn't know who he meant.

"Yes, her."

Jean's hand fluttered and she set the book on the desk.

"Her," he repeated. "I see you took it." He picked up the book.

She set down her cup, her hand shaking. Tommy knew everything. There was no point in being secretive. "I didn't think it should be in his office right now."

He smiled. "Of course not. Let me take it."

Maybe he was right. No one would notice it with him.

"It will be our little secret," he said, putting his finger to his lips.

"So you knew everything," she said, the bourbon making her voice a husky whisper. "Keeper of secrets?"

Tommy blushed. "Well, I don't know. It wasn't put into so many words. We would go out for a drink, but he'd break it off early, to go off somewhere, and I didn't think it was home. It was only a suspicion. I suppose for you, too?"

She shook her head, and drained the cup. He poured a third drink. "Not a suspicion. I knew. Because of that book. It was on his desk one day when I was waiting in his office. I opened it and saw . . . her childish scribblings, little love notes between the poems." Her hands were calm now. It was starting to be a relief to talk about it.

"I don't pretend to understand such things. Since Nina left for the brighter lights of L.A., Eros has been a mystery to me. Maybe it always was."

Maybe she left because you call it "Eros," Jean might have thought.

"I'm sorry, Jean. Maybe I should have said something." His pale blue eyes were soft.

"No, it wasn't up to you."

"Did you confront him?"

She shook her head. "I thought maybe it was just her imagination. A fantasy. Even though I had the impression she wasn't the fantasy type. I waited. Just waited. But maybe it's time I talked with him. Get it all out. Maybe we can start over. In a new place."

His eyes widened. "You must feel like you're drowning here."

She laughed into her cup, because it was so true.

"Jean, it was only one of those midlife things, don't you think? I know, it's a betrayal. And if it was that unforgivable, should you even stay?" He looked at her tenderly. "You have to decide, what do *you* want?"

That was the question. "What I want is for him to tell me. Not to make me guess. Not to make me accuse him."

Tommy poured a final round. "Well, you know I'm a friend to both of you. Whatever you decide. But maybe it's something to consider, moving on."

She took the last sip of her bourbon, feeling woozy, wondering what was real and what was the alcohol. "We've had too much to drink." The small bottle was half empty.

His smile, like a naughty child's, remained as he tucked the bottle back in the drawer. "We'll talk again."

She rose on wobbly legs, thinking she'd better walk a while before driving home. She glanced back from the doorway. Despite his bald spot and gray mustache, Tommy looked so like a little boy.

CHAPTER FIFTEEN

As others from the search parties gathered round, I was able to drift into the background. Various police arrived. We were told to get back. I both wanted and didn't want to look at the skeleton. Through the crowd I saw a bright pink dress, and a skull with red hair, its braid dangling. A woman from the coroner's office gently tucked the braid under the skull on the stretcher. When they'd taken the body away, I left and called Scott from my new cell. He picked me up by the woods, somehow understanding just where I was from my stammered description.

We went to my home and I made us a lunch of canned lentil soup. I stirred the soup in the bowl, wishing it weren't the color of Cassandra's bones.

"You're sure this was Cassandra?" he asked.

"I think so. The people around me were convinced. So how do you think it relates to Diana?"

He frowned. "There's no reason to think it does. Not at all."

I forced down a spoonful of soup. "I don't know. Two young women, both students . . ."

Scott set down his spoon and gave me a firm look. "How many years apart? Five? And they had nothing else in common? We have no idea if Diana was murdered. She might be sunning herself on a beach somewhere right now."

"Out of nowhere, without telling anyone? Scaring her family to death? She wouldn't do that."

He nodded. "But there's still no reason to try to connect them. I know it's human nature," he said more gently now. "It's irresistible to look for patterns. Because we're story tellers. People, I mean. We look for patterns. But life is more random than that."

He finished eating as my soup went cold. He was right, but if I was wrong to look for a connection, I thought he was equally wrong to be so sure there wasn't one. He was too insistent.

He seemed to sense my thoughts. "The point is . . . I don't want you to drive yourself crazy over it. It won't be good for you."

I bristled at his condescending concern. "I'm fine."

"I don't mean . . ." He sighed with frustration. "I'd say that anyway, not because of your condition."

I wasn't mollified, but I didn't argue. He stayed awhile and we kept an eye on the news reports. Pretty soon Cassandra was definitely identified. They were looking for her old boyfriend, a known drug dealer.

When Scott had to leave, he put his hand on my shoulder. "I can't control you, but please take me seriously." His hand felt heavy.

I knew what mattered to him: to be trusted. "I'd like the same," I said.

His jaw tightened. "We'll talk again soon." He left, both of us feeling the other didn't get it.

The landline rang a few minutes later. The caller ID was Diana's Aunt Jackie, but her brother Greg's voice greeted me.

"I saw on the news about this girl they found. Is there anything you know?" His voice was sad, pleading.

I told him what little there was.

"I'm sure you understand how upset I was that night," he said by way of apology.

"Of course."

He lingered on the phone, but there wasn't more to say. "You'll tell me if anything comes up? I'm depending on you."

"I'll do my best."

After we hung up, I resolved that no matter Scott's concern, I would do what I could to figure this out and help Greg.

As it grew dark, I focused on my schoolwork. I felt I made good progress on it, investigating Henry James' mentally ill sister and the conditions of madhouses in the nineteenth century. I sat at the kitchen table with one light on, the rest of the house blurring into dusk. I contemplated those days when madness was almost a death sentence, when mental wards were rife with disease and despair. So many conditions were lumped together under that word, "madness," a word that evoked fear and revulsion. Yet Poe and others had lent it a kind of romance as well. The mad artist, the mad poet, were icons of genius. Well, I did not feel like a genius.

I heard a car but didn't pay attention to its stopping. When a loud knock thundered at the door, I jumped. I opened the door to Deputy Polozzi and let him in. I went around and turned on the lights while he waited, standing in the living room with his pad; once again he wouldn't sit. He stood over me while I sank onto the couch.

"We ID'd Cassandra Sommers," he stated.

"I heard it on the news," I said, eager to know whatever information he had. "Is there any link to Diana?"

"That's what we're wondering."

I felt vindicated, wishing Scott were there to hear that.

"Did you know Cassandra?" the deputy asked.

"No, I never really heard of her."

He wrote in his pad, his pen scratching like Ann's. "You were never in a class with her?"

"No. I think she was—the news said biology. And it was before I was here."

"Where did you live before you came here?"

This seemed strange. "Outside Utica."

"Do you have friends who knew Cassandra?"

"I don't think so. Not as far as I know."

"Cassandra went to Utica College."

I started to feel weird. "I heard that too." Scott and I had met there, but it wouldn't have been at the same time Cassandra was there. But . . . actually it could have been.

He looked like he was deciding what to ask next.

"I really don't know anything," I said, my voice weakening. I reached to turn on another lamp, and the bulb blew, the flare blinding me for a moment.

He didn't blink. "I'm wondering why you asked about her the first day you came to me."

That was it. It was true, I had asked. "Well, my roommate was gone and I heard once that a while ago a young woman disappeared. It only made sense to wonder." As he paused, regarding me, I raised my voice. "It only made sense."

His face was impassive, but he closed his pad. "Please don't upset yourself. We're just following every possible lead." He turned to go, and I was glad to walk him out. At the door, his look fixed on me, drawing himself up with feet planted, he said, "Right now, we just try to make connections. You asked about Cassandra. You were there when we found her. Diana was your roommate. So far, you're the only connection we have."

When he left, I collapsed at the table, my knees shaking.

CHAPTER SIXTEEN

I sat in the waiting room outside Ann's office, a magazine in my lap. I loved looking at *The New Yorker* before our appointments, skimming the articles and poring over the poems.

"Jealousy, the dark heart of love that isn't love, but need,
A love that never comes to seed."

I caught my breath. I didn't know Diana had been published in *The New Yorker*. The line leapt out at me again. "Jealousy, the dark heart of love that isn't love, but need,/A love that never comes to seed." The line from Diana's poetry book. But the rest of the poem wasn't the same. When I came to the end, the byline stated, "Dan Hellmann." I shivered. It was unmistakable. Professor Hellmann had plagiarized Diana's work.

"Wendy?" Ann stood in the doorway of her office. I fumbled with the magazine and put it back on the table. Once inside, I sat down and said, "I found Cassandra's body." I spoke lifelessly and kept my eyes locked on the books behind Ann's head.

"What?"

"Cassandra Sommers. I was with the search party."

She set aside her pad. "Are you all right? Why didn't you come to me right away?"

I was surprised at her question. "It didn't occur to me. We had this time scheduled."

Ann shook her head. "Well, you're here now. What happened? I read that Cassandra was murdered. They found a bullet in her skull."

"I think so. I feel so numb." I continued to stare at her bookcase.

Ann pushed up her red-rimmed glasses. "I worry about you."

I looked at her, startled. I couldn't remember the last time someone was worried about me. When I'd been put on lithium three years earlier, my mother had said something like, "All's well that ends well." Not worried at all.

"Does that surprise you?" Ann asked.

"Kind of. What are you worried about?"

"You just told me that you found someone's body. That's major. Don't you think?" There was an ironic smile on her face. Did she find it funny?

I pulled a tissue from the box next to me and balled it in my fist.

"Do you feel guilty?"

My eyes flew open wide, zooming upward. The ceiling seemed to fall toward me. "Why would I?"

Her voice sounded far away. "Because you do tend to feel guilty. Survivor's guilt. It's very common. What is it? Wendy? Look at me." The bottle of water on the desk beside Ann's elbow glistened. "How have you been sleeping?"

"Not too bad."

"Remember, lack of sleep with no loss of energy means trouble."

"Right. I've been pretty tired." I shifted in my chair. I was so thirsty. I was silent a few moments. I wasn't sure where to take the conversation, but I felt a strong resolve to get to the point I'd always wanted to make. "I want a new future. I want a future. . . . For the past few years, the future has seemed closed to me. Even going to school is repeating what I've done before. I want a new future."

"What do you see in this future?"

"I want to teach." My voice rose loud, surprising myself.

Ann lowered her head, looking at me over her glasses. "But you got a grant in order not to teach."

"I know." I started shredding another tissue. "But it was a big part of me. I put everything into it. Getting certified was hard. I was starting to have some problems with mania when I was in school.

It was tough to get through it. I was diagnosed soon after I finished student teaching. This was going to be my life."

"Did you enjoy teaching?"

That was the question. It had been nightmarish. "I can't judge that because I was having problems all along. If I just had another chance."

Ann smiled. "You know the definition of insanity."

"But I wasn't well. Now I'm well."

"But you got a grant not to teach. Doesn't that tell you something?"

It tells me I'm terrified. I crumpled the shredded tissue that was growing moist in my hand.

Ann's face was bright as she leaned forward. "You need to define what you want in a way that's under your control. You say you want to be an adult. What does that look like to you?"

It felt like a final exam. "I can't see it. But I don't want everything to stand still or go backwards. What I see for the future is that I'm an adult, that I'm making good decisions, and I'm respected, and trusted, and I have responsibility and I don't screw up everything."

"You still might screw up some things."

"And I'll be able to handle it and bounce back."

Ann picked up her pad and made note of what I said.

"Do you think it's possible?" I asked.

For the first time that session, our eyes met. Ann's eyes seemed hard. "Of course it's possible. Anything's possible. What we have to find out is why you, on some level, don't want it. If you don't feel like an adult, maybe some part of you doesn't want to be an adult. Or doesn't want to perceive yourself as the adult you are." She flipped a page in her notebook. "Maybe you aren't ready to talk about this experience of finding Cassandra's body?"

"I'm not sure."

She waited as if I might say more, then shrugged as if to give up. "Would you like to pick up where we left off?"

I wanted to pick up my life where *it* had left off. I wanted to go back, start over. I wanted to spend this session talking about my decision to come back to school and whether it was right for me, or if I had done it only because I was afraid to grow up and be independent. That was the kind of thing my brother had said. Maybe Ann was on the right track. I was scared. I was afraid to see myself as an adult. This was the moment when I could admit that, and we could really talk about it.

"Where we left off, yes." I said. I felt better just anticipating we would talk about it.

"This trauma with your mother and your uncle's death. You said your grandmother would talk about it?"

I started. This wasn't what I expected. I'd forgotten this was where we'd left off. The insistent wind rattled the aluminum window frame, while the radiator hissed. A bright streak of cold sun highlighted Ann's sharp face.

"When we went to church, she'd tell us to pray for Uncle Johnny."

"And your grandfather became a secret drinker."

"Oh, no. I don't think it's that likely, from what little I knew of him."

"But you don't know."

"He died when I was two."

"Given that your mother ended up marrying an alcoholic . . . It's a common fate. How else do you think this accident affected your mother?"

I wondered how I could get us back on track, but I kept going. "I've always been afraid to ask her about it. She's never brought it up. I think hearing about it so young really affected me. Made me fearful. And maybe passive, too. Like, there's nothing you can do. It's going to happen. I have a great fear of accidents. I feel so helpless about the whole idea."

"It's going to happen. . . ." Ann took off her glasses and set them on the desk behind her. "Do you think your mother felt this way too?"

Then I remembered something strange. "You know, there was a funny thing I never thought about. When I was child, it seemed like pretty often, there'd be a dead robin in the road, hit by a car. And whenever we saw one, my mom would pull over and take it out of the road and lay it on the shoulder, so it wouldn't get squashed by passing cars. I don't know why so many robins got hit on that road, but I feel like this happened enough times that it made an impression on me."

Ann looked at me and didn't reply. The radiator's hiss got louder.

I felt tremulous. "When I was a kid, we never wore seatbelts. We just never buckled up. It seemed like, a few times, my door wasn't closed all the way. I didn't pull it shut hard enough. So my mom would slow down for me, and I'd swing it open to pull it shut. That happened a few times."

"She would have you open the door?"

"Yes."

"With the car moving?"

"She'd slow down. Yes, with the car moving."

"What do you think that means?" Ann asked.

I started to shiver. "I don't know. I feel like my life was in danger all the time when I was young. I mean, my brother and I weren't supervised. I feel like I wandered around a lot with no one looking after me."

"Your life was in danger?"

"It feels like it. Do you think . . ." My throat was dry, and I coughed violently for a few seconds. There was no water for me. "Do you think my mom was trying to recreate the accident, so that she could rescue me at the last minute, sort of?"

Ann slowly nodded.

Tears fell down my face. "Is my mother crazy?"

Ann exhaled and beamed at me. "Your mother has a personality disorder."

In that moment, her words felt like a beacon of truth. "Am I crazy too? Aside from being bipolar?"

"You have a dissociative disorder because your mother has a personality disorder."

"How do you know? About my mother?"

"I've known a long time."

"How?" I asked, choked with tears.

"You never talk about your mother. Therefore you're defending her. Therefore she has a personality disorder."

I slid off the chair onto the floor. I put my hands over my face, shaking and sobbing. Ann stood up and bent over me, pressing her hands on my shoulders. "I feel like I'm with a baby, all pink and new," she said.

It must be true. I wouldn't be crying like this if it weren't true. And the snow makes it true.

I cried for a bit. Then I talked about ways it seemed like my mother was crazy. Ann was kind, encouraging, and strangely excited, a happy lilt to her voice. The half hour went by quickly. It seems strange now, this time slot, this half hour to revel in tears and trauma. Then she checks her watch, your time is up. You dry your tears. You leave to face the world again, and the hallway is the same, the traffic is the same, so is your house with its humming and ticking.

After the session, I decided to go for a walk. I was always a walker, and often avoided driving to campus. Downhill away from campus, then up again. Crows clamored in the corn stubble fields. A hawk stood sentinel in an old oak tree, blinking in the sun, and a dove mourned. A feeder in someone's yard hosted flitting nuthatches and cardinals. The wind had died down and it was warming, the snow melting into the drainage ditches. I unzipped my coat. I wasn't paying attention to where I walked, until I realized I was in front of the Hellmanns'. The white exterior, bright in the sun, made the windows especially dark. Coyotes howled in the woods behind the house. I stopped, feeling slightly disoriented.

Suddenly there was a flash of red. A pileated woodpecker flew onto a nearby tree. I had never seen one before. It was a huge black and white bird, larger than a crow, with a long beak, and a crest the brightest red I had ever seen. It hopped up the trunk. I watched it a long time, transfixed. When it flew away, I followed it. It flew from tree to tree. I followed it up Cooper Hill Road to where it became County Route 20. Then it flew overhead and into the dark woods on the other side and disappeared. I turned away from the trees toward the rolling view, tinged with the pink sky. It was getting dark, and if I walked a little farther, I'd be at the spot where I hit the deer. I decided to keep going; I felt pulled to the spot again.

The bend was easy to pick out, a green Victorian house up ahead on the forest side, and the ditch and stubbly field on the other. The snow was melting from the field into the ditch, a black current trickling down the hill.

Then I saw it.

I almost fell, couldn't think what to do. Just then a big car pulled up beside me. Deputy Polozzi got out.

"Good evening, Miss Zemansky. I got a call. It might be a stretch to call it harassment, but you know, hanging around outside people's houses, it makes people nervous."

I stared at him blankly and pointed at the bicycle tire poking through the melting snow.

CHAPTER SEVENTEEN

Dot's Café was busy in the early morning, noisy and bright with red and white tiles. I imagine this scene from what I was told later, on a gloomy day, a confession over cold coffee, in a voice jagged with the shame of the past and the weight of decisions yet to be made. A story that seeped into mine and disappeared again like a curl of smoke.

Dan Hellmann wasn't hungry. Tommy's plate was stacked with pancakes and bacon. As Tommy buttered the cakes and poured on the syrup, Dan felt ill at the sight.

"You've got to eat something," Tommy said as the server refilled their coffees. "Bring him an English muffin," he said to her. He turned to Dan. "They're good here. Coffee on an empty stomach won't do you any good." He took a bite, careful not to get syrup on his mustache. "Mmm. And the bacon is so crisp. You sure you don't want any?"

Dan shook his head. The noise of the café was a dull roar in his ears, but Tommy's precise, high voice cut through the din.

"You look pretty ragged. How are you?"

Dan shrugged. "How should I be?"

"It's closure, isn't it? In a way?"

"It doesn't feel like it."

Tommy set his fork aside. "Tell me how it feels then. And lower those shoulders. They're up to your ears."

Dan took a deep breath. Tommy was right. "I've got knots on top of knots."

"I know. Write about it. Use it. Go to your office, close the door, and pour it all into a wonderful poem."

It was the kind of thing he'd say to a student, and now he knew what awful, callow advice it was. "I can't. I feel like I'll never write again." Dan laughed in despair. Life was *life*, not fodder for some egocentric poem.

"That's what I was afraid of. Don't shut it out, don't shut down. That's not who you are."

"What am I? I'm a killer. Everyone I touch."

"Of course not." Tommy waved his fork. "Look at all the good you do. The conference on Blake. Your poems in *The New Yorker* put this little hole on the map. Teacher of the Year twice. And what's her name—Beth Lincoln, her novel published straight out of the gate, because of you."

"I didn't do that much on it."

"You coached her the whole way. You know that." He swallowed another big bite of the pancake. "You're feeling bad now. Of course. It's understandable—a vibrant young woman is dead. But it's distorting your vision. Don't lose sight of yourself. The poet, the teacher."

"The lecher, the cheater."

"Everyone needs to feel loved. *Everyone.* Do you feel—" The server brought the English muffin and Tommy put his finger to his lips until she left. "Do you feel loved these days?"

"I didn't care enough. I used her."

"To fill a void. Besides, wasn't she the one using you, for her career?"

"I don't know."

"To fill a void. A void that demands to be filled. Especially here, in this Siberia. This exile. We're all lonely. It sucks the life out of you. You only wanted to breathe. To come up for air, for God's sake. So she gave you room to breathe for a little while. There's no shame in that. But remember, that spark that you think she gave you was inside you all along. That's what you forget. The real spark is inside. Sure, feel the guilt, feel it all, but in the end, that gleaming coal is inside you. So write it. Pound the keyboard and scream it out."

"There should be an end to it."

"This is it, isn't it?"

"An end to words. An end to writing it all down."

"You know better than that." He finished his bacon and pushed the plate away. "Ugh, these heavy breakfasts. I always overdo it." He rubbed his hands together and turned back to Dan. "So what will you do about her?"

Dan started. Diana was dead. What should he do about her? "About her?"

"The girl, Wendy."

Dan squinted in confusion. "What do you mean?"

Tommy smiled. "The note. The note you just told me about. That she sent to McGill." He licked his lips. "You can't stand for that."

"Oh, you mean . . . But . . . You think? You're sure she did it?"

"Of course I'm sure." Tommy's smile was like that of a parent amused by a naughty but charming child. "You know she did it. Who else? Who else would do that?"

"But how would she know?"

"She was Diana's roommate. Of course she knows. She probably knows everything."

Dan meant, how would Wendy know he'd applied to McGill? But when Tommy spoke those words, they burned, and the color red leapt out to him from all around. Of course. Roommates. Notes. Of course. He would have to do something, before it escalated.

"Oh, and speaking of that. You aren't serious? You're tenured for God's sake. And what about Jean? Is she on board with this?"

"We have a lot to talk about."

"Tonight let's get a drink at Stanimer's and go over it. The whole plan. It's too noisy here to think." He tapped Dan's plate with his knife. "Your muffin is getting cold."

Later, in his office, he did try to write. But he could never write out of guilt. When he argued with Jean, or if he accidentally hurt his daughter, the words could never come. He sat at his desk and stared at the blank screen. A precarious stack of papers slid onto the floor. In the tight office, he twisted reaching for them, his back spasming. He rose in slow motion, gingerly sitting again, the pain like an ice-cold knife in his side.

There was a tap on the door. He inwardly jumped, the tap so familiar, Diana's tap. Jean poked her head in. "Hi. Are you writing?" Her face was gentle, softly tired.

"Not getting anywhere."

She entered and took the other chair. "You must have heard by now."

He nodded.

"I'm sorry." The exhaustion in her voice communicated there was much to be sorry for.

They looked at each other in silence. He felt the weight of secrets between them. He wished she already knew. He wished he would never have to tell her. Maybe she did know. He waited for her to continue.

"I know she was a shining light in the department. Everyone expected a lot of her, didn't they? A bright young thing?"

Maybe she did know, and now he was irritated that they were pretending.

"At least it . . . well, wasn't a serial killer. An accident this time. That's what they're saying. A hit and run. It was bad that night. If it was that night. But she wasn't there. She wasn't at our place."

"No."

"You didn't go outside. Unless, it was when I went out for the wine."

"I didn't go outside. I didn't see her." Now it was obvious she knew, but she was still playing this game. "You didn't see her either?" he asked. If she could torture him, he could torture her back.

But she smiled defiantly. "No. You know I didn't. Or maybe I followed her, right?"

He shrugged. "You dented the car that night, if I remember."

Her smile had a hint of victory. "Sideswiped a mailbox. I had a drop too much."

He realized with a start that perhaps she was a little drunk, even now. He waited for more, but she rose.

"At least I know you'll be home tonight," she said, buttoning her coat.

Maybe now. Talk. Have it out. She stood as if waiting for him to speak.

He stretched his arms. "Tommy wants to take me out for a drink. He wants to convince me not to leave. I won't be late."

Her look made him hate himself, and she left.

CHAPTER EIGHTEEN

After I got out of the deputy's car, after I rushed inside to vomit, I called Scott.

I sent my mother an email. She wrote back, "Sorry about Diana—you weren't close, were you? This sounds like great material to fuel your writing. Will you be responsible for the whole rent now? I can send you some money to cover the difference." I hadn't thought about the rent. Personality disorder or no, sure enough I soon had a check from her.

Scott stayed with me most of the next few days, patient with my long silences. That Monday I went to keep my regular appointment with Ann, but when I got to the health center, I found that she had to cancel over some conflict, a car repair. It wasn't public knowledge that I was the one who found Diana, so she didn't know. Strange how unimportant I considered myself, that I didn't try to reach her or let her know.

When I got home, there was a voicemail from Scott on my cell—which I was still getting used to carrying around. "If anyone needs a break, it's you. Come to Stanimer's tonight. There's an open mike. I'll pick you up." I was hoping he was still performing. Either way, I could enjoy his company and forget about finding dead bodies for a while.

Stanimer's was the only bar in town. I had never been inside. It was dark and smelled of the cigarettes that were smoked there years before. We squeezed between small round tables crowded with both students and locals. The students were loudly possessive of the room.

A red-haired woman waved to us from a table by the little platform stage, and Scott led me to meet his friends. There were Madeleine and her fiancé Mike, "M & M." Madeleine was perfectly made
up with arched brows and red lipstick. Daniel Quinn was there too,
wearing a brown trilby. I stumbled over saying "Hello" and "Good
evening" simultaneously. Mike stood up and shook Scott's hand.
He was a programming student, clean-cut with short brown hair
and looked like an all-American football player, one from the 1950s.

"Are we late?" I asked as we sat.

Madeline waved her hand. "Nothing's started yet. What are you
singing?"

Scott tugged on the collar of his flannel shirt. "A Robert Burns
song called Ae Fond Kiss."

"Sounds like classic Scott," Daniel said.

Scott turned to me. "You had a guitar, that you bought at a pawn
shop. Whatever happened with that?"

"I learned one song, Scarborough Fair, but it hurt my thumb so
much to press it against the back of the neck." I showed him how
I held the guitar.

"That's all wrong. I'll help you."

Madeleine nudged Mike. "Why don't you do something romantic
like that?"

"Hey, I can make a mix tape with the best of them."

We laughed as I glanced at Scott, wondering how he felt about
the allusion to romance. He busied himself tuning the guitar.

At the microphone, a lanky, thin-haired man, about thirty-five, in
an Ed Hardy skull T-shirt under a navy blazer, and looking like he
expected to be doing more with his life, welcomed the crowd. Then
he nodded toward Scott. "And now, an old favorite of ours who
hasn't been here a while, Mr. Scott Garrison."

I applauded with the crowd, some of whom hooted and cheered.
I wanted to concentrate on him, and while he sang, I thought
how this handsome, talented man singing before an appreciative
crowd was my old best friend. He began:

"Ae fond kiss, and then we sever.
Ae farewell, alas, forever.
Deep in heart-wrung tears, I'll pledge thee.
Warring sighs and groans, I'll wage thee."

A brief shadow flickered over the stage as people entered, cross-
ing the spotlight. I looked toward the bar, where two men faced
away from the stage. Hellmann was slumped low over his drink,
and Kind was whispering in his ear. *Diana, I almost forgot about Diana.*
It had slipped my mind like a coin slipping out a hole in my pocket.
The bicycle tire, warped and twisted, sticking out of the snow. I'd
stood there pointing at it, and at first the deputy didn't see it. He
was saying something about harassment or scaring people; I didn't
know what he was talking about. "Her bicycle," I croaked. He
looked, and slogged through the snow down the ditch. When he
pulled on the bicycle tire, a small hand broke through the snow. An
angry look came to his face. He rushed up to his vehicle. "Get in,"
he said, flinging open the door. He leaned in the front and radioed
for help. I watched him trudge back down the slope and brush the
snow away from her, revealing her blue face and wet hair, revealing
her as carefully as an archeologist, so that her features gradually
appeared like a fossil in the strata, like a picture being developed.
With delicate fingers he cleaned the snow off her eyes and lips, and
her head appeared like one of those statues where the body is unfinished, and only the head is detailed in the marble.

Then there were more police cars and a useless ambulance, outside of which the paramedics smoked cigarettes and shook their
heads and chatted while they waited for the police to finish investigating the scene. There was little evidence left in the road which
had been snowed on, salted and plowed several times. The deputy
and a paramedic finally disentangled her from the bicycle and lifted her onto a stretcher, covered her tightly, and slid her into the
back of the coroner's van to take to the morgue. The officers put
the crumpled bicycle in the back of one of their vehicles. The
deputy drove me home without saying anything until he pulled

into the driveway. Then he asked, "Did you know she was there all along?"

"No, I just found her. Maybe she was leading me. I was just walking."

"You didn't follow her from the party?"

"No one saw her at the party, remember? No one believed me." I sat slumped over, my stomach full of ice, clutching my mouth as if my lungs would fall out.

On stage, Scott sang:

"I'll ne'er blame my partial fancy.
Nothing could resist my Nancy.
But to see her was to love her,
Love for her, and love forever."

A memory came to me. It was one of those arguments where I felt disoriented and at a loss, the last conversation I'd actually had with Diana. The Supreme Court had an abortion decision at hand, and Diana had said, "Everyone has a side. No one listens. No one wants to face it with real compassion."

I was in the kitchen, she was on the couch, and I was chopping an onion when I answered, "It's hard for me because I was raised in a family that was kind of pro-life, even though otherwise we were very liberal and feminist and all that. I was raised to have this cold, logical belief that a baby is a baby. And it took me a long time of thinking, to feel, maybe logic isn't everything. Maybe compassion has to overcome that sometimes." This was the first and only time I had ever stated my views on the subject. I forced myself with all my will to overcome my inhibition, my fear of "taking up space," as Ann called it. To express myself.

But Diana took me by surprise. "What about compassion for the mother? Compassion enough to let her have her child and support that and not force her to abort her child?" Diana was shouting. "Force her to make a choice between her own life and its?" Then she sprang up from the couch and went to her room, slamming the door.

I stood still at the counter, the onion stinging my eyes, blindsided. The one opinion which I thought was reasonable and was sure Diana would agree with—or even simply accept—had somehow been a horrible mistake. I was shaken by her anger.

The coroner revealed the answer. *Now I understand,* I thought, as if to her. *You were having a baby, and you were going to keep it. You wanted support, philosophical support, to back you up. But why didn't you tell me? Just tell me. Why hide behind a debate?*

Scott sang:

"Had we never kissed so kindly.
Had we never loved so blindly.
Never met, and never parted,
We had ne'er been broken-hearted."

Diana stayed in her room and I went out to a movie alone. When I got home later that night, Diana had left for break. In my room was the small painting of the rose on my desk, her apology. I left for Christmas break early the next morning, never speaking with her again. *No one feels they can talk to me. No one confides in me. Why? Am I so unreasonable? So neurotic? Why don't people trust me?*

Scott sang:

"Fare thee well, thou first and fairest.
Fare thee well, thou best and dearest.
Thine be every joy and treasure,
Peace, contentment, love, and treasure."

I must change. I must become sane and trustworthy and grown-up. I must learn how to act like an adult, think like an adult, like a real person. I must kill the Buddha, whatever that means, I must kill the Buddha.

I looked back up at Scott. His voice was excruciatingly sweet, and in the stage light his high cheekbones and firm jaw were gorgeous, even sexy. He repeated the first verse to finish, and the crowd applauded wildly, with whistles and cheers. I snapped out of my trance.

Scott smiled and waved to the crowd and then winked at me. I felt like an infatuated fan. When he came back to the table, he bent down and kissed my cheek. I knew it was because he was buoyed by the applause, elated at having performed well. It wasn't romantic.

"I feel like I should ask for an autograph," I said.

"You should put out a CD," said Madeline. "It's not hard these days."

Scott shrugged and smiled, and we ordered a round of drinks.

A tall, thin blond woman walked up to our table. She was wearing tight, expensive jeans with high-heeled boots and a designer leather jacket. "Hi," she breathed to Scott. "I wanted to say how great that was."

"Thank you," Scott said. He looked up at her, not shyly at all, to my chagrin.

"You aren't from here, are you? I'm Lenore."

Of course you are, I thought.

"I'm from Utica," said Scott. Then I realized his tone. It was polite but guarded.

Lenore continued. "I represent a folk label out of Buffalo. I'd like to give you my card." She extended her hand.

Scott took the card. "Thanks, but I wouldn't be interested."

Lenore gave a small, confident smile. "Well, think it over. Good night." She ambled away with a slow, swinging gait as if she were ice skating.

I stared after her and then turned to Scott, who was smiling to himself as he slid the card into his pocket.

"Uh-oh," Madeleine said with a wink at me.

Scott shook his head. "Not my type at all."

"Are you crazy?" I exclaimed.

Scott laughed.

Madeline turned to me. "So, Wendy, what's your story? How do you know Scott?"

I flushed at their expectant faces. "We were best friends years ago in college. Then we lost touch. Kind of a falling-out. This semester we ran into each other again, and here we are."

"Great story," Daniel said, lifting his wine glass in a toast.

"That's so romantic. You really have a hold on him," Madeleine said.

I looked away, blushing. They were assuming a romance. I didn't know what to say or where to look.

We ordered another round. Shadows passed in front of the spotlight again, the two professors leaving. Seeing me turn my head, the others noticed. "Oh, it's Hellmann and Kind, how weird," said Madeline. "He seems too conscious of his good looks, the way he wears his hair, you know, a little long. There's just something about him, almost creepy."

"Dr. Kind is the creepy one," Daniel said. "So prim, so prudish."

I shook my head. "I think Dr. Kind is very nice. He always has a funny joke."

"Is he gay?" Mike asked. "I got that vibe, but I can't really tell."

"I think he's never had a sexual thought in his entire life. At least, I hope not," Daniel said. Everyone laughed.

Madeleine shook her head. "What are you talking about? He's married. Or he was."

"That's right," Daniel said, with a baffled expression.

"Doesn't his ex-wife write for a TV show?" Mike asked.

Madeleine nodded. "She's a show runner for one of those crime shows. *Law and Order*, or something."

"No, *Dexter*," Daniel said.

"What's *Dexter*?" I asked.

"Who's Dexter?" Mike asked. The bar was getting louder.

"Is his partner Sinister?" I asked.

They looked puzzled. Scott said, "Dexter means right in Latin, and Sinister means left."

They groaned. "Dexter is a serial killer who kills serial killers," Daniel explained.

"I may not know Latin, but I know tautology. It's a tautology!" Madeleine shouted above the noise. We were all getting slightly drunk, except Scott who had stopped at one glass because he was driving.

"I love *Dexter*!" said Daniel.

"Tautology!"

We toasted tautology.

"I saw his wife last year," Madeleine continued. "She was in town settling some business with him. She was very LA. She was wearing a cropped leather jacket with chinchilla sleeves. Chinchilla sleeves! It was awe-some."

"Not fur," Daniel said.

"In the words of Patton, God help me I love it."

"Do you remember the Halloween party?" Daniel asked. "*That* was awesome." I asked why. "We were supposed to dress as our favorite poet. Hellmann came in a ruffled shirt and frock coat as Keats. He was beautiful. And Kind—" Everyone laughed and nodded. "Kind came in a gray wig and a fisherman's sweater and cords, and said he was Dr. Hellmann."

I had to laugh. It felt good. Why had I skipped that party? I could have been having fun. I remembered Diana that night, dressed as Christina Rossetti in a white gown. She didn't come home until almost morning.

"Under Pressure" started playing over the sound system, and I tapped my fingers against the table. Mike picked up the beat and drummed the tabletop, our glasses shaking slightly. We all sang the chorus with exaggerated David Bowie accents. Scott looked around nervously as if afraid we were making a scene, but Daniel slapped him on the shoulder as if to say, "Loosen up," and then even Scott joined in singing. I realized that, like me, Scott was usually tense. It was nice to see him relax.

When the song ended, the music switched to something softer. We toasted 80s music and quieted down, as another round of drinks came by.

Madeleine took a big sip of her Riesling and pointed her finger in the air. "I shouldn't tell you this. But Carolyn told me he made some kind of pass at her at that party."

"Kind?" Mike asked.

"Some kind of."

"No, you mean Dr. Kind?"

Madeleine nodded. "She didn't want to make a big deal of it."

"She must have been mistaken. What did he do?" Daniel asked.

"It was a weird thing. He didn't touch her or anything. He just said something weird."

"For Christ's sake, spit it out," Mike said.

"Is this appropriate?" Scott asked. "We shouldn't spread rumors."

Mike belched loudly. "That's what I think of that," he said to Scott.

Madeleine put her hand over Mike's mouth and continued. "Apparently, Kind asked her if she'd be interested in him if he were the glamorous Dr. Hellmann. Or something like that. She said something like, not even if you were the glamorous Keats. And he said, 'just kidding.' And it never came up again. They just pretended it didn't happen."

That was what we did in those days.

The lights flickered. "Final call," Mike said. I'd had enough, but he grabbed a quick beer and insisted on buying me one more glass of wine. I was feeling warm, not used to drinking or the attention. "Thanks. It's been a while since I felt like I wasn't annoying people."

"Nonsense," Madeleine said. "Who do you annoy?"

I finished my drink, hesitating, but feeling uninhibited now. "For example, the night Diana disappeared, I thought I saw her at the Hellmanns', on their patio. They acted like I was crazy. Didn't want me talking about it, since I could have been mistaken. I just wanted to do the right thing. It could be important in figuring out who killed her."

Their mouths gaped. Madeleine put her hand over mine. "It was an accident, honey. A hit and run on a blizzarding night. She wasn't killed, not in that sense."

"It just seems all connected. It can't be a coincidence. Her and Cassandra."

Daniel shrugged. "They've already arrested Cassandra's boyfriend. He was in Florida and has a rap sheet a mile long. There's no connection. Is there?"

Scott said, "The universe is all coincidence. Chaos and coincidence. Atoms collide, and anything can happen." He seemed to be
speaking to himself, gazing down at the table.

"Of course, though it wasn't on purpose, she *was* killed, by whoever hit her," Daniel said.

"You're right," Madeleine said. "I just meant, not murdered."

I saw Scott throw a look at Madeleine, as if to say, enough, be
quiet about it now. Daniel seemed eager to talk about it. "I suppose
it's even possible that whoever hit her never even saw her, in the
snow. It was a blinding storm. But you'd have to know, wouldn't
you? That's a bad stretch along there. Always deer running across
the road at that spot. She was hit like a deer." Scott gave Daniel a
dark, frowning look, but he didn't notice. "That's the funny thing,"
Daniel went on. "Diana's name being Cerf."

"What do you mean?" I asked, suddenly feeling hot, my hands
sweating.

"Since Cerf means deer in French."

The room made a strange tilt, the same tilt it made years ago
when a therapist diagnosed me as bipolar. *A deer. I hit a deer. She was
at the drugstore.*

Scott said, "This has been a rough time. Maybe we shouldn't play
detective."

My ears were ringing, the bar seemed so loud. I don't remember
paying and leaving, saying good night. Scott drove me home in the
dark and I made a great effort to talk as if everything were normal.
The curves of the country road hid the dark way ahead.

"Watch for deer," he said.

My brain skipped a groove. "I hit a deer a couple of weeks ago.
At four o'clock." *It was a deer and she was alive. She went to the drug store.
What was the time on the receipt?*

"You drove by yourself to Ohio and back? I would have worried
about you if I had known." His tone was so light, so easy.

"You always took care of me."

He put on a CD. A wild reel of pipes and drums played, filling my
head with its driving rhythm.

"Tell me about what you're studying," I asked. *Talk, say anything.*

He warmed to the topic. "Sometimes it's as simple as where to dig a well. Other times there are hard choices. Some people ask if it's right to bring the modern world to remote tribes, but we can't create cultural zoos, either. I was inspired by a man who walked across Africa. He was doing a simple thing, bringing people the formula of salt, sugar, and water, to feed babies who have diarrhea. The tendency is to withhold water from them, the worst thing you can do. But that's different from my work. The field is wide open."

He talked at length and I fought through the fog of my spinning brain to ask intelligent questions. The conversation turned to physics, quantum mechanics, I hardly knew how the conversation got there. He spoke eagerly, happily—this was our old friendship. "It's not just that the state changes, the future changes, but there is no fixed past." He was saying something about atoms and electrons.

My breath trembled in my throat. "No fixed past?"

"The past changes as we look at it."

Maybe I can change the past. Maybe I can do it over. "But there's cause and effect. Something causes something to happen. There's a permanent change, it ripples into the future," I said.

"Maybe not."

Maybe I can retrace my steps. "Do you think we can travel to the past? And relive it?"

He glanced at me. "People think the past is always better. But it seems to me that things do get better. I wouldn't go back. I wouldn't go back for anything." He reached over and squeezed my hand. I felt nervous, his taking his eyes off the road, his hand off the wheel. "You did have such a beautiful singing voice in those days."

"Really? Thanks."

"We should sing together at Stanimer's sometime."

"Maybe."

We were past the woods when we crested the hill, and the fields opened up around us and below, like a white, rolling ocean, lonely and anonymous in the moonlight. My identity was given up to this place of hot green summers and winters as cold as the gleam in

Satan's eye. *This is where people disappear.* Something seemed to hop along the ditch. A small child in a gray coat.

"Did you see that?' Scott asked.

"I thought I imagined it." I clasped my shaking hands.

"A great horned owl. Haven't seen one in years."

"Oh."

We pulled into the driveway and he walked me to the door. The air was moist and cold, and we could see our damp breath in the night.

"Thanks for the ride."

"Sure, no problem."

I leaned against the door and he stood close. His white skin glowed in the moonlight, his lips purpling in the dimness.

"I don't want to take advantage of you," I said.

"You can take advantage of me, as long as you don't take me for granted." He had a faint, rueful smile.

I stared at him, my eyes growing wet. "I did. I did take you for granted. Oh, Scott."

He pulled me into his arms. "The past isn't fixed," he said.

He drew back and I gazed into his face and saw everything. His eyes were open wide and there was a softness and tenderness to his look. And—*hope. He loves me. He always loved me. What's wrong with me? How could I not have realized it? And now he's hoping, and I can't invite him in, because I don't know, I don't know. I don't know the time on the receipt.*

He leaned down and gave me a brief kiss. I didn't kiss back.

"I'm sorry. I'm not feeling well tonight. I, I have a splitting head-ache." I felt dizzy, and I hated this, I hated the timing of it.

He rolled his eyes, smiling ironically, and I knew he was chiding himself, knew that he was feeling shot down and blaming himself, not knowing anything I was thinking and feeling.

"I'll explain everything later," I said weakly.

"What's to explain?" I hated the sharp note in his voice. "Good night." He turned and left, not waving from the car as he drove away.

CHAPTER NINETEEN

I was starting not to be able to sleep. Ann had told me several times, "Lack of sleep with no loss of energy means you're in trouble." That's the beginning of mania. But here's the thing: I was exhausted, and for that reason I didn't worry. I lacked energy—so I couldn't be manic.

I tried to write, sketching out a story, about the end of civilization, everything gradually shutting down. In the end an ambulance's siren makes a lonely wail on a street impassable with snow. Sitting alone, I read it aloud. Then I read it aloud again. My voice sounded soft and hypnotic in my ears. I read it aloud again. To my surprise, two hours passed. *I'm fine, because I'm exhausted.* It was dinnertime but I wasn't hungry at all.

I went to the phone, hesitating, then got out the scrap of paper with the number on it and dialed. "Hello Mark, it's Wendy."

He turned down some music in the background. "Hi." He sounded like he welcomed my call. "You must be psychic. I was about to call you." I felt warm at that, and he continued. "The art show. I've arranged it at the gallery for April. If you want to be a part of it? At least, I'll have to come by for the paintings."

"Sure, that's great. I'm glad."

"Thanks for the idea. How are you?"

The care in his voice lifted my spirit. "I'm okay, I guess." I swallowed. "I wanted to ask you something. Greg said you saw Diana recently, since November." I clenched the phone tightly.

My heart sank as his tone changed entirely. "Well, that's none of your business. But what about it?"

"I'd like to know which day it was. When she was last—"

He cut me off. "You should obviously know it's all I've thought about. I don't need you going over this."

"I'm sorry. I'm just trying to piece it together because—"

"I did tell the sheriff. They know all about it. She was through with me."

"I understand."

"No, you don't." His voice was hard. "Just drop it. You can't keep going into it. You want to play detective. You think you can understand. You can't. There's no explanation for any of it. It just happened. It just happened, Wendy. And you should forget it. You're going to piss off the wrong person with this. You're going to get hurt."

Was that a threat? I tried to speak, but my voice was lost.

"So, forget it. I'm sorry to be rough on you. But it's hard enough right now. Good night."

"Wait. There's something else. I don't know what to do about it, but I saw this poem by Dr. Hellmann in *The New Yorker*. He stole a line from Diana, from her book."

He paused, considering it, and suddenly sounded friendlier again. "You should go to Dr. Hellmann. Go straight to him and ask him about it."

"Really?" It was the last thing I wanted to do.

"Yes." His voice softened. "Thanks for telling me. I appreciate it." He hung up.

I lay awake, waiting for morning. I had the goal of piecing together Diana's last day, so that I could find out for sure when she was last alive, when she went to the drugstore. I was starting to feel a little better, that the flash of panic I'd felt, simply because her name meant "deer," was absurd. But still, I wanted to know. There had been that email from the art professor, so Diana might have met with her then. The art department was in a small wing of Kennedy, the building they shared with the science department, an afterthought. In the morning I got into my coat and boots and somehow I was there.

The wing was bright, student art covering the walls. Professor Andrews' office was dominated by an Escher print of infinite staircases. She was a petite African American woman with long braids and strong hands. She held my hand and squeezed it affectionately.

"Call me Cynthia. This must have been awful for you," she said as we sat down.

Her sympathy took the weight off my shoulders; immediately I felt I could confide in her.

"Thank you. The thing is, I'm trying to find out what Diana did on her last day. It's a long story." The professor nodded as if I didn't need to explain. "Did she see you that day?"

"Let's see." She opened a page on her computer. "I did have an appointment with her. Yes, it must have been that day. Oh, how terrible."

"What time was the appointment?"

She clicked on the date to open it. "It was at two o'clock and I had another appointment at two-thirty, so it would have ended then."

"Was she on her bicycle?"

She raised her eyebrows. "I don't know. I suppose she might have been. She was wearing a backpack. I remember because it was sort of funky, and I admired it. She said she bought it off the street in Chicago. I couldn't help but wonder why I'm not in a place like Chicago where I can buy funky stuff off the street." She smiled. "But we all wonder that. Anyway, that's probably all I know."

"You don't know what else she was doing that day?"

"Maybe if you tell me what you do know, it will jog some memory."

I had to decide whether to mention the Hellmanns' party. "I thought she was going out that night. And she went to a drugstore."

"Hmm." She closed her eyes a moment. "That's right. She mentioned she was quitting smoking, and had to get going to an appointment at the health center for advice. So that was probably the next place she went." Cynthia glanced around her desk. "There's something. . . . Yes. She joked I should teach Dr. Hellmann how to clean his office, since mine is so tidy. I think she had just come from him."

I had been holding my breath, and now I let the air fill my lungs. "That helps a lot. Thank you so much."

Cynthia walked me to the door, giving me a little hug. "Don't go crazy, Wendy. Don't let this obsess you."

"I know. But I have to find this out."

"I hope you'll find peace."

"Thanks."

I left. Down the hall I passed a classroom. Something caught my eye through the door. Jean Hellmann stood in the front of the room, wearing purple gloves, holding up a brain. She happened to turn her head. Our eyes met, the brain squishy in her hands. She glared at me. From inside someone laughed, and Jean turned back to the class again. I hurried along.

It was sleeting outside. The slush was gray, and greasy underfoot, especially just inside the door of Caspar Hall, the linoleum puddled and slick. A janitor backed toward me. It seemed like technology should have improved by now on the mop and dented bucket, but he swirled the stringy mop across the floor in long, slow swipes. I tiptoed around him.

Dr. Hellmann's door was open, and I leaned in. He was talking to Dr. Kind, who was perched lightly on the corner of the desk. Kind turned to me, his face so affable, his smile so welcoming.

"Here she is now," he said. This surprised me and I felt my expression turn vacuous. He sprang up. "I'll leave you to it." He pointed a finger at me and clucked his tongue as if there were a message in it, and left abruptly as I started to say hello.

Hellmann rose from his desk and closed the door. He cleared his throat as he sat again. I took the other chair. He was looking at me with a certain intensity. He looked older than he had before, fine lines in his cheeks, his mouth drawn tight. Everything seemed so gray: his hair, his face, his sweater. Like everything was made of ash. There was the faint smell of cigarettes.

The room felt so small and crowded. My mission to reconstruct Diana's last day was slipping away from me in a cloud of self-doubt, but I was there and had to say something. I wiped my mouth with my hand. "I wanted to ask you about Diana."

He raised his hand in a gesture of "stop." But he didn't speak. A weird amount of time passed while his hand stayed frozen in the air. Then a guttural sound came from his throat. "You want to talk about Diana?"

"I've been wanting to find out . . ." I was losing my nerve.

He suddenly opened his desk drawer with a bang and took out a scrap of paper and a pen. "Here. I want you to write something. You're a note writer, right? Want to write a note?" He threw the paper and pen in front of me. "Pick up the pen."

My hand was stiff with fear as I fumbled with the pen.

"Write this down. Ready?"

I moved my head somehow to say yes; my neck felt loose and wobbly.

He dictated. "He knew her *very well.*"

I scribbled it down with jagged letters. Gripping the pen, I waited for more. Somewhere in the walls, steam pipes hissed.

"Is there more?" I asked.

"Is there more?" he sneered. He grabbed the page and closed it in a book.

"I don't understand." Anyone else would have asked what was going on, easily, but just stating that took all my courage.

"Don't you?" He exhaled loudly through his nose, a punctuation, pulling in his thin lips until his mouth was a white line.

I was so embarrassed by the sense of accusation, that I knew my red face looked as guilty as he thought I was, of whatever this was about. I probably had a crazed smile on my face, a smile of utter embarrassment that looked instead as if I was enthused to have so utterly displeased him, my mouth wide open, my cheeks bright. I felt so disconnected from my body, my brain so baffled and frightened, my face so gleeful and mocking. I tried hard to make my expression match my thoughts, but my breath only made a staccato sound, almost like laughter.

"Are we done?" he asked.

I stumbled to my feet. "Is anything wrong?" I squeaked.

He was up and opening the door and I was there, too. He blocked me a moment and whispered, "I don't know why you're gunning for me, but I won't play your little game."

I was out the door with a slam. Shaking, I crept around the corner to Dr. Kind's office.

I knocked and opened the door without waiting, catching him red-faced as he fumbled to put out a cigarette. They had just banned smoking in the offices.

"You shouldn't barge in," he said with a cough, smoothing his bow tie and straightening himself. He took a sip of coffee from a school mug.

"I'm sorry." My voice was too loud, panicked.

His face grew concerned, his pale eyes wide. "What's the matter? I know things are terrible now, but you look worse than usual. Please, sit down."

"I just saw Dr. Hellmann. He was upset about something. I don't even understand."

"He asked about the letter?"

"What letter?" I fell into the chair. A space heater rattled, spitting warm air into the little room.

"Someone wrote to a university where he applied to teach. A newspaper clipping about Diana's disappearance and a suggestion that he had an improper relationship with her." He smiled, his head cocked to the side.

"I had no idea—how would I know—where he was applying? Why would I think they were having an affair? Diana wasn't seeing anyone."

He raised his eyebrows with interest. "Well, you are a letter writer, aren't you?"

My heart pounded. "Not like that."

"No?"

"I would never do something like that."

"Of course not." His smile was gentle, regretful.

I had never thought my tendency to write a little note could be this self-destructive. "I guess . . . I've really damned myself."

"I believe you."

Did he believe I didn't write the letter, or that I had damned myself?

He continued. "I know you need to express yourself. I'll tell you what, if you ever feel like unburdening yourself, write to me, not him. Leave him alone. He's been under stress. You can write anything to me."

"Thank you." It meant a lot, that invitation, the sense that it was okay.

"Why did you come? What did you want from Dr. Hellmann?" He made a gesture of "just between us" and relit his cigarette, the pearly vapor making a halo over him.

I liked that he was confiding in me, letting me keep his secret about smoking. I struggled out of my coat, my turtleneck damp with sweat. "I was trying to establish what Diana did on her last day."

"Why?"

I shook my head. "Maybe no reason. Just wanting to piece it together."

He sat forward, seeming interested. "That's a bad stretch of road. You know the night of the party, our friend Jean got a DUI."

"Mrs. Hellmann?"

He nodded. "Sideswiped a mailbox when she went to pick up more wine. We were a thirsty group. Most embarrassing." He shrugged. "Could have happened to any of us." He took a drag and slowly exhaled, looking up at the ceiling. Then he stubbed out the cigarette and clapped his hands against the surface of the desk. "All right, then." He gave me a questioning look as if to ask if we were done.

"There's something else. I don't know what to do about this. I think Dr. Hellmann might have plagiarized a line from Diana. I'll show you." I took out Diana's book from my bag and opened to the page. "This line was in *The New Yorker*, in a poem by Dr. Hellmann."

Kind glanced at the page and snapped the book shut. "My dear, don't be silly. She stole it from him."

I took a deep breath. "But this poem was only just published. Her book is from last fall."

"Where did you see it?"

"At the health center."

He waved his hand, chasing away the last of the smoke. "Those magazines are months old."

I furrowed my brow, trying to remember. I'd thought it was the latest issue, but I could have been mistaken.

"That girl . . ." He sighed. "The late, lamented John Gardner said there are only two stories: someone goes on a journey, or a stranger comes to town. . . ." He seemed lost in thought. "Why did she come here?"

"I do wonder. It's funny, I'll always think of her in winter."

"Winter . . ." he muttered. Then he focused on me. "Do you know the difference between honesty and disclosure?"

I shook my head.

"I know you want to be honest. But that doesn't mean you need to disclose everything. Do you see the difference?"

"You're right! That's so true." That note to Dr. Hellmann about needing the grant, about being bipolar, was totally unnecessary. I saw that now. I felt better than I had in a long time.

"Do you know what it really is, always to be self-conscious and worried what people think of you? Think about it. Really think."

The pink walls of the room seemed to pulsate. Then the breath caught in my throat as it hit me. "It's paranoia, isn't it?" He slowly nodded. It was a stunning realization. "You're my hero right now! I really needed that."

He chuckled a little puppy bark. "I just worry how much your jumbled thoughts interfere with your work. Your last paper was a comedown. You were so good, but I fear the work is getting too much for you."

"My literature review?" I had started to get up, wanting to leave on the high note, not wanting to hear any criticism.

"I have to reject it."

My rumpled coat half on, I sank down. I must have looked a mess. I felt confused and disoriented. I had never had a paper rejected before. The literature review was just a thesis statement and annotated list of sources. What was there to reject?

"Gothic literature and mental illness," he said with a disapproving sigh. "Someone already did the same paper last spring. It's well-trodden ground. I want originality."

I didn't know what to say. He'd been so warm and caring a moment earlier. Now he seemed so matter-of-fact. So pitiless.

"You have flashes of brilliance. But you can't rely on that. It's all about consistency. You had a flash of something and got published. My first novel, *Mother's Milk*, was reviewed in *The New York Times* when I was twenty-five. They said it was a work of subtle genius. My second novel is still in the drawer. You don't want that, do you?" He pushed aside some papers, laying his hands open on the desk. "There are two ways to teach. I want you to know this because someday you will teach. You can be a judge, merely scribbling red ink on a paper and doling out the damnation of a poor grade. Or you can really teach. Not tell, but show. Come to me with another theme and we'll go over it. You need to sharpen your thesis statement and draw stronger conclusions. You were so good before. You can be good again. Come back to the light, Wendy. Come back to the light!" He called to the ceiling, jocular, acting.

I laughed, and he joined me. Maybe he was right. He was trying to help, trying to take care of me.

"Now run along like a good girl. You have a lot of work to do."

I beamed at him in gratitude and left, surprised at how cold it was in the hallway after his womb-warm office.

CHAPTER TWENTY

The next week, February started with a snowstorm that closed campus for three days. Snow fell for forty-eight hours straight Tuesday and Wednesday, thick and heavy, filling the air like a Biblical plague. It was accumulating too fast to keep up with plowing, particularly the campus parking lots. I was off the hook, not having to go to my classes that Thursday. I spent the days reading and listening to the radio.

I finally went out to shovel the driveway Thursday afternoon when it stopped. Scott had emailed offering to do it, but the driveway was short, and I needed the exercise. The snow was wet and heavy, and soon I ached from my lower back down my trembling arms. The county plow had made a wall at the end of the driveway, and I regretted underestimating the job, but I got it clear enough around the two cars, Diana's and mine.

I'd heard the phone ringing from the driveway, but ignored it. Once I came in, I pulled off all my sweat-soaked clothes and plopped down in the living room naked, the draft cooling off my flushed skin as I played the message.

The voicemail was Diana's brother Greg. They needed to arrange getting her car and belongings. After a shower, I called him back and, feeling like some kind of Hercules, I offered to drive the car with Diana's things to Chicago myself and fly home.

"Really? You'd do that? Because that would be great of you. It was going to be hard for me to take the time off work. I was going to drive straight through. But if you could do that, of course we'd pay you. And if you spent the day, I'll take you to the Art Institute, and maybe a show. All on me. You know, see *Nighthawks* and *American Gothic*. That would be so nice of you. When can you come?"

He was so grateful that I couldn't change my mind from the impulsive offer. I also wanted to get away, get far away from this town, the Hellmanns, everyone. He gave me the address on the north side of Chicago, and I booked a flight from O'Hare to Syracuse to come home. I'd leave the next morning, spend Friday night on the way at my mother's, arrive in Chicago Saturday evening, spend the day Sunday seeing Chicago, and then come home Monday morning. I wouldn't even miss any classes, though returning to class wasn't exactly a priority anyway.

I spent the evening packing Diana's things. On the phone I'd asked Greg about the art show at the gallery, and we decided the paintings would stay behind for that. There wasn't a lot more: two suitcases of clothes, including the one that was never unpacked, paints and brushes, books, a small amount of silver and turquoise jewelry, school papers, a clock that made bird calls at each hour, boots and sneakers, and the laptop. Her belongings were spare and practical.

I thumbed through a sketchbook. Diana sketched people she saw in public, on park benches, in the union. There was a self-portrait, a cartoon of Diana flying on a broomstick over snowy hills, with the caption, "He called me the witch of winter." I wondered who called her that.

I stopped at a drawing of me, bent over the table writing. I remembered Diana drawing while I was composing the note to Dr. Hellmann. I didn't know I was the subject. At the bottom of the sketch, Diana had written, "Our heroine falls on her sword." I hadn't shared the note I was writing with her, but there were balled-up versions all around. And Diana had tossed one at my head, saying, "Commit nothing to writing, Wendy."

I put the sketchbook into a box and reached into the last dresser drawer. Among the paintbrushes and pens was another object of similar size. It was the EPT. It never occurred to me Diana would save it in the drawer. Still blue. A sharp breath of grief caught my chest. I put it back in the drawer.

Was it possible to really know someone? Should we have been closer? We had cooked together, Diana teaching me vegetarian recipes and encouraging me not to worry about my weight. It was a warm, supportive relationship. Maybe it didn't need to be more. Not that it could be, now.

The next morning I took the keys from the hook and loaded up quickly. Before I left, I went to the calendar on the kitchen wall and drew a smiley face on the date, as Ann had suggested. This was the most grown-up thing I had ever done.

Sitting in the car, holding the keys, I felt tense, my heart beating hard. I'd hardly driven all winter, since the night I'd hit the deer. I realized I'd begun to dread driving. I counted to ten. *Come on, get on with it. It's not hard.*

The roads and highways to my mother's house were easy and familiar, uncrowded, moving from the hills to the broad flat expanse of the thruway. It had only been a few weeks since I'd made the drive for Christmas. As the white landscape rolled by, numbness stole over me. I drove all day making minimal stops and arrived at my mom's in Dayton in the dark.

Her ranch house was set off from the road, concealed by a row of pine trees. I pulled up and tramped through a thin layer of snow to the side door, giving a few rapid knocks before leaning into the kitchen and calling, "Hello? Mom?"

My mother emerged from the pantry holding a large cast iron skillet. She lowered her arm with a strained smile. "Wendy, my God, what are you doing? I saw a strange car pull up."

I laughed. "Were you going to hit me with the frying pan?"

"It's a good thing I don't have a gun. You shouldn't do that."

My laugh stopped short. *You would shoot me?* "I sent you an email I was coming," I said, puzzled.

"You didn't say you'd be in a strange car. What brings you here?"

I explained about returning Diana's car and belongings. She didn't seem happy to see me. She put the pan on the counter and picked up a cigarette burning in the ashtray. The smoke made a

little cloud over her head of short gray and blond hair. Her glasses
hung from her neck on a beaded chain, making her look older. It's
strange now to think she was only in her fifties.

She puffed the cigarette. "That's right, you emailed me something
about her. She died in an accident?" Her face turned more genuine-
ly concerned. "Are you okay?"

"Sure."

From the other room a loud TV show emitted gun shots. "Let
me turn that down."

We went into the cramped living room. When I was a child we'd
had a big house, and added to that lifetime of stuff was the house-
hold she'd recently inherited, when my grandmother died. It was a
constant battle to sort and get rid of things.

"Have you eaten?" she asked.

"No. Do you want to go out?"

"I don't like people watching me eat. There's still marmalade."

She made me toast with marmalade and coffee. "Mom, do you
think I'm creative?"

She lit another cigarette. "I don't know what creative means."

I took a sip of the weak coffee. "I felt like I didn't teach well because I wasn't creative enough."

"It wasn't you. One or two at a time, of your own kids, is one
thing. But a whole roomful of thirteen-year-olds has got to be the
most horrible situation anyone can face. People who like to teach
are people who like to control people, give orders and be obeyed.
You're not like that. You're soft."

"I'm not assertive."

"Assertive isn't enough. You're assertive. You're not Hitler. You
have to be a secret Hitler to teach."

I laughed. "I thought teachers were nurturers."

"That was your mistake. You should teach college, not kids."

I hadn't thought about that. "Go on for a PhD?"

"Well, you don't want to be a school junkie."

I sighed. Which was it supposed to be? "Peter said something like
that. But to teach college, I'd need a PhD."

Her look brightened. "If you want that, then go for it. It's a noble profession for a writer, to teach college. It's almost the only way. You should do it."

I nodded, my mouth full of crumbs and marmalade. This was always her desire, that I pursue writing.

"Oh! I found something of yours. Speaking of writing. It was wonderful. Let me get it." I wondered if she'd found some crappy old poem of mine or something. She rose and went to her bedroom, returning with a manila envelope. "Remember? I didn't get a chance to mail it to you, but here you are."

I smiled over what was inside: the "opera" Scott and I had written together in college.

"I didn't tell you, I've met Scott again. He's in school with me now."

My mom beamed. "I always thought you should be together."

I read over the lyrics, studying his handwriting next to mine. My eyes grew wet. It hit me. *I love him, I do love him, I've always loved him.* "Mom, do you have any idea what I should do, what I should be? How I can grow up?" I laughed through the tears in my eyes. "What I should be when I grow up?"

She stabbed out her cigarette and lit another in one motion. "You're a writer."

"No, I'm not. I had a flash of something once. I don't think it's what I was meant for."

"Why isn't writing enough? I've been working on my mystery novel for ten years. If I were your age and starting over, I would jump at the chance. Anyway, it sounds like you've settled on a decision. You'll get the PhD and teach college. Done."

I dried my eyes. She was right. I didn't know if I wanted to write, but pursuing a job as a professor was the obvious thing to do.

"Do you have laundry you need done?" she asked.

It was true I had packed quickly and not all my clothes were fresh. She did my laundry. Though my mom had always been a feminist, there was a streak of an old-fashioned housewife in her. She ironed everything.

As the laundry spun, she put on *CSI*, a show I wasn't very familiar with. She had told me before how much she liked it. So I was shocked at how gruesome it was. She was fascinated, and approached it with a clinical eye. I was glad when it was over.

She folded my clothes and put them in the spare bedroom. "I thought you didn't like violence." I called to her. It was something we shared.

She returned to the ironing board, her face still bright with fascination for the show. "I don't like *suffering*. But in this case, they're dead. They aren't suffering."

I glanced at the murder mysteries lining the room: Agatha Christie, Ruth Rendell, P. D. James. People cleanly, neatly dead. No suffering. I also thought: no emotion. Everything distant and detached. That was how my mother liked things.

"I've been having the worst nightmares lately," she said. "That I'm pushing people into ovens. Just awful images and feelings."

I don't think you want to write a murder mystery. I think you want to kill someone.

With the TV off, there was only the squeak of the ironing board. She was actually ironing my pajamas.

"What do you think, about my future?" I asked.

She finished, and the hideous screech of the ironing board as she folded it up seemed to be my answer.

"You can't think about the future until you let the past die," she said.

*   *   *

I lay awake, waves of thoughts flooding over me, my mind wandering into dream territory, though it didn't seem I was sleeping. All the cats dying all the time, my mother's cigarettes, my dad's drinking. Always playing unsupervised, the car door not quite latched. Dead robins in the road.

The next morning in the bathroom mirror, exhausted, my face was distorted. Instead of my mother's high cheekbones, my temples stretched wider, my face square like my father's. I thought, *In the mirror, her face had lost her mother's bones.* Something had shifted.

In the years since, I've discovered a pattern that if I go for a very long drive, it can encourage mania. I don't know what it is, maybe something about my eye movements watching the road, the dull roar of the tires, the light. This long drive wasn't good for me.

And there was something else. This was my first time seeing my mother since Ann had declared she had a personality disorder. This suspicion, this fear, bled deeply into my subconscious. Rising out of the awful dread was a bizarre paranoia.

I turned my head from side to side. My eyes seemed to stretch into my temples, alien. Again I felt the loss of my mother's face. I had lost her.

I went to the kitchen to take the lithium.

"Would you like devilled eggs?" my mother asked. "I always find they're worth the trouble."

It occurred to me that the strong taste of devilled eggs could disguise poison, which was what was happening on the TV. Mom had turned on some murder show where Diana Rigg was poisoning her children. I was surrounded by murder.

"You still take medication?" she asked as she made the coffee.

"Sure, I have to."

"Isn't there a point where they shake your hand and say goodbye?"

"Not really."

My mother shrugged. "It's all a racket," she murmured.

We ate, and soon I headed to the door. There was a strange moment. Mom went to the calendar pinned to the cupboard door and pointed at the dates. "So this is today. And you'll be in Chicago tomorrow, and come back on this day?" She pointed to Monday.

There was a slightly frightened look on her face, I thought. I wondered if I was looking disoriented, and she didn't want to address it, but wanted to make sure I knew where I was.

"Yes, I fly back Monday." I put on my coat. We didn't hug; we weren't huggers.

"Do you want me to call you when I get to Chicago?" I asked.

She seemed to shake off whatever had concerned her. "I'm sure you'll be fine."

A few hours later, I did not feel fine. Living in the country all my adult life, Route 90 coming into Chicago was like nothing I had ever experienced. The six lanes of traffic were circles of hell, taxis zipping by right and left. A stretch black limo created its own lane on the shoulder, spraying slush. Following the signs to stay on 90 meant thinking I had to change lanes, then discovering I didn't need to change lanes, while every time that I managed a decent following distance a car jumped in to fill it. I didn't know if I should get into an express lane, then the express lane was closed with barriers, and I had no idea whether to slow down for the continuously merging traffic. I knew I wasn't supposed to do that, but the stream of cars trying to get in was a constant threat. To top it off, I hadn't memorized the directions which I thought I'd somehow be able to glance at while I drove. No way. I clutched the wheel, my knuckles white.

I found myself in an exit only lane with no possibility of getting out, wanting to scream with panic, desperately wishing I weren't alone, wishing for Scott to navigate. It was impossible to watch for all the traffic at once and read the signs. I continued down the exit, terrified of getting lost. I was in the left turn lane and then onto the first city street I'd ever been on. There was no gas station or parking lot to turn into to stop and get my bearings. A taxi behind me honked the instant the light turned green. "I'm sorry, I'm sorry," I mouthed. There didn't seem to be a street sign on the corner to check where I was.

A city bus went by, labeled Diversey. When an oncoming ambulance wailed and everyone stopped, I had a moment to look at the Mapquest directions, realizing with a wave of panic they were for getting off at Irving Park. But as I was able to stop and think, I remembered something Greg said on the phone. Chicago is a grid. Go west and north. Pulaski runs north-south and Irving Park runs east-west. I had turned left, so I was heading west. If I kept going west, I would hit Pulaski. Then right, north to Irving Park. Maybe it wasn't so hard. Maybe it wasn't a nightmare, as long as I could find a street sign.

I glimpsed the dense city as I drove, signs combining Korean, Spanish, Polish. Electronics stores with burglar bars on the windows, bedding stores with blankets of Disney characters hanging out front, Thai restaurants, taco places, ten-dollar hair stylists, laundromats, and money-wiring places.

Orange cones narrowed the street and I bumped over the ridges of an unpaved section, wondering how a bus could squeeze through the lane. When a bus did appear, I was afraid to try to pass. A car honked. Holding my breath, I swung around it.

The blocks stretched on, and I seemed to hit every red light, but each stop was a chance to take a breath. The view widened with a parking lot on my left and a Golden Nugget on the right, its lot dominated by a huge white stretch Hummer, like some kind of mutant beast. The sign said Pulaski and I turned right, feeling giddy to have found it. A blue and white police car stopped traffic again, followed by a blaring fire engine.

At last I reached Irving Park and could follow the written directions in snatches. I turned onto the last street. It was crowded with parked cars on each side. My last worry was finding a place to park. When I saw a spot there was a hydrant. I would have been willing to park far off and walk, but didn't want to inconvenience Greg.

Two folding chairs sagged in the street in front of the house. I idled in the street, glad no one was coming from behind, as I figured out what to do next. Then Greg came out of the house, pulled up the chairs, and waved me in. I hadn't parallel parked in years, but it came back to me. When I shut off the car, I slumped, hands on my face, shaking and fighting off tears.

CHAPTER TWENTY-ONE

Greg opened the passenger door and got in next to me. "What's the matter? Are you okay? Were you in an accident? The car looks fine."

I wiped my face on my sleeve and straightened up. "I'm okay. I just didn't expect—the traffic, the highway, the streets. I've never been in a place like this." I laughed. "I can't believe I made it." He handed me a crumpled paper napkin from his pocket, and I blew my nose. "You must think I'm an imbecile. I feel like a child."

"Not at all. I didn't think about it. I'm so used to it here. But I don't blame you at all. I don't even own a car."

I wiped my face on the clean side of the napkin. A car drove by, the headlights catching Greg's big brown eyes with a sparkle. He had grown fashionably scruffy facial hair that wasn't quite a beard.

"You don't own a car?" I had no idea you could live without a car.

He shrugged. "It's a pain the city."

We got out, splashing through the icy puddle by the curb. I was surprised at just how cold it was, my fingers tingling. My toes got wet from the puddle. Back home there was snow, but not this ice and water. Salt crunched beneath our feet.

Greg's side of the street was lined with brick buildings two and three stories tall, each a little different, very close together with a tiny square yard in front. On the other side were bungalows. The one directly across was still decorated for Christmas—times a thousand. White lights outlined the roof and windows and wound up the path to the door. Penguins marched beside a Santa in his sleigh inside a huge plastic globe. Candy canes and nutcracker soldiers were strewn in front of Snoopy on top of his doghouse dressed as Santa, Woodstock at his feet as an elf. Mechanical deer turned their heads toward the red-nosed Rudolph, and a pair of ice skaters spun on a silver pond. It was all crammed into two hundred blazing square feet.

"Wow."

"At least they turn it off at midnight. And maybe the light scares away the rats."

We entered a vestibule at the foot of a staircase. I hadn't pictured the inside to be like this. It wasn't a single-family home, but had three condos, one on each floor. Our tread echoed from the worn wooden stairs to the third floor.

"It's a good thing I'm used to walking up a lot of hills," I said.

Greg laughed. "These places don't have elevators. I think zoning only requires them with four floors."

He opened the door into a short hall lined in bookcases, leading to the living room. Beyond the tiny hall, the room was spacious. At the far end, a kind of bay with windows on three sides overlooked the bare trees and yellow streetlights. A blue and white floral carpet anchored a gray velvet sofa and an Eames chair eccentrically upholstered in pale lime green leather. Original 1920s woodwork framed the space with a built-in mirrored buffet on one side. At a large round dining table, a couple was opening takeout food.

Diana's mother hugged Greg and extended her hand to me. "Hi, Wendy. I'm Kristen. We ordered Thai, I hope you'll like it." Kristen was petite, like Diana, but slight rather than buxom. Blue eyes shone in her pale, taut face, her dark hair swept back in a sleek ponytail. She seemed young to have two grown children, and I remembered that I was a little older than Greg and Diana.

As I took her hand, I realized it was still only two weeks since her daughter's body was found (they did not know I was the one who'd found her), and grief was raw in Kristen's face. I wondered if I should say something, like, "I'm sorry for your loss," but somehow it seemed better to stick with the present. The dinner, the drive, the immediate moment. She was looking at me with bright determination in that way.

The man beside her was opening a bottle of white wine. "Hi, I'm David," he said. He looked a little worse, his shoulders stooping as if under the weight of his grief. The cork made a crying sound as he twisted it out of the bottle.

"It's nice to meet you." I searched for something to say. "I've never had Thai food before."

Kristen looked confused. "Never had Thai food? How is that possible?"

Greg chuckled. "She's from the middle of nowhere." Turning to me, "You have a big day in store tomorrow. City life. You're in for a treat. You'll want to move here."

David put big spoons in the various takeout containers while Kristen set out a stack of plates and forks. I hadn't eaten since the toast and marmalade at my mother's that morning and the Thai food smelled delicious. I was ravenous.

"Please help yourself," Kristen said.

I restrained myself from taking a huge helping. I noticed Kristen took only a few dainty spoonfuls. As we sat down to eat, I responded to Greg. "I don't know if I'd want to move here. It seemed overwhelming coming in."

He waved his fork. "You can adjust. What do you do in New York, watch the cars rust? Watch the paint dry?" We laughed.

"What do you do for fun there, Wendy?" Kristen asked.

I struggled to answer. "Sometimes I drive to Syracuse and walk around the mall."

Kristen looked confused again. "And that's fun?"

"Well, I don't know. At the mall I treat myself to Panda Express."

They laughed. "I hope this is better than Panda Express," Kristen said.

"Yes, it's wonderful."

"And, what else?"

"The university put on a play last fall."

Greg laughed. "*A* play, *a* play. We have two hundred theaters in Chicago."

"Really?" I chewed the chicken Rama, the peanut sauce rich in my mouth. I couldn't imagine living here, a place so full of cars and traffic, honking horns and sirens.

"So, you write?" David asked.

"A little. I used to."

"What about?" Kristen asked. "What's your medium?"

"I had a humor class as an undergrad. Actually my mom just gave me a copy of something I wrote back then. My friend Scott and I wrote a little opera."

"Oh, we must hear this!" Kristen said.

My eyes met Greg's from across the table. There was an affirmative look in his eyes like he wanted very much for me to do so.

"It's right in my bag, I'll get it." I quickly got it out of my suitcase and brought it to the table. "So, it was an opera, *Ballad of the Cow Tippers*."

They were laughing immediately. "Cow tippers?" David asked.

"There's a legend, and I don't know if it's real, that bored teenagers in upstate New York go into farmers' fields and rush at the cows and tip them over. It's called cow tipping."

They laughed more. I cleared my throat, picked up the page that shared mine and Scott's handwriting, and began to sing:

"Don't cry for me South New Berlin,
The truth is, your mom's a Holstein.
So don't go tipping,
That cow you're tripping
Could be your mother,
Could be your mother.
Go ask your brother
If she's your mother. . . ."

Amid joyous laughter and applause, I finished it and went on to the Lactose Intolerance Song:

"Touch if you will my stomach,
Feel how it trembles inside.
That's all because of the lactose,
That's why my side is so wide. . . ."

The "opera" was about twenty minutes long, and, after gaug-
ing once more that the Cerfs' delight was genuine, I performed
it through. Kristen was wiping tears from her eyes by the end. I'd
forgotten the fun it all was years ago to do this kind of thing.

"You have to bring this to a fringe festival," Greg said.

"That would be perfect for fringe," Kristen agreed.

The idea of fringe festivals and two hundred theaters seemed
more magical than real, though I was realizing it was true. I helped
clean up. As we wiped down the counters and loaded the dish-
washer, I knew that Diana hadn't been mentioned yet, and I felt
some apprehension about when and how she would come up.
I was letting go of my dread about what time Diana had been
killed—it was a silly, crazy fear. But I still wondered how she had
spent her last day.

As we finished cleaning up, we talked about other things instead,
plans for the next day and Greg's schedule for the week. It turned
out Greg was an actor. We sat in the living room, and Greg told me
a little about his career while a cable channel played calm music in
the background.

"I get a lot of readings, and I just closed an improv show. I have
some auditions lined up next week."

"And this is full-time, or do you have a day job?" I asked.

"Sure. I'm not Equity. I work at a bar and at Starbucks."

I took the glass of wine David handed to me, thanking him. "I
went to a Starbucks once."

They looked at me agog. "Once?" Greg asked.

"Yes, in Binghamton. The coffee was so strong."

They all laughed. Kristen, in the Eames chair, sipped her wine,
and with some effort said, "Diana tried to tell us it was nowhere,
but I never realized."

We turned quiet as the soft music played. I swallowed the dry wine, grasping for what to say. I didn't want to say, "I'm sorry." Sorry wasn't the word.

"She was a great talent," I said. "A strong presence."

Kristen nodded, her face partly hidden behind her glass of wine. She closed her eyes, took a sip, and then a deep breath. She seemed to clear her head, turning to Greg with a fierce, determined look.

"So what are you auditioning for, honey?" she asked.

At the time, I thought this was strength, and that Kristen was the one from whom Diana had gotten her strength, her determination. But maybe it wasn't strength to turn off her feelings. Maybe Stoicism. In the moment, I admired it, as my mother had raised me to admire controlling emotion, turning it off.

Greg talked about the upcoming play, and the conversation turned to theater and the arts for a while, until Greg rose to put on his coat. "Would you like to walk me to the bus stop?" he asked me.

"Sure." I put on my coat and followed him down the stairs.

At the bus stop on Irving Park, he took my hand. "Thank you. You've been great for us."

"What do you mean?"

His eyes glittered in the streetlights. "While you were singing your funny songs, mom ate twice as much as usual. I appreciate that. You might have noticed she's anorexic."

"I didn't realize."

He nodded. "My dad's a doctor and here we all feel so helpless. Especially this past month, I think she's lost another five pounds. But she was better tonight. Ordering in like that and even eating rice. It was great to see. So thanks."

"I don't know if I did anything special, but you're welcome."

"You did." The icy wind picked up. "If you want to head back, you don't have to wait in the cold."

"I want to. I wish . . ." He looked at me expectantly. "I shouldn't bring it up. But I've been wanting to know . . . how she spent her last day."

He didn't look shocked, as I had feared. "I've been doing that, too, going over it. Yeah. I have some idea. That bastard Mark lied about not seeing her. He saw her that day, the day she died. She said so in her last email."

I looked up at him in surprise.

"I've been reading it over and over. She was chattier than usual. Changing her schedule, seeing an art teacher, going to the health center to help her quit smoking. And then the argument with Mark . . . But you know, let's forget about it. Let's not do this. We'll have fun tomorrow. She'd want that." He gave me a quick hug as the bus pulled up. "So I'll see you after breakfast, Wendy. Sleep in—we won't be going too early. Good night."

He got on, and I nervously walked back up the deserted street. The Christmas house was dark.

CHAPTER TWENTY-TWO

Scott stopped at the library to look up the story that I had gotten published in *The Iowa Review*. He took it to a carrel and settled down to read, smiling, my deep voice in his head. This was the me he used to know.

"The Dostoyevsky/Tolstoy Papers"

Dear Count Tolstoy,

I'm writing to tell you how much I enjoyed your book *Child-hood*. Until recently I was an engineer in the army. I quit nominally for my health, but really because I hate math. What I want to do is write. Do you have an agent? Should I try to get one? Will an agent understand Death? Thank you for your time. Yours truly, Fyodor Dostoyevsky.

Dear Mr. Dostyevsky,

Thank you for your letter. I hope I spelled your name right. Your handwriting is a little hard to read. I would recommend you get a secretary, or marry one, before you get an agent. Not because of your handwriting (though a secretary would help on that score as well), but to organize your work. A wife is good for that kind of thing. An agent will come in time. How are you talking about Death? A physical death, or a death of the spirit? Is the promise of Heaven's reward at the end? Always leave them laughing. People want some redemption. Good luck to you in your endeavors. Yours truly, Leo Tolstoy.

Dear Count Tolstoy,

Thank you for the advice. My name is D-O-S-T-O-Y-E-V-S-K-Y. You missed an 'o.' Everybody does. I saw your picture today hanging in the bookstore. You have a great beard. How do you keep it clean? I use Doc Elgor's beard grooming powder, but I'm not satisfied. I fear it smells of cabbage. As for a wife, I'm on my second marriage and we have been on a long honeymoon, seeing Europe. I would like Europe better if it weren't so proud in its corruption. Materialism is seen as progress, as an end in itself. I think that is related to my conception of Death. I blame their Church. Only our dear Orthodox Church is free of the slavery of material concerns, don't you agree? Yours truly, Fyodor D.

Dear Fyodor,

Sorry about the name thing. I think we can be on first names now, agreed? To answer your first question, I use Old Ivan's Rose Oil to keep my beard clean and soft. I agree it's hard not to smell like cabbage, especially for a vegetarian like myself. But I must disagree with your religious view. All established church is a mistake, and against Christ's teaching, which is simple and plain. The priests only keep us mired in fearful superstition, and obedient to the government. I'll forward you some literature. Yours truly, Leo.

PS I don't really like to use "Count." I don't believe in status.

Dear Leo,

Thank you for your tip about the rose oil. I've seen it at the store, but it's a little expensive. Money is tight. My wife has been harping at me to ask you for a little loan. I've given up gambling—you know how one gambles in the army—but it's taking me a long time to write my novel (can I look for an agent before it's finished?) and now my wife is with child. I shouldn't bother you about that, though. I can't agree with you about religion. Our Orthodox Church is what makes the Russian people uniquely mystic and philosophical. It's the experience of it, the glittering icons and haunting prayers through the haze of smoke. We are a people singular in our morbidity and faith, and it makes us think, during these long Godawful winters, about eternity in a way no one else does. Other people have fun. The Europeans have opera, and the rabid maniacs who call themselves Americans have sport. We don't have sport. We have ontology. We have no preaching. We have the silence of snow as our prayer, and our Church echoes this silence in a beautiful way, echoes the silence of God, our winter God, in a dream of eternity. I hope you'll agree. Yours truly, Fyodor.

PS Could you perhaps lend me ten rubles? My wife is reminding me right now. She is getting annoying about it.

Dear Fyodor,

I've enclosed ten rubles. You don't have to pay it back. I'm sure your wife is charming. My wife is an old hen, all clucks and feathers. I understand your feeling about the Church. But you have been seduced by it. Recently I was overcome with an understanding of Christ's teachings. I reject all organized society, both church and government. It is enough to be dumbfounded by existence. We are alive! It is wondrous. We can know each other. We are all human, and yet we are fooled into making war, into being tools of a machine that teaches that anyone is less than we are, that some are better than others. We must oppose this machine, even the Church. It is all simple with Christ. Tell me, why do you write? To contemplate Death? Contemplate Love. Love is eternal. Yours truly, Leo.

PS I would recommend that you publish a few short pieces before trying to get an agent interested in your novel.

Dear Leo,

I am no tool of a machine. I think for myself, and my views deserve respect. I have contemplated the mysteries of our dear Church for a long time. When I was in a Siberian prison, The

Bible was all I had to keep myself going. A kind woman sent me one. I don't need other literature to educate me. You sound like a socialist. I don't know if you realize that. I write in haste as my wife is in labor. Yours respectfully, Fyodor.

Dear Fyodor,

I'm sorry if I offended you. Letters are a poor way to communicate, and we come off differently than we think. You came off very defensive in your letter. I was only trying to share with you my joy in the Word. I'll leave it if it offends you. Congratulations on the baby. Still your friend I hope, Leo.

Dear Leo,

I'm sorry I was defensive. I was being overly touchy, perhaps I was nervous about the baby. I'm besotted with our little Sonya. She has changed me. I thought I knew love, but I didn't. I feel that the blinders have been removed from my eyes, and I see myself, so stupid and proud, I see my shameful faults now, and I understand that I require forgiveness. Love is forgiveness. This tiny baby loves everything she sees. She loves her tiny fingers and toes. My hand is so big and dumb wrapped around her. We are all fools and sinners, as we grow in the world, and it is our duty as Christians to be born again like this baby and see the wonder of the world around us. I hope you will forgive my pride. Yours sincerely, Fyodor.

Dear Fyodor,

I am glad to hear from you. I think we are not so far apart. You're right, Christ asked us to be like children, as do all the great teachers. I've been reading about Buddha lately and enjoying what he says. My wife rolls her eyes at it. She is content to kiss her crucifix and ask no questions. That is what I was trying to say before, I'm against religion that represses all questioning. I think you are on the right track. But perhaps it isn't for me to evaluate your faith. Your faith is between you and God. I was wrong to imply otherwise. Take delight in your beautiful baby. Try to remember this happiness when she is a teenager. Yours truly, Leo.

Dear Leo,

I'm sorry it's been so long since I last wrote. I am wild with grief. Sonya lived three months. I have been sobbing like a woman every day. Where is God? How can there be a God who would let this baby die so senselessly? What good are doctors? They did no good. I see nothing but ugliness everywhere I go, the grime and rags of the people I pass, the greasy windows, the shapeless ghosts of trees. There is no beauty in the world. I thought I knew Death. I thought I understood it uniquely. I didn't know Death until I knew Love and lost it at once. Where am I to go? What is the point of life now? ~~The future is~~ Yours truly, Fyodor.

Dear Fyodor,

How my heart goes out to you. When you crossed out "the future is," I feared for your life and soul. I don't know if my poor words can touch your grief. All I can say is this: You only know Death because you knew Love. What is mourning? It is a contemplation of Love. It is a contemplation of the experience of having been loved. A baby is the embodiment of Love, pure and simple. You not only loved, but experienced Sonya's pure love for you. Now she has gone to Heaven, gone from love to Love. Be joyful because she taught you love. Remember that love in your grief; it is the only reason you grieve. Rise from your bed of grief and see the world through her eyes again, as you did once. Let it prepare you for that future you crossed out, a future where there will be those who still need your love, and where God waits for you as patiently as an oak. Put aside the vodka and drink bracing tea, and find strength in the common and mundane beauty of existence. And keep writing. I will pray for you. With love, Leo.

Dear Leo,

Thank you for your letter, though I can scarcely take it in. My writing has taken a dark turn. I think of murders and violence. I hope by the end of my novel there will be redemption. I understand people want that, but it's hard. I'll try to remember it. Your letter is a comfort and I thank you. What are you writing now? Also, can a novel be too long? I worry about that. Yours with love, Fyodor.

Dear Fyodor,

I'm glad I could help, if only a little. I've been very busy lately writing about a woman who is unhappy, and can't help but choose to be so. It too is dark. Sometimes I think I should try to write with more levity and humor. Most people don't know my humorous side. My friends say I'm hilarious. Anyway, as I come to its completion, I won't have time to write to you for a while. As for your novel, it can be as long as it needs to be. I'm glad you are interested in writing again. Yours, Leo.

Dear Leo,

I finished my novel today. I think I found the redemptive ending it required. The novel took a lot out of me. Perhaps I exorcized some demons. I'm starting to see the world again, still perhaps less beautiful than it was for those brief three months, but sometimes I see a child playing with a delighted dog, or hear a woman singing as she hangs her wash on the line—a beautifully mournful peasant song, or I see glistening cabbages in someone's kitchen garden growing through the frosted ground, and there is a glimmer of hope that there is a God. I will continue to try to see Him. I look forward to reading your next book. Thank you. Love, Fyodor.

PS Can you recommend me to your agent?

This was the me that he used to know. When we'd met, he was the odd man out, the engineer in a humor in literature class. I'd said, "You're an engineer? Then you're important. You know how the world works."

It was a weird friendship, because it was quickly so close, so intense. One day he tried to drop a hint, and I quickly replied, "You're like a brother to me." And he was sure now that I'd forgotten about this, (I had, so selfishly), forgotten that small moment in the mists of time. He stayed like my brother.

And he stayed in the friendship. He dated, moving in with someone later. When she pushed him out, after he'd spent a year fixing up her house, he decided women only took him for granted. He'd done his best, switching to contacts instead of glasses because of this girlfriend, always giving in to what she wanted. Women. A small bitterness rose in him.

He lost his job. It seemed like everything in his life was falling apart. So he started over, returning to school. But staying distant, removed, afraid to trust. And then I appeared again. He'd tried to forget me, but there it was: That sensation of peace. The feeling he could say anything to me, and I'd understand.

He couldn't take not being understood, especially by me, the one person he could count on. Our argument had enraged him, triggered his abhorrence of being misconstrued, overlooked. Now he knew he was the one who had been mistaken, not seeing the signs of my illness, not realizing what I was grappling with.

Now what? He knew one thing. He was not going to be taken for granted again. I was going to have to show I cared. I was going to have to fight for him. He put the book back on the shelf, feeling tired, his arms heavy.

No. This was a repeat of last time, when he'd abandoned me. It was selfish. Maybe I just wasn't into him, was that something to blame me for? Maybe we could only be friends, but a close friend was still a good thing to have.

The library windows were dark, and a quiet murmur pulsed in the background as he fell into thought. I'd been reasonable back then. Maybe emotional, and impulsive. But still basically sane. I seemed to have declined so much. I was not the same, not the same person who made him laugh, who wrote this story. The loneliness of the past few years filled him with longing and nostalgia. He wanted me back, wanted back the old laughing Wendy.

CHAPTER TWENTY-THREE

I lay in Diana's bed, exhausted but alert. The room was green and white, fresh and clean. It was small and somewhat bare because most of her things had been in New York. I felt funny taking Diana's bedroom, but it was the only spare room, and Kristen didn't betray any emotion about it.

I hoped I would sleep, but most of the night my thoughts tumbled, scattered, at moments seeming deeply meaningful and then gone into static. In the morning just as I was at the bathroom door, David stepped out. I had been about to walk in on him.

"Morning," he said with a curt nod. "Did you sleep well?"

"Yes, thank you."

I didn't want to occupy the bathroom too long, but after the sleepless night, the hot shower felt good. I smoothed on some scented lotion from the shelf since Kristen had said to use anything.

As I pulled on my pajamas, there was a rapid knock on the door. "Diana? Diana, is that you?"

I opened the door. Kristen's pale face glowed with frantic anticipation, her fist still raised to knock on the door.

"It's me, Wendy."

She stood frozen, her eyes wide but unconscious. David rapidly came and put his arm around her shoulders, taking hold of her fist to lower it.

Kristen's expression melted into confused grief. "Oh yes, of course. I'm so sorry."

"It's all right."

David wrapped his arm around her waist. "It was a dream."

"Yes, a dream, of course."

"Let's get you some coffee." He walked her away to the kitchen.

I dressed and came out to the living room. Kristen was sitting at the dining table drinking black coffee, a small glass dish in front of her with seven almonds in it.

"I got out the sauté pan, and there are eggs in the fridge," Kristen said with forced brightness. "There's cereal. Please have anything you like, help yourself."

There were bananas on the counter. "How about if I make us banana omelets?" I asked.

Kristen caught her breath with a smile, her eyes wet. "I used to make those." She broke off before finishing, "for Diana," but I felt that was what she meant. Kristen wiped her eyes, still forcing a bright expression, jumping up to get out the vanilla and cinnamon sugar. "That would be lovely. You'll need a big breakfast."

David came out of the bedroom straightening his tie as I sliced the banana. "That looks good. I have to meet with that committee. Enjoy your omelet." He gave Kristen a peck on the cheek and left.

I thought it better not to try to give Kristen a big serving, dividing one three-egg omelet. I recalled reading somewhere, that some anorexics were actually foodies, and hoped the dish was appetizing. Kristen took small bites, eating slowly. She seemed to enjoy the taste, letting it linger.

"I'm off to my yoga class at the gym," Kristen said when we'd finished. "Please make yourself at home, and don't worry about how late you get in tonight. I think Greg has plenty of adventure planned for you. Here, I'll put on the music."

She put the TV back on to the New Age music station and soon left. Tired already from all the strain and not having slept well, I thought about going back to bed. I stretched out on the couch with that weird feeling of being alone in someone else's house. I closed my eyes, but sleep didn't come. The music channel displayed peaceful images of flowers and trees, and as my eyes opened and closed, I read various inspirational messages on the screen. "Focus on your potential instead of your limitations." *I should do that.* "If you cannot find the truth right where you are, where else do you expect to find it." *Yes. What is the truth? Is it here?* I started to dream and forgot my dream instantly. "The water the cow laps turns into milk. The water a snake licks becomes poison." *I was thinking of something. I knew. I knew something. What did I know? Winter.*

The lock turned in the door with a click. Greg called a greeting and went down the hall to the bedroom. I followed. He had brought up some of Diana's things from the car.

"Let me help you," I said.

"Thanks. I think we can get the rest in one more trip."

The day was bright, cold, and windy. There was only a thin layer of snow on the ground, but the wind felt like ice water pouring on my head. My hair was still damp from the shower, and my scalp ached with the cold.

I grabbed a suitcase while Greg got the rest of the boxes. I panted from the effort of carrying it up three flights. In the bedroom, he stacked everything neatly in the closet and closed the door.

"We can deal with this later on," he said. "Are you ready? You have a hat and gloves? Don't tell me you won't wear a hat because it messes up your hair."

"No, I have a hat." I pulled it down over my ears, but I hadn't brought gloves.

Greg looked through the drawers in Diana's white dresser and took out a fine pair of green leather gloves wrapped in tissue.

"I couldn't," I said, almost drooling over them.

He pressed them on me. "It's okay. It's cold out. I gave them to her, I can lend them to you. I guess she was saving them." He gave me a grim smile.

I pulled them on. They were beautiful, lined in cashmere, and fit tightly to my slender hands. I felt like a model. I ignored the guilt. "Thanks."

The bus was scheduled in five minutes. We jogged down the sidewalk, dodging patches of ice. The blue and white bus was just pulling up. Squeezing between a stroller and a shopping cart, we headed to the back. I was hoping to look out the windows as we rode, but they were too grimy.

"I've never ridden a city bus before," I said.

"Yeah, they actually have paved streets, and lights at the intersection. And there's sliced bread. Do you know about sliced bread?"

I laughed. It was a short bus ride to the train. He led me up the steps to the Brown Line platform, where we huddled in a small heated shelter that was full of pigeons. It all seemed complicated.

"I could never find my way around if I lived here."

"Of course you could. You made it to the house, remember?"

"How do you know which train to take and which way to go?"

He shook his head with a smile. "It's not rocket science. The Loop is downtown, south, and Kimball is the end of the line to the north. There are only two ways the train can go. It's not a wormhole. It's simple."

When the train roared up, I grabbed a pillar, fearing I was going to be sucked under the wheels. At least the windows were clean, as I watched the city go by below. "There's quite a lot of brick," I said.

"Well, we had that fire."

"Right." We crossed the river, red bridges paralleling the track into the distance, the train narrowly careening by skyscrapers that seemed only inches away. "Oh my God!"

"What is it?"

"It's like we're going to hit the buildings!"

He snorted. "Okay, Dorothy."

The skyscrapers were all different. Some had ornate Victorian carvings, others were brand new, straight black monoliths or blue glass curvilinear towers. We passed a couple of colleges as the train bent around the loop, and I wondered about Diana rejecting them in favor of North Carthage.

Where we got off the train, the air smelled of chocolate. It was a short walk to the Art Institute. The only art museum I had been to was the tiny one in Utica, and this one was massive, never-ending. The colors of the Impressionists pulsated. *Sunday in the Park* was a huge canvas; I felt I could hear the crowd by the riverbank. Van Gogh looked down at me with regret.

I wanted to see *Nighthawks* so we went up the marble stairs. Eternally distant, the man and woman sat apart in the lonely diner.

"Edward Hopper is my mother's favorite painter," I said. She would like that—the isolation, the loneliness. I wondered if I was drawn to my own isolated life in New York for the same reason my mother was drawn to Hopper.

"They had a big show of his, a couple of years ago. The final painting in the show, the culmination of his work, was the bare, empty corner of a room. Just light, bare walls, a floor. Nothingness," Greg said. "Diana loved it. She said if she had more courage that's what she would do."

I thought of my meeting with Professor Andrews, Diana's plans to switch to art. "But she did have courage."

He nodded, looking away, wiping his eyes with his sleeve before recovering.

We went to a nearby Russian restaurant for lunch. It was softly carpeted, dark, with white tablecloths and red cloth napkins. He insisted I try a cosmopolitan, and the cranberry juice in it was fresh and light. I had borscht and stuffed eggplant.

I was still thinking about Hopper and my mother as I ate. I started to try to explain, stopped short, feeling tangled, and said, "My family is just weird."

Greg tilted his head. "So, whose isn't? My mother is anorexic, my father spends all his time at work. I'm only twenty-four, and I'm in recovery from drinking. We're all a mess. But we get on. The thing that hurts me most about Diana . . ." he stopped and swallowed. "Was that I thought of her as the one completely sane person in our family. The rock. And then God knows why, she went out to that black hole in the middle of nowhere, and managed to get pregnant. What was that about? And get killed out of stupidity. I mean, what happened to her? Did she finally crack? Did we pressure her too much? She was the genius of the family." He raised his hand absently, his voice breaking. "It was not her Fate. It shouldn't have been. She was destined for more. She was our hope and dream. Maybe it was too much." He slowly lowered his hand to his chest, his gaze somewhere over my head.

I waited, searching for something to say. I, too, wondered about all of it. "So she never said why she left for New York?"

"She once said she wanted to see if she could survive, where there was nothing." He sipped his glass of Russian tea, his food almost untouched. The restaurant seemed to go silent. "Of course, she didn't."

"Didn't what?"

He grimaced. "Survive."

I reached for his hand. "I didn't mean to make you talk about it."

Greg squeezed my hand, meeting my eyes with a firm nod. "No, it's okay. I knew it would be hard to come here today. I like to think while I'm looking at the art, she's looking at it too, through my eyes. I know it's silly, but it helps. And it's nice to show someone new around." He took a forkful of carrot salad, forcing himself to eat. He took a deep breath and smiled. "But she was funny, too. Did you ever see her funny side?"

I started to laugh, remembering. "One night we were watching PBS, and she was complaining Ken Burns had the hairstyle of a twelve-year-old boy. And she started reciting a Civil War letter: 'Dear Martha, the rats have eaten the shoes off our feet. Dear Martha, to keep our feet warm we keep them in the porridge . . .'" Greg's laughter made me laugh harder, remember more. "And then it was fashion, and women who wear flannel pajama pants in public, like children on their way to a drive-in movie. And there was some makeover show called *What Not to Wear* she had seen—"

"I remember her watching that junk sometimes!" his eyes shone, the memories like finding pieces of treasure.

"Yes! She said the hosts always wanted to put their hapless victim into a jacket with a 'nipped-in waist.' You had to have a *nipped-in waist*. She said in Chicago it was always either Arctic cold or blazing hot as hell, it's never the right temperature for a jacket, but for those two days a year when it's sixty degrees, she had her jacket with a *nipped-in waist. . . .*" Our laughter died away and we sat, each in our private memories.

I sighed. "What you said before, about her being your rock. I see that. I feel like she was so grown-up, and if I could grow up, there's some mystery I can solve. I'll understand it all when I grow up."

Greg shook his head. "That's a funny hang-up. Of course you're grown-up. We all feel that way."

Ann had said that, too, but it didn't help. "I know. . . ."

"A lot of people say trying to become an actor isn't very grown-up. I'd think grad school and teaching and writing is grown-up."

"I'm not teaching now. I tried a few years ago. I failed at it. And then . . . I spent two years delivering newspapers."

"Newspapers? Like throwing them on the porch?"

I shook my head. "In the country, with the houses acres apart, it's done by car. It's done by adults. Adults on their lowest legs . . ."

"Come on. . . ." he put his hand on mine. "I think everyone has a year like that. The year of their worst job. It's totally normal."

I sighed. He had a point. I let his hand stay on mine for a few moments. Around us the restaurant made a low buzz.

He looked me in the eyes. "I think I know what the thing is. When I started college, I was writing a screenplay, as bad as any freshman would write. It was all talking heads. My teacher said to me, people don't change by sitting around talking. They're changed by experience. So you, you live in this isolated environment, and you haven't been employed a lot. It seems like, you haven't had experiences, you haven't had *opportunities*. You know, to socialize, to interact with people and discover your own maturity."

I held his gaze, thinking how much he must have been through, recovering from drinking, struggling with a difficult career, his mother, and Diana's death. He had pinpointed it exactly. "I never thought of that. Thanks. Thanks a lot." I laughed. "That was worth years of therapy."

I did what I could to steer the conversation to something positive, asking Greg all about his acting life in the city. His mood lightened as he told me stories about improv classes at Second City and devising new works.

"I have a surprise for you this afternoon," he said as he paid the check. "I got tickets to a sold-out show. You'll love it."

We walked a few blocks in the icy wind, and I felt exhilarated now by the tumult of new experiences and the bracing cold. We took the Blue Line, which stayed underground, and came up to a small, ornate theater. Inside it was all black, the walls and floor, and the seats on three sides looked down on the performance area. "So this is a theater? It seems so small."

He looked surprised. "This is a good size for a black box theater. I've been in some that only seat forty people."

"I think of a theater as having a stage and a curtain, and the audience all in rows in front of it."

He chuckled. "A high school auditorium?"

I laughed, blushing. "I guess so."

Opposite our seats were metal cages, the set a skeleton of steel pipes. Everything was so stripped-down and exposed, but the show, about the life of Harry Houdini, was anything but minimal. The cast played instruments and sang, taking on multiple roles, and the star did magic tricks that took my breath away. When he escaped from the water tank and somehow changed places with another performer, I was agog.

When it was over, I was rooted to my seat, not wanting to stop applauding. "That was amazing! I couldn't believe it! I've never seen anything like this."

Greg put his arm around me. "This is theater. Come on, let's go to the used bookstore."

"On a Sunday night? It's after five o'clock."

He smiled. "They're open until eleven."

There was still plenty of traffic out and people in the streets as we arrived at the huge store. Greg browsed the drama section and picked up a book of monologues. I looked over literary criticism and picked up a book about the Brontës. An older woman approached us. Greg quickly introduced Pat, a playwright. Pat was in her fifties, her face free of makeup, her hair short and white, a stack of books in her arms. "Hi, Wendy. How do you like Chicago?"

"I feel like I'm in Oz," I said with a laugh.

"Where are you from?"

"Upstate New York."

Pat's smile grew wide. "So am I. Do you know Utica?"

"Yes."

"I went to school there."

"So did I!"

Pat shifted the stack of books in her arms. "You should move here, come to Chicago. It's a good place to start over."

"Driving here was terrifying."

She nodded, her big earrings catching the light. "Well, of course. But it's really very livable. How can you fault a city that smells like chocolate?"

Greg asked what she was buying. She'd picked up a book on female Pulitzer winners. "It's inscribed, the author dedicated it to a friend, and now it's here," she laughed. "Never overestimate your importance." Pat winked, and we went to the register. At the door, she clapped Greg on the arm and gave me a hug. "Hope to see you again, soon. Very soon."

I no longer felt the cold as we made our way home. That night in bed, I felt elated. Maybe I could move here. Maybe I could start over. I tried to sleep but was wide awake all night.

The Cerfs and I said goodbye early the next morning. They thanked me profusely for going to all the trouble, and I thanked them just as profusely for the magical day.

Kristen pulled her cardigan tight around her tiny body. "Stay safe," she said, her voice strained. Unable to completely push down the emotion, her face reddened.

David put his arm around her. Then to my surprise, she reached out and pulled all of us into the embrace. The moment of silence was our one tribute to the departed. Then the moment passed and she quickly waved us out the door.

Greg rode with me on the Blue Line to O'Hare.

"Well that's simple, the train actually says O'Hare," I said with a laugh.

"Who's picking you up in Syracuse?" Greg asked.

My heart dropped twenty feet. I had completely forgotten to arrange to be picked up. This was before Uber and Lyft but even so I wouldn't have considered taking either, or a cab, for the two-hour drive. "Oh, just a friend."

"Scott?" he asked.

I stared down. "Yeah, Scott."

"Give him my best."

We said goodbye at the top of the stairs leading out of the subway. Greg gave me a tight hug.

"Oh, the gloves, I almost forgot." I started to take them off, but he held my hands.

"Keep them, please. I want you to have them."

I took a deep breath. I did love them. "Thank you. Thanks so much for everything."

"Thank you. Take care of yourself, Wendy."

On the flight home, my mood sank. This trip had shown me the possibility of a different life. There was a world out there I scarcely knew, museums, plays, late-night used bookstores. Pat said it was livable. People could get along without cars. The air smelled like chocolate. It was magic. But more than that, I had a glimpse of myself as someone else. I had been competent. I drove that long difficult way by myself, it seemed like I had said the right things, I hadn't walked in on David in the bathroom, thank God. I'd gotten Kristen to eat a little more food. And maybe it was good for Greg to open up, too. He seemed happier by the end of the night.

I had been different, an adult. I hadn't apologized once in twenty-four hours. I'd seen a new side of myself. But now I was going to have to call Scott from Syracuse and ask him to pick me up. I felt like a child again.

It didn't help when I called and heard his exasperated sigh. "What time are you getting in?"

"I'm in Syracuse now."

"What? Why didn't you call from Chicago?"

I felt even more stupid. I had wanted to put it off as long as possible. "I had to get on the plane."

"You know it takes two hours to get there."

"I know. There's a Starbucks. I'll just wait."

He sighed again. "Fine. I'll see you when I get there."

I went out to the curb far ahead of time not to keep him waiting, and when he pulled up I hopped in the car so quickly he barely had to stop. We rode in silence for a few minutes. I wanted to tell him all about Chicago, but the excitement was lost in his sour mood. After a while, I spoke. "There's something I want to explain. Why I was weird the other night."

"You don't need to explain." His jaw was tense.

"I want to. But it's . . . weird. When I heard that Cerf meant deer. I had this idea. This thing hit me. I hit a deer that night, the night Diana was killed."

"So?"

"I had this idea that maybe I actually hit Diana and had a delusion that it was a deer."

He hit the brakes as a car cut us off, and I jerked forward, feeling like I might throw up.

"Sorry," he said, easing up on the brake. "I can't pull over here, but let's get you home and talk. We'll talk about it then." After a pause, he reached for my hand. That was all I needed. "How was Chicago? Was it interesting?"

I told him about the traffic and the museum and the late-night bookstore. "We saw a great show about Houdini. And *American Gothic* and *Nighthawks*."

"I've always wanted to see *Nighthawks*. I'm glad you had a good time."

When we pulled into town it was dark. He asked if we could go to his apartment first. His place had his familiar stamp, everything so compact and orderly. We sat on the couch. I almost felt I should nestle in his arms. We weren't there yet.

"Sorry I was abrupt on the phone," he said.

"I'm sorry I put you to this trouble."

"No, you don't understand. It was no trouble. I wasn't upset at that. I was upset for your sake, that you had to wait so long for me to get you. But all I did was make you feel bad. I'm sorry."

I gazed at his face so full of tenderness. "We seem to have the same issue over and over."

"I know." He smiled. Then he put his arm around me and pulled me close.

"Dr. Kind said I was paranoid."

"And now, what is this, thinking you hit Diana? That you imagined hitting the deer? Are you okay? Are you becoming manic? I know you've been under a lot of stress. I can't imagine what you've been through."

"I'm okay. It was a passing thing. A strange thing." I didn't tell him that I'd hardly slept the past week or two. I should have.

"You're sure you're okay? You seem okay. Would I be able to tell?"

"Actually I feel like I've never been better." And that statement should have been the first hint.

"There's something I need to tell you. I got an internship in Syracuse for the rest of the semester. I'll be going back and forth, so I won't be around as much. I hate to leave you now."

"Did you just have to drive to Syracuse, twice in one . . . ?" I looked at him in shock.

He put his finger on my lips. "Please don't worry about it. Not at all."

I sank into his arms, smelling again his green soap. His chest was warm through his flannel shirt.

"I'm nervous about it, about this internship," he said with some hesitation.

"Why?"

"I never told you how I lost my job." He tightened his arm around me. "I was a civil engineer for a town downstate. They had extra funds they didn't need, that they wanted to spend. So they decided to build a road right through the middle of a park. Just to spend the money. I ended up testifying against them in court."

"Did you stop them?

"Yes."

"You're a hero! What are you nervous about?"

"I didn't tell them about it at the interview. I was going to, but I lost my nerve. They're bound to find out. I told them I left to go back to school."

I sat up, putting my hands around his neck. "If they don't value you for what you did, you shouldn't work for them."

"I know, but what do I say if they ask why I didn't tell them?"

I cocked my head. "That you were too modest. Didn't want to toot your own horn."

He smiled, took my hand from his neck, and kissed it. "You've been through a lot. I wish I had a whiskey to give you. Actually, I think I have an old bottle of red wine." He got up and went to the kitchen.

I glanced around at the orderly room. It was dominated by a large bookcase. Stretching, I got up and read the spines, arranged by subject. Math books, physics, structural engineering, Shakespeare, poetry. Then I stopped. There was a thin black volume with nothing on the spine.

"Hey, what about your old guitar?" Scott called from the kitchen. "I can help you. Let's get going on that."

I slid out the book and opened it. My heart pounded. "Some Mr. Flannel Shirt tried to get my number," she had said. He knew her, well enough to have her book. The floor felt uneven beneath my feet. At the sound of his step I jammed the book back on the shelf.

He came in with the bottle and glasses. "It's a modest, unassuming wine with hints of gravel," he said with a joking smile, that fell away when he saw my face. "What's the matter?"

I didn't know how I must have looked. "Nothing. Just tired. Maybe I should go. Actually this afternoon is my regular appointment with Ann, so . . ."

My heart ached at the disappointment on his face, but he didn't argue. It was a short drive to my house.

When we pulled up, he put his arms around me. "I need you to be okay. I feel like I let you down, years ago, when you needed me."

In the dark car his voice was soft and caring, and I tried not to shiver in his arms. "It's okay. It's good to see you again."

"Yeah."

In the pause that followed, I nervously wondered if he would kiss me. The moment passed and I got out of the car. We waved to each other and I went inside.

CHAPTER TWENTY-FOUR

"How are you, since they found your roommate?"

This was my first visit to Ann since I'd found Diana's body. I struggled through telling her the truth, which wasn't in the press. That "they" weren't the ones who'd found her. Ann's face went from gentle concern to utter bafflement.

"Why didn't you call me?"

"I was supposed to see you the next week, but you had a conflict."

"You didn't have to wait."

I felt embarrassed, as if I had done something wrong. My face grew hot. "I don't know. I guess I didn't want to bother you, outside our regular time."

She sighed. "It's no bother. I thought I told you that before." Every word and sigh and expression only made me feel that I had done something wrong.

"Are you mad at me?"

"Why would I be mad at you?"

The question only made me feel she was irritated. I didn't know what to say. My mind flashed to what I'd said to Scott earlier: *We seem to have the same issue over and over.*

Ann set down her notepad and faced me squarely. "You're here now, so tell me what happened."

There actually was something on my mind, the thing that really bothered me. "The reason the deputy found me was because Jean Hellmann called the sheriff. Because I stood outside their house for a minute. I was watching a bird. A pileated woodpecker. That was all. And she decided I was stalking her or something."

Ann waited, expectantly. She gestured as if to say, "Well?"

"It upsets me. To be treated like that."

She furrowed her brow. "That's your takeaway, after finding your roommate's body?"

I didn't know what to say. I *was* upset by it. Maybe it was trivial in comparison. I felt my confidence ebb away as I looked at Ann's face. I felt her disapproval.

She must have seen some need in my expression. "It sounds like Mrs. Hellmann overreacted," she said.

That helped, and I nodded vigorously. "Right. Exactly. Thanks."

Ann waited again. There was a long silence.

"Maybe you need more time to process it all?" she asked, picking up her notebook.

"Maybe." I wondered what she wanted, how she wanted me to react. Maybe it was weird. And maybe I couldn't process it all. I had just come from seeing Scott, finding Diana's book there, and that was uppermost on my mind.

"You remember Scott," I started.

She raised her eyebrows with a questioning expression.

"I'm in love with Scott. I think he loves me, too."

"Scott?" Ann looked puzzled.

"My old best friend. I told you about him. The one I had that fight with."

She looked tense a moment, then amused, that amused look of being embarrassed to have forgotten and then remembering. "You've barely mentioned him. An old boyfriend you recently reconnected with, right? The one who treated you so badly?"

I nodded then shook my head. "He was never my boyfriend. Just my best friend. He didn't treat me badly. It was just a misunderstanding."

"Never your boyfriend? But you're in love with him?"

"And he loves me." Even if he'd lied about not knowing Diana.

"How do you know?"

How could I explain? In the small, shadowy room, I sank into my thoughts. It was just there, always. His concern. His loyalty. And even when he had broken things off, that wasn't disloyalty, it was pain. Pain because that was how much I mattered to him, that I could hurt him that much.

"Wendy?"

"I just know."

She looked away and sighed almost inaudibly but I could see her chest move with it, in her black turtleneck. She raised her small hand. "You know, if you have sex with him, you can't get pregnant."

I already knew this.

She continued. "Lithium causes a hole to form in the heart of the fetus."

I knew this so well that I felt bored for a moment and let my mind wander, thinking of Scott and how much I loved him. I think a faint smile crept onto my face.

"Wendy, are you listening to me?" Her tone was sharp, and I focused back on her. I had offended her.

"Yes, I know about the hole in the heart. Um. Thanks."

"I'm concerned you're getting caught up in something. Something you're not ready for."

When I had told her I didn't feel like an adult, she had always emphasized that I was one. Now was she saying I wasn't after all?

"I have to be ready sometime, don't I?" I was practically a virgin. Did she know that? Had I told her? I couldn't remember. I didn't want to talk about all that. "I'm ready to spend my life with him. He's my soulmate."

"Wendy . . ." I wished she would stop saying my name. I hated the sound of my name. "Listen to yourself. You meet a man and you're ready to marry him? A young girl would feel that way."

I wanted to shout, "I'm a woman! I'm an adult!" And it was because of my love for Scott that I could feel that way. But I was also collapsing inside. I just sat there. Outside, the trees were whirling and arching in the wind, almost bent over double, the roar of the branches like a train.

"How well do you know him?"

"I've known him for years."

"Weren't you apart for years?"

Long enough for him to get to know Diana? Share her poetry? Date her? "It's like we were never apart."

"It's been, what, six weeks?"

Another lull. I was thinking of a windy city and trains and how I would like to take Scott to Chicago and show him this impossible world where people did magical things and went to plays and bookstores. We needed to get out of this desolate place I once loved but was starting not to love anymore.

"Let's talk about something else." It took a lot of courage for me to say that.

"You want to avoid the topic?"

What seemed like avoidance to her was my attempt to take control of the conversation, to set my own agenda, but I couldn't say that.

She turned a page in her notebook. A page backward. "So let's see where we left off. We were talking about your mother. You told me your grandfather was a secret alcoholic."

The room tilted. She had put her own words into my mouth. "No, I don't know if he was. He died when I was two."

"What did he die of? Was it alcohol-related?"

"Colon cancer."

Her pen scratched the paper as she wrote that down. I didn't know if colon cancer was related to drinking or not. I had a strong desire to leave and be with Scott. I had to make up for running out on him. Maybe I'd have the courage to ask him about the book. That's what I wanted from Ann. I wanted to tell her I'd seen Diana's book on his shelf, and I had to screw up the nerve to ask him how well he knew her.

"So, I was just in Chicago," I started, "and Scott picked me up at the airport."

"Why were you in Chicago?"

"Oh." I wanted to tell her this. "I did something very grown-up. I drove there, to bring Diana's car back to her family. It was probably the most adult thing I've ever done."

"Just driving to Chicago?" She must have seen my face. "Oh, that's great!" Her face brightened and filled with a smile that looked phony. A smile a bit like my mother's.

We ended up talking about the trip to Chicago and then I walked home, battered by the wind. I was lost in fearful thoughts, of whether Scott had been lovers with Diana, if he was actually the father of Diana's baby. A big car slowed down next to me.

"Would you like a ride?"

Dr. Kind's friendly face was irresistible, and I hopped in. The car was warm and very clean, the ride in the plush leather seats smooth as silk. I was surprised by the lack of cigarette ash and smell. What I could smell was his warm cologne, something like plums and spice.

The walk to my house was short because I could cut through a stand of trees, but to drive we had to loop around the university. Still, it wasn't too far.

"Nice to get out of that wind," I said.

"I see you walking a lot. I drive by you all the time. You live up Grange Hill? Is it the Kulik house?"

"That's right." I was surprised he knew of it, but he must have lived in the area a long time.

"You know it's haunted, don't you?"

"My house?"

He nodded, turning his head toward me. Throughout the short drive he made me nervous by turning his head, taking his eyes off the road for what seemed a bit too long. But he drove with confident ease, his hands light on the wheel. "Old Mrs. Kulik died there," he continued. "Now she haunts it. Ooh-weee." He made a ghostly sound.

"Was she murdered?"

He shook his head. "One would wish for a better story. No, it was very boring. Just a heart attack." He thoughtfully stroked his mustache. "How would you like to die?"

I giggled. "I haven't thought about it. Suddenly, I guess. How about you?"

"Not alone."

"Of course. No one wants to die alone," I agreed.

"Yeah, I'm taking someone with me." Dr. Kind turned around to look at me again with wide eyes, and then laughed his puppy bark laugh. "You must forgive my absurd sense of humor."

I laughed. It was a pretty good line.

"How is it with you and Scott?" he asked. I was surprised at the question. Why couldn't Ann just ask me that? "How is the journal coming?"

"Oh! The journal! It's coming along great!" We really needed to work on that.

"Great! I thought you two would be a great fit. The same kind of aesthetic, the same sensibility. Actually, it's none of my beeswax, but you two could be a great couple."

It felt good to hear that. "Yes. We care for each other deeply."

"Ah, really? I'm glad to hear that. I think you need each other. He would be good for you. Yes, very good for you. So many girls make mistakes with loving the wrong person. But Scott is a fine young man. Don't let go of him." We pulled into my driveway. "And to think, I got you two together."

I had just unbuckled the seat belt, and I stopped to look at his cheery face. He had gotten us together, that was right. "Bless you!" I said, giving his hand a squeeze.

He gave a modest wave of his hand and I bounded into the house, full of love. Bless you, Dr. Kind. Bless you indeed.

CHAPTER TWENTY-FIVE

"Have you all read *The Turn of the Screw*?" Dr. Kind asked the class. "It was originally seen as merely a ghost story. Then Doctor Freud came along, that old charlatan."

I had skipped Hellmann's class that morning, lingering in the hall until I saw him leave the opposite way. I still needed to figure out how to deal with it, but avoidance would work in the meantime. I focused on Dr. Kind's warmth and humor. Dr. Freud, an "old charlatan"—I giggled in response.

Carolyn said, "My problem with the book is that I don't find the governess sympathetic. She's so annoying, the way she controls the whole situation, and is obviously so crazy."

I raised my hand. "I understand it's easy to think she's in control, but she isn't. She isn't in control of herself. She's mentally ill. She has no control."

"Does the protagonist have to be sympathetic?" Dr. Kind asked.

"But she's so *irritating*. She's so crazy, and I think she *is* in control. Look how she's controlling poor Mrs. Grose," Carolyn said.

"You're not in control when you're mentally ill," I repeated. "You're actually a victim. She's a *victim* of mental illness. Wasn't Henry James's sister Alice actually mentally ill? He based it on her, right?" I didn't usually speak up in classes, but I felt safe here, happy to be involved in a lively discussion after another long, sleepless night.

Dr. Kind cleared his throat. "Think of the poor governess in Victorian times. She has little choice in life. Constrained by duty and society, her only sense of importance, of prestige, is in her care of these little brats."

Carolyn nodded. "Yes, you can see her ego is enormous, maybe that's what irritates me so much about her. She's so self-important, thinking she's a hero. She's pure evil. She's evil in her big ego and her delusions about saving the children, when it's clear her problem is sexual repression."

"You can't say she's evil," I said. "No one is to blame, not when you're mentally ill."

"You can't absolve her of responsibility," said Carolyn. "She killed the little boy. She killed an innocent boy."

Dr. Kind chuckled with his little barking laugh. "But the children are so manipulative of her, too, playing games with her and throwing her off balance. She might not actually have done it—it doesn't say—but I personally don't mind if she kills the little twerp."

The blood rushed in my head. I couldn't hear the class for a few moments. *I personally don't mind if she kills the little twerp.* More students chimed in, as they discussed the modern Freudian views of the story, which Dr. Kind disparaged as merely fashionable and apocryphal.

After class, I followed Dr. Kind out of the room.

"Yes, Miss Zemansky?"

"I need to start discussing my future."

We went down to his office, passing the forlorn rubber plant starved for water at the bottom of the stairs. As I sat opposite his desk, my glance went up to a plastic smoking skeleton on the shelf behind him, next to some kind of small animal in a clear box.

"What's that?"

He turned his head. "A llama fetus. It was a gift on a trip to Argentina." He shrugged and smiled.

"This semester seems like it's going on forever," I said.

"Is this your last semester of classes?" He sat, taking a cigarette out of the drawer.

"Yes. Then I have to write a thesis." *And rewrite that lit review,* I thought with some resentment.

"On what? Do you have a topic?" His tapped the cigarette absently against the desk.

"I don't know. Something about the heroine in Gothic fiction."

"Ah. But there are no heroines in Gothic literature. Only victims."
He smiled, his pale eyes squinting. The gray mustache twitched
above his smile.

"What about survivors?"

"Well, mere survival is hardly heroic."

"I think it is."

"You don't mind?" he gestured with the cigarette and lit it when
I shook my head.

The space heater crackled like a hearth, the pink windowless
room like a cocoon. I opened my backpack. "I'd like to ask your
opinion." I pulled out the slim black volume. "I have this book, the
one of Diana's poetry. I was thinking the art gallery might want to
display it with her paintings. I want someone to have it, for it to
belong somewhere. She threw it away. I don't know. I'd like to do
something special with it."

He took the book from my hand and held it lightly. "The gallery
probably has everything arranged just so."

"Do you know of a special place for it? In the library or something?"

"I'll take it for now. I'll think of something." He smiled and put it
on the bookcase below the smoking skeleton and the llama fetus. It
seemed to disappear in a haze. "Was there something else?"

"I'm changing my mind about my goal for school. Originally I was
planning to teach high school. But now I'm thinking of going on
for a PhD, to teach college."

"Are you ready? It takes real stamina to work on a doctorate. En-
durance."

"I have to do something. I'm not really good with young kids. I
don't know what else I can do with an MA in English."

"Perhaps you could write a blog." He chuckled dismissively.

I felt myself redden. "I think I can do a PhD."

"And besides, you'll certainly have to teach, and you seem to avoid
teaching. That won't look good."

"But isn't the grant good on a resume?" My voice felt weak, my
throat tight.

He ignored the question. "Where were you thinking of applying?"

I hadn't thought much about it. I considered, thinking maybe it was time to leave home. "Could I get into a big school, like UCLA? Or Northwestern? I like Chicago."

He laughed. "Good luck."

The good feelings ebbed away. It seemed strange, this undermining. But maybe he was right. It was his job to know these things, to be able to evaluate students. My eyes scanned the shelves behind him. I'd lost track of Diana's book.

"It does seem a little overwhelming. But if I do a good job on the thesis . . ."

He leaned back, his arms behind his head in a satisfied pose. "We'll see. Perhaps you'll surprise us all."

"I thought I had . . . flashes of brilliance?" I whispered around the lump in my throat.

"Of course. Yes, if you want to go to Northwestern, we have a lot of work to do. You need to write not just any thesis, but a fabulous one. Something that could get published. Not Gothic literature. No. Because it has to be something current. Semiotics. Psycholinguistics. Something postmodern, as much as I dislike the milieu."

His interest cheered me, and I started to take out a notebook, but he gestured not to.

"You have to discuss it with Dr. Hellmann. Isn't he your adviser?"

My blush deepened. "I'm still avoiding him. Things are strained between us. I'm not sure what to do."

He tilted his head with a tsk. "Oh yes. Your letters."

"That I didn't write."

He smiled, taking a puff of the cigarette. "Let me talk to him. I'm sure this can be straightened out."

I exhaled in relief. He would take care of it.

"If you feel compelled to write a letter, send it to me instead, okay?"

"Thanks, you said that before. I'm sure I won't. . . ."

There was a pause, and his look felt like he was reading my mind, my past, my future. The corners of his lips smiled, but his eyes were sad. It was a look of humor and pity. Like he knew that no matter what, I was a failure. That he sympathized, but it was sympathy mingled with contempt. He didn't have to say a thing.

A fly landed on the desk between us. In a motion too quick to follow, he jabbed the cigarette right onto it, a black and red bit of lava was all that was left.

I felt like I was that fly.

CHAPTER TWENTY-SIX

And then it started.

I awoke early to the bluish dawn light that glowed softly on the ceiling. I stared at the ceiling, at the corner where it met the wall, and the corners disappeared into the chalcedony shadow. I thought about the word chalcedony, a bluish-gray quartz; I had picked up that word as a teenager and always liked it, holding it in my mind as if I held the stone itself, a lucky stone smooth in my palm.

I felt full of the dim blue light, and when I switched on the lamp, its yellow glare was jarring. I switched the lamp off again and went to the window. The landscape still expanded as it always did, serene and bucolic. I felt connected now, not isolated. These hills joined my world together, and in between the milky sky and the gleaming snow fields, it was an oyster, and my little house a pearl. It was a secret. This country so far from everything was a secret land, it was the inside of a snow globe, it was a whole little world.

This made sense. I turned away from the window. I was afraid of Diana's empty room, and felt I must go into it and face the fear. The door was shut and latched. *I must leave the door shut until she speaks to me. She will speak. This is the pearl, the center of this place.*

In the living room, stacks of books leaned precipitously. *I need a bookcase.* I tapped down the cellar steps. The landlord had scraps of wood and tools. *I can do this.* Plywood feet, two lengths for the sides, molding for rails, no back needed, the thick wood heavy enough to support itself. I measured, cut with a crosscut saw, and hammered in long nails. In two hours it was done. But it was too heavy and awkward to carry up the stairs. I was panting over it. Scott would have to help me carry it up later.

I had no appetite and ate nothing, swallowing my lithium with a little tea. I felt *so healthy, so well*, energy welling within me. There was something I needed to do; I tried to remember. I paced restlessly, then remembered I needed to call the deputy and ask the time on the receipt, just to be sure, absolutely sure. His card wasn't on the table anymore. I searched all the tables, dumped my purse and searched the wallet. It was not to be found. I felt someone had taken it to make it hard for me.

I decided to walk to the sheriff's office. Why not? I had so much energy, anyway. It was only four miles. It didn't seem too cold, though the thermometer on the porch said seventeen degrees. The road crunched loudly under my feet. I swung my arms, then started singing at the top of my voice. A horse dashed a long distance toward me from across a field. It raced up to the barbed wire fence and I stopped.

"Are you okay?"

It bent its neck to the side as if saying no.

"Are you cold?"

It bobbed its head up and down.

"Sorry." I walked on and it followed me to the end of the fence.

The hill went down steeply to the village. In front of Stanimer's, I was stopped by the biggest headline I'd ever seen on the local paper: RABID DEER FOUND. Hot and cold chills vibrated over my skin. I walked into Stanimer's.

It was early and only a few people were there. It was almost as dark as night inside, the cigarette-scented air humid. At a table near the bar sat two hunters in camo. I went up to them. "Excuse me, may I talk to you a minute?"

They were an old man and a young one, possibly father and son. The old man had a beer in front of him, and the young man was drinking coffee. They both had about three days' growth of beard, the young man's dark and the older man's silver. A pool of light fell on the table, highlighting them like the saints of an icon by candlelight.

"Sure," said the older man.

I rubbed my face. "A few weeks ago, I hit a deer. Three hunters stopped and helped me. I'd like to try to find them."

The young man was staring away from me, seeming uncomfortable, but the older man smiled, his teeth broken and gapped. "There's a lot of us," he said.

"I know, but could you please ask around for me?"

He shrugged. "I guess I could try."

I took out a pen and a slip of paper and wrote my cell phone number down for him, and details about the accident, thanked them, and left. It was much colder outside now. The wind had picked up, dangerously swinging the Stanimer's sign. The rutted snow on the edge of the sidewalk was frozen. It was too far to walk all the way to the sheriff. I climbed back up the hill home.

I got the mail on my way in. There was a postcard from my old high school, asking me to participate in a fundraiser. Mr. Fellowes sprang to my mind, unbidden, my English teacher who had lost a young daughter. Years after high school, during a manic episode, I'd written him a crazy letter about death and mourning, thinking I was helping. It was one of my most shameful secrets. I picked up a pen.

"Dear Mr. Fellowes,

I hope you are well. It has been some years since I wrote you that crazy letter. Please forgive me. I have bipolar disorder, and I wasn't well. I'm on medication now. I am in school working on an M.A. in English. I used to be undecided between history and literature, but I made my decision for literature. Again, I'm very sorry about the letter. Yours truly, Wendy Zemansky."

I addressed it to him at my old school, and I had to mail it immediately. I paused. Was this right? I needed a sign. I thought about emailing Scott.

Scott had set up an email address for the literary journal we were supposed to be working on, and as I looked in my inbox I saw that he'd forwarded me the submissions. The first one jumped off the screen. "So Right," by Wendy Born. *Born!* This was clearly a sign.

Now I know that coincidences to normal people are nothing. Occasional occurrences maybe worth a laugh of surprise at most. But coincidence to the mentally ill means one thing only: hell. It seemed impossible to be meaningless.

So, it was urgent to mail the letter to a teacher I hadn't spoken to in years. I was hardly aware of putting my coat back on and going out the door. I didn't feel the wind as I walked, nor time pass by.

The post office was dark and shadowy after the bright glittering daylight. I bought a book of stamps from the old man behind the counter, and he took the letter and stamped it in front of me. His stamp thudded like a slaughterer's mallet. *When your only tool is a hammer, every problem is a nail*, I heard Diana say. *Commit nothing to writing.*

But this one is okay, I told myself. This will redeem the others. This will cancel them out.

As I walked back home, I was not aware of the distance, of time passing, of the bitter cold. Suddenly the air was filled with large, fluffy snowflakes, materializing like magic out of the bright golden sunshine. *Oh Earth.* This letter would be okay, *because it's always the right thing to apologize*, I insisted to myself. *And because it's snowing. It's snowing because I did the right thing.* And as I walked, I felt very well. Even elated.

CHAPTER TWENTY-SEVEN

"February 20, 2007
Dear Professor Kind,

Sometimes Diana rushes into my thoughts as if she flew into my mind on wings. I remember her poetry. Her words were like darts, pinning me to a truth I didn't want to face, and then when the most feared thing happens, the fear melts into a relief of arrival, a clearing of warm flowers in the sun. She brought you through the anguish of anxiety and dread into a place of calm repose. She knew what she was doing, writing like that. But she threw it all aside. One of the last things she ever said to me was to commit nothing to writing. Once, the first time I was manic, I couldn't stop writing. And one thing I kept writing were little notes of warning because my brain was splitting between a sane mind and a deluded one, and the sane one was warning me saying, "Beware of unilateral communication," meaning letters. But I was under a compulsion to write, my manic activity. So that now I fear every time I write, that it's a sin, a real mortal sin. But then I feel sometimes, "This time it is right and will redeem all the other times." And don't we write for redemption in the end?"

"February 21, 2007
Dear Professor Kind,

You once said something about the womb of the intellect. I sense that. It must seem like being in school forever, to be a teacher. Something has to detach to rise above that.

I meant to say, you seem very close to Dr. Hellmann. I see you sometimes around his office and in the union. So I hope you can convince him to take my side, or at least to pity me. No, I shouldn't ask for pity. I don't know why I say that. Just to give me the benefit of the doubt."

"February 21, 2007 4:00
Dear Dr. Kind,

What I wonder is what Diana was sacrificed for. To die in the snow in winter, like the Aztec children sacrificed in the water but not of the water, she was sacrificed in the snow but not of the snow. Yet spring doesn't come. The wind lashes my windows with stinging darts of snow. March never goes out like a lamb, unless it's a sacrificial lamb."

"February 22, 2007
Dear Dr. Kind,

Maybe my sanity is a sacrifice. Maybe to journey to the truth and meaning of it all, the hidden meaning, I have to go into the horror house. Is that my Fate? Maybe I have to give up success, respect, relations, family, profession, to go into the cave. But will I come back? I go through life so naked and unprotected. I used to pride myself on being so open and naked in the world, but only an infant is naked. I fear I will never reach adulthood. I envy young women who know how to tie a scarf, who are calm and self-possessed. Diana was like that. Yet her self-possession didn't protect her. There is no security anywhere. The world is a fragile place where anything can happen. A place where nightmares can come true at noon in the bright sun. Easter is coming and slaughter is carried on the wind. My therapist's name is Ann Wolfe. My mother's maiden name is Shepherd. I must be the sacrificial lamb.

If I unlock Diana's mystery, then I can bear the guilt of surviving her. I am the lamb and it should have been me. I seek meaning where others seek justice. Justice only imprisons us all.

Thank you for giving me permission to communicate with you. It helps. I feel you and I are very much alike. I can't say how. I just sense it. Thank you for being there, Wendy."

CHAPTER TWENTY-EIGHT

I managed to sleep for an hour, before I woke from dreaming of Uncle Johnny, and the face of the driver who hit him was Diana's painting, the long teeth in smears of yellow and gray. Outside there was only the faintest tinge of dawn color on the horizon. The road was deserted. It had stopped snowing, and Venus was rising.

I walked down the hill. The lights were on in Dot's Café. Otherwise all was empty. I walked out of town. When I passed a farm, I heard the milking machine from inside. *Mother's milk.* A crow landed in the road ahead. It was sipping the blood of a dead raccoon, roadkill. The snow and the crow and the blood reminded me of an Irish legend I'd read, the story of Deirdre. She had looked out her window at a crow sipping blood, and thought, I shall marry a man with skin the white of snow, hair the black of the crow feathers, lips as red as the blood. That was Scott; he looked just like that. I had always loved him, all along, since the beginning, but I was too dysfunctional to realize it before.

But now I'm well. I've come back and I'm well, so well. The farms disappeared and tree-covered hills rose on either side. The trees were thin and bony, black and wet. In the damp air I could see my breath. I began to sing, my voice ragged, the steps booming in my ears.

There was movement ahead. A pair of eyes glowed in the dawn. I stopped, and so did the dog, a German shepherd, running loose, as they all did in the country. It was on the other side of the road, growling low. I took a step, and it gave a lurch as if about to jump. I froze again, then took another step. The growls grew louder. I was afraid if I ran, it would chase me and attack. I walked on tiptoes, avoiding its eyes. I lowered my head, shrank myself and looked down, submissive, silently begging for it to see I was no threat.

I kept going. The growling continued, but then it was behind me, and I was past it. I breathed deeply in relief as sweat trickled down my sides under the down coat. The road started downhill and the going was easier. I wondered how far I had come out of town. At least three miles.

A bird swooped, brushing my head. It was diving for my eyes. I put my hands over my face. *There must be a nest nearby. But that doesn't make sense, it's winter.* But the bird kept coming at me. I walked unsteadily, arms shielding my face, barely able to see. The bird flew at my face, over and over, grazing my head. I ran blindly up the next hill, legs heavy in my boots.

The bird was gone at last. The woods and fields stretched below me in the sunrise, the few barns and houses dark and despondent. No cows were out. The world was snow and mud, tangled trees, and the gritty, sludgy road going on and on. Nothing stirred.

I can't do this. I have to go back. I was breathing heavily from the race up the hill and my fright. I turned around, but I couldn't go back that way, not with the loose dog. I was trapped, trapped in the open. I looked around, staggering. A dirt logging road went off to my left between the trees. I headed to it.

The road went deep into the woods, which quickly turned from poplars to ash and hemlock. A few ash stumps lined the road where they had been harvested. It was darker and colder in the shade of the wood. A frightened grouse crashed through the branches, flying up and away. I dug my bare hands into my pockets, the hair damp on my neck. I thought the logging road would come out to Route 20; I had seen the other end of it before. I was circling around the town.

I jumped at another, louder crash. It was a deer, its antlers grazing the black branches. Then a rifle shot, followed by another, echoing around me. Hunters were out, and I was in the thick of them.

"Hello!" I cried, but my voice was hoarse. "I'm here, don't shoot!"

I strained to spot their orange vests. There was no color in the dark wood. Another gunshot rang out. I started to run, my heart exploding. I tried to scream, but my voice didn't come.

I'm dreaming. This is a dream. Wake up, wake up!

The sounds of the rifles came closer. By running I was only drawing their fire, I probably sounded like the deer I was running with. Then I slipped on some leaves and fell on the hard clay ground.

As I lay there panting, paralyzed, a large doe stepped onto the path ahead. She stepped gently, serene. She caught my eye and stared. I stared back. She was beautiful and dreamlike, a peaceful void in this hurricane nightmare.

The doe nibbled a twig. Her fur was rough and mottled, her big tongue swiping at the shoots. Chewing delicately, she lifted her head to keep an eye on me.

A gunshot rang out, and the bullet whizzed over my head. Time slowed down. I expected to see the doe hit, that she would fall at my feet. *And I drew the gunshot toward you.* But the bullet struck the tree and the doe turned and fled.

"Don't shoot!" I shouted at last. Male voices rose. Orange vests were moving toward me now. An old man with a rifle stepped onto the road and then ran toward me.

"Jesus, are you hit?" he asked, bending over me.

I sat up, shaking. "No."

He swore. "You gave me a big scare, lady. What the hell are you doing out here?"

"Walking." I stood up. "I'm headed for Route 20."

The man shook his grizzled head. "I know better than to argue. Take this." He took the orange knit hat off his head and gave it to me.

"Thanks. Am I headed the right way?"

"Sure."

I felt he would have said that whether I was or not. I pulled the cap over my tangled hair and kept walking. They held their fire a while. Then I heard a few shots, but far away. There was light through the trees, and I stepped out onto Route 20.

I was at the top of the hill. The first house I passed was an old
Victorian, turreted, with a large porch. Dark green with black trim,
it looked better kept than most of the other old houses. The hem-
locks around the porch were neatly bundled in burlap against the
wind. One light was on upstairs. *An early riser.* I wondered if I could
knock and ask for a glass of water. The black door loomed like the
entrance to a cavern. A fanlight in the door gleamed like a single
eye. I decided not to.

At the end of the driveway, the mailbox wasn't quite shut, and I
closed it against the swirling glitter of snowflakes. Gold and black
peel-and-stick letters, neatly fastened along a straight penciled line,
said "KIND, RR 3, BOX 14."

A crow flew past, onto a rock, drawing my gaze. The rock was
smooth and curved. Not a rock at all, but a headstone. There were
several of them, surrounded by a black wrought-iron, ankle-high
railing. It was a family plot next to the house. There was one headstone, bigger and newer than the rest. I stepped over the rail and
walked up to it. "Eloise Koval-Kind. May 18, 1929–November 7,
1998." *He lives with his mother's grave.* The snow was tamped down a
bit in front of the stone. The crow hopped down and picked up
a cigarette butt. Shivering, I was starting to feel the cold. I had to
get home.

I came to the bend where I had found Diana. Now it was hard
to tell anything had been there. The ditch was filled with snow. For
a moment, I thought a voice called my name. I listened. The wind
sighed in the trees.

I knew the angle of the view at the exact spot. The woods were
behind me and fields spread out before me, bisected by a wind-
break hedge, pink in the sunrise. Venus sparkled by the moon. I
looked at the ditch, for some sign, some clue. But everything was
gone, not even a shard of broken glass.

I stepped a little closer. There was something, a glint of red like
a coal. I picked it up. It was an earring, but not Diana's. It was my
own, which must have come off the day I found the body. *I find
death, I find myself. Are we twins, are we one?* I started to slip the earring

in my pocket, but then dropped it on the ground to leave it there, as an offering.

I kept on, knowing I'd pass Dr. Hellmann's house as well. When the white stucco façade appeared, I lowered my head. Trying to ignore the house, I almost walked into his mailbox, RR 3, Box 13. No lights were on.

Past the orchard, down Cooper Hill, then up Grange Hill Road. Then home, home at last. I was hot and sweating. I passed my car, the cracked windshield glaring and accusing.

CHAPTER TWENTY-NINE

The fine snow fell like tiny pins. There was black ice on the road, and I fell, hitting my elbow. The frigid ice hurt my hands as I pushed myself up. I went into the union, bought a bottle of water from the machine, and guzzled it. Someone waved to me in the corner of my eye. To my disbelief, Daniel was giving me a friendly wave and motioned me over.

I slumped across from him.

"What's the matter?" he asked, blue eyes surprised and concerned. He looked so calm and neat, so kempt.

"I think I'm becoming enlightened."

He smiled. "I went through that. I got over it. You'll get over it."

I smiled back. "You'd make a good father."

His smile broadened. "They do let us adopt. But really, are you okay? It must be hell for you."

I was startled by the word hell. *Am I going to hell? Am I in hell right now? I've died and I didn't know it and now I'm in hell?*

"I don't know."

"Have you talked to anyone about everything that's happened?"

I nodded quickly. "I have Ann, at the health center. She cured me."

"Really?"

I nodded again. "And now it's like everything makes sense for the first time. And I'll never be crazy again. And there won't be any hurt, because when everyone understands everything, there's no hurt. There's only forgiveness."

A sad look crossed his face. "I think there was a time when I thought that way."

"Don't be sad! I think you and I feel the same. And we were both touched by Diana, that's why."

Another sad look. "I'll confess to you."

Confess?

"I had a negative view of Diana. To be frank, I thought she was a bitch. I said so behind her back. I feel kind of guilty about it. You don't expect people to die. Not young and tragically. And she wasn't really a bitch. She just had high standards. These weeks of thinking about it all, I realize I've grown to like her. And it's too late." I reached for his hand. He gave me a smile of relief. "You'd make a good therapist. You have that soothing voice."

It still touches me that he said that. Maybe somewhere beyond all the illness I was someone real, someone people could talk to. Maybe there was an adult in there. I squeezed his hand. "You didn't treat her badly. You were supportive, when you went to her reading and wrote that note on her program."

He shook his head, "No, I wasn't at the reading. I couldn't go. I regret missing it."

"Are you sure? The note said, 'Keep writing, Dan.'"

He shook his head. "I would never say 'Dan.' I'm Daniel."

Something sank inside me. "Maybe I don't know everything."

He smiled wanly. "I know the feeling." Then, his face brightening, he snapped his fingers. "I almost forgot, I really need to talk to you about something. Yes, you'd be perfect! Listen—" He tapped the table with his coffee cup. "I found out yesterday my father is sick. It might be serious, and I need to go home. I'll stay until spring break, but after that I don't know if I'm coming back this semester. I teach Intro to World Lit. Can you take over my class?"

I almost knocked over his coffee in surprise. To teach. To have that chance again.

"I can pay you of course. It's easy. All the lessons are planned. The first one after break is William Butler Yeats. You know him, everyone does. You can do it, can't you? You're only taking two classes, right? It would help me out so much. I'd really owe you one."

I hesitated. I wanted to, but I was frightened. "I don't know."

Daniel's eyes widened in encouragement. "You have a background in history, which is ideal, especially for Yeats. Right?"

"Carolyn is good at poetry."

"She's a good *writer*, but this is analysis, which to be honest I don't think she does as well."

It was flattering. He really wanted me to do it. "Can I let you know later?"

He shrugged, disappointed. "Okay, but please let me know soon. I won't ask anyone else until you answer."

"Okay, I will. Thanks."

He raised his cup in farewell. "I'd better go. You look tired. Take care of yourself."

"Thank you!" As we rose, I kissed him on the cheek. His face was pink, and he gave me an embarrassed smile.

I walked, the ice crystals in the air shining like fairies. A pair of headlights came up behind me. I stepped to the side and slid into the ditch. The car sped by, the driver oblivious. I skidded slightly with each step on the slippery road, my legs wet.

Finally at home, I made a cup of tea and took my lithium. I'd eaten almost nothing all week. On the computer there was an email from Scott. "I've got to go to my mother's tomorrow to take care of some things for her. I'll see you Sunday night, unless you're busy, NBD." I puzzled over the initials and finally thought of "No big deal." He was still hurt at my rejection.

I slept deeply for three hours. When I got up, I drank two large glasses of water. The water tasted like poison, and I felt it was time to die. My failure should end now. I checked my email again.

This time there was a message from the English Department: "Don't forget! Tonight is the Late-Night Poetry Slam at Stanimer's, at 10:00. Come read, or sing, or dance. Come play! Find romance! (Okay, that's just because it rhymes.) Be there, or be square!"

My eyes were heavy as I read it over, deciding to go. I lay down, but kept waking up, afraid to oversleep and miss it. Minutes went by like hours, and hours like minutes.

I recalled the story I'd started about the end of civilization, and got up to work on it. Usually my handwriting was jagged and hard to read, but as I wrote the story in my notebook, my handwriting danced on the page, growing more beautiful and calligraphic with each word.

When I finished, I read the email from the English department again, wondering about reading the story at the open mike. But it seemed like they'd want a poem. I tried to write a poem about the earring I'd lost. This made me think about jewelry, then fashion. There was no fashion magazine dedicated to jewelry. I should start one. I researched online, ordering a jewelry making kit. *I should make things, I should do things.* I started ordering craft kits, cross-stitch, a model plane, glue, beads, accessories. When I'd spent two hundred dollars, I stopped. I looked at the time and jumped up. It was time to get to Stanimer's.

I put on my coat and the orange hat and trotted down the hill, feeling light, a second wind propelling me. Voices and light spilled from the bar. It was a wonderful feeling, to participate, and not be alone twenty-four hours a day. *I'm almost human.*

It was crowded, and the heavy coats on the backs of the chairs narrowed the aisles even more. Voices crackled through the shadows and the pools of orange light, ceiling fans chopping up the sound. Fake candles twinkled on the dark wooden tables. There was a hearth with a gas fire on one side, warming the already over-heated space.

Over the hearth was a large painting of deer. The deer faces seemed to be frowning, judging me. I reached toward it, thinking I wanted to take it down, when someone spoke.

"Wendy! Hi!" She had red and black striped hair and big glasses, her face wavering in the indistinct light. "It's Carolyn. It's so dark in here."

"Of course. Of course, I know you."

"Come join us."

Madeleine, Mike, and Daniel were in a booth. "Hi, there's plenty of room," Madeleine said. A waitress added a chair to the end of the booth.

I looked at Daniel, feeling awkward, my face warming. "I haven't been sleeping much at all. I know I was weird earlier."

He gave me a relieved smile, waving his hand. "Of course, that's understandable. How could you sleep with everything that's happened?"

I bobbed my head. "Yes, of course. That's it."

Carolyn turned to me. "I heard you and Scott are editing the literary journal. I'd like to submit if that's okay."

"Of course. Scott set up an email for submissions. I'll ask him. Where is he? Oh right, he's at his mother's farm. I talked to a horse Monday."

Mike laughed. "Did it talk back?"

"Kind of. Maybe it was magic." *Magic. The witch of winter on her broomstick. Who said that? Someone said that recently.* I gazed at my companions, who kept talking. I couldn't follow the conversation, but felt content in a little bubble.

Madeleine put her hand to her cheek. "Darn, I've lost an earring."

My eyes flew open wide. "So did I. And it made me think, how I'd like to start a magazine."

She gave me a puzzled look. "You're doing the literary journal."

"No, I mean a magazine about jewelry. There are magazines about making your own, about beading, but there isn't one like *Vogue*, about high-end jewelry. I think there's a niche for it. It writes itself. You could have a gem of the month column, profiles of wealthy women and their jewelry, jewels in history, Hollywood jewels. It would be easy as pie."

Madeleine's smile was strained. "Sure. You know a lot about jewelry?"

I felt my face redden. "Not really. But it would be easy."

"Sure," Madeleine said.

"I would buy it," said Carolyn.

For a moment, I felt angry. They didn't think it was a great idea, they were humoring me. Before I could speak, the waitress came with drinks, setting water in front of me. I gulped the water all at once. *Poisoned.* Mike said something about his brew. *Witch's brew, the witch of winter.*

"There's something I've been trying and trying to find out about."
My voice sounded far away. "Just before break, Diana was determined to switch her major from English to studio art. Do any of
you know why she would do that?"

They sipped their drinks and considered it. Mike said, "She was
so good at writing. I bet it wasn't enough of a challenge for her.
She wanted to take on something harder. Use the other half of her
brain."

Madeleine agreed. "She was someone who pushed herself."

Off a cliff. "But maybe she was running away from something."

Carolyn shook her head. "She's not the type to run away."

I pressed my fist to my forehead. "Not that she was afraid. To
spite someone. To punish someone."

The others in the booth frowned and looked down at their drinks,
but Daniel turned with an alert, interested face. *He always did want to
solve it, too.* "So, who was she punishing?"

I looked into his blue eyes. "Whoever killed her."

Carolyn gasped.

"Really, honey, you were saying this before, and I thought we . . ."
Madeleine said.

Daniel said, "We'll never know. Let's not drive ourselves crazy
over it."

I looked at the quiet table, suddenly realizing again I was being
wrong and crazy and making them uncomfortable, even Daniel.
"You're right. I'm sorry. I forget myself." That's the thing, you see.
It's not a continuous thing, this madness, but something you're slipping in and out of, moment to moment.

The MC took the stage and microphone, his chunky metal brace-
let glinting in the spotlight. "Welcome to North Carthage State
University's Semiannual Poetry Slam. Is it Semiannual or Biannual?
Twice a year?" A few voices called out "Semiannual," and he chuckled. "We have a list of wonderful poets and writers here tonight.
So let's get started with some mood music." A guitarist strolled up
to the stage, playing a classical piece while the crowd quieted and
settled in for the reading.

Next, the MC introduced Carolyn, who turned to me and whispered, "This is what I'm submitting." She took the stage and recited four poems. I tried to pay attention, but various images kept pushing my racing thoughts: Wolves, jaws, ice and blood, *the gray fog slipping soft on the bones of trees, brown leaves littering the hidden path. The path that leads to destiny, leads to death, but in the unseen breath words awaken and give an afterlife, a memory, a ghost that said, 'I love you' once, and once heard, is heard again.*

As the night stretched on, I felt increasingly agitated, though I sat very still, my eyes almost unblinking. I wanted to recite something. I wanted to stand before everyone and reveal the secrets of the universe.

Daniel was the last one signed up to recite. He was humorous, his poems all wry observations on life's small absurdities. With his thin hair and neat goatee, he seemed older than he was, and full of wisdom, his voice crisp and sardonic. I was able to hear most of what he said, and laughed loudly, shaking with mirth, hot and sweating. When he was through, I slid out of the booth and stood to applaud.

I remained standing. I wanted to go up front and ask to recite. My chance was slipping away. The MC took the microphone again. "Well, it's quarter to midnight. We have fifteen minutes. Anyone else want to take a stab at fame and fortune?"

I took a lurching step. In the corner of my eye, I thought Madeleine made a gesture for me not to go. Standing near the stage, Daniel winked. I took a few more steps. There was still a moment to change my mind. A moment to sit down again.

But the MC saw me and gestured. "Here's someone, I think. Are you coming up?"

"I think so," I said. There was scattered applause. I stepped into the spotlight, hotter than ever. The crowd looked inviting. I felt happy in front of them; they were all so friendly.

"What's your name?" the MC asked.

Then I spotted a face, less friendly. A face with pursed lips, frowning in the shadows. Dr. Kind sat stiffly, his arms folded.

"Diana the huntress," I said.

There was an uncomfortable silence.

"No, I'm Wendy. Wendy Zemansky. But you can call me the witch of winter."

"Okay," he said. "Wendy, are you going to recite for us?"

"I'm going to tell you the secrets of the universe."

There was some laughter and applause.

"Great," he said. "What is the secret of the universe?"

I looked out, my mind going blank. I was staring straight at Dr. Kind, though I was trying not to. I swallowed, wishing I had more water. "I think you can kill a woman with kindness," I mumbled. "Yes, that's it. A woman is killed by kindness."

There was another uncomfortable pause with a few giggles. I thought I heard someone whisper, "She's drunk."

"I'd like to sing a song. Just an old song."

"Sure, we can close with a song. Are you okay?" the MC asked.

"I am the best I've ever been!" I opened my mouth, and the song poured out. My voice was rich and clear, even thrilling.

"Oh I wish, I wish, I wish in vain
That I could be a maid again.
But a maid again, I'll never be,
Till apples fall from an ivy tree.
Oh, love is pleasin, and love is teasin,
And love's a treasure, when first it's new.
But as love grows older, then love grows colder,
Till it fades away, like the morning dew.
There is an ale house, in the town,
Where my love goes, and he sits him down.
He takes a strange girl upon his knee,
And tells her things he once told me.
Oh, love and water make a young girl older
And love and whiskey make her old and grey.
But what cannot be cured, love, must be endured, love,
And so I am bound for Ameri-kay.
Oh love is pleasin, and love is teasin,

And love's a treasure when first it's new.
But as love grows older, then love grows colder,
Till it fades away like the morning dew."

The audience applauded wildly because, frankly, my singing was fantastic.

"That was for Diana," I whispered, unheard. I bowed quickly and got off the stage.

"That was fabulous!" Carolyn said.

Daniel kissed me on the cheek. "Now it's my turn," he said, referring to the kiss. "I was afraid for a second."

I shook myself. Nothing mattered. We gathered our coats and paid the tab.

"Oh, Wendy," Daniel leaned close. "Did you decide?"

I clutched his hand. "I'd love to teach your class!"

We shook and I bounced out. I walked briskly home and threw off my clothes to take a long shower. In my pajamas in front of the computer, I wanted to write a book, a book about my life. I wrote two sentences and stopped. I didn't want to do it if I couldn't write it all in one night.

CHAPTER THIRTY

Writing and writing. I sat at the kitchen table surrounded by balls of crumpled paper.

"Education is experience and reflection upon the experience. Socrates and Jesus Christ were killed because they were great teachers. In using parables, Jesus provided experiences to be reflected upon. Socrates forced people to deal with their real experience, not theories. . . . Everything in our society is opinion. 'I read it in a book; it must be true.' Layers of opinion on opinion. We go through life wearing thick gloves of opinion, touching nothing real. Experience is disappearing from our lives. . . . In the beginning was the Word, and the Word was with God. God is the experience, the Word is the reflection upon the experience. . . . Everything that changes is in some way alive. The rock that erodes into ocean sand is alive. Everything is alive until it decomposes into the atomic state. Cremation is the best way to bury the dead, returning their bodies to the atomic state. Take them off the respirators, this is what their minds are doing, racing further and further into enlightenment.

A child died in my mother's womb the year before I was born. Maybe the ghost was in there with me. Maybe I am a ghost. This is my Fate.

Mom had a miscarriage after Peter. Then I was born. I made up for the miscarriage. I am she who returns. I am the prodigal daughter. I came back. I make up for things. That is the mystery of my birth. Every birth has a mystery, but few know their own stories.

Why was I insane? I don't know. I am haunted by a ghost. I am the ghost in my mother's womb. It is my Fate.

Life is an illusion. Time is a construct. Clocks keep track of nothing, it's all an illusion. This is a world of illusion.

I know what happened to Jesus. Joseph rejected Mary when she was pregnant, then took her back. That detail makes the story so real. Why did he reject her? He was not the father. Then he took her back. Because he found out she was raped. But they couldn't prosecute it. She was raped by a Roman soldier. A secret. It drove her mad. His mother was crazy, mad with this secret horror.

Joseph was a wonderful father. He died when Jesus was thirty. Jesus went into mourning.

Building his furniture. Sanding and sanding in silence. Thinking, thinking, thinking. Mourning is the contemplation of the experience of having been loved. Then someone told him. Joseph wasn't your father.

That love. All that father's love. And Joseph was never obligated to love him at all. A father's love without the obligation. Jesus understood this literally. God's love is the love of a father for his child, without the obligation.

Mr. Fellowes, my teacher. Loved me that way. A father's love without the obligation. His daughter died. Years later, I wrote him that crazy letter. The trees told me, the grass whispered it through the breeze.

Jesus knew it was all literal. If we love each other like a parent does a child, without the obligation, and then we die, our children mourn this way and achieve enlightenment. That's what it's for. People can only go into enlightenment contemplating the love of someone who died. Without that love and without true mourning there is no enlightenment.

But Jesus couldn't tell the truth, because his mother was still alive. He had to keep her secret. So it all had to be veiled in parables, for her sake.

Why was I chosen to understand this? I am thirty. Am I the
Messiah? What is my Fate, to be sacrificed? It is my Fate to be
sacrificed."

I sat at the table rolling a penny between my fingers. Waves of
thought rolled over me, gliding like water over sand. It was getting
too dark to write, and I stopped when I couldn't see the writing
anymore.

"What if I am the Messiah? Will I be attacked and killed? I don't
want to die that way, a sacrificial lamb, a hunted deer. It was a
deer, I know I hit a deer. I didn't hallucinate it. Diana was still
alive then. She bought the EPT and the shovel. She was still
alive."

I sat for a long time in the dark, thinking about Diana, trying
to remember our conversations, feeling that if I just knew Diana,
knew the things Diana never confided, I would know the meaning
of everything.

I turned on the lights, the yellow florescent kitchen light like an
acrid taste in my mouth. When I opened the copy of *Frankenstein* to
read, Deputy Polozzi's business card fell out. It was just before five
o'clock; maybe he would be there. I called.

"Yes Wendy?" he answered.

I swallowed, my throat dry. "Hi. I've been wondering, trying to
establish the latest time Diana was alive. If I was wrong about seeing her that night. Can you tell me the time stamp on that drugstore
receipt I gave you? If it's no trouble?" Just having Polozzi on the
phone calmed my pounding heart.

"I guess. But I'm not at the office. Can I call you back in a little
while?"

"Sure, thanks."

I lay on the bed, catatonically still. There was an explanation
for everything. All these people were strangers to me. Their lives
were locked doors. There had to be a key. Why didn't I know

Diana better? Why couldn't I talk to Ann? Or my mother? And I knew I was deeply afraid of what was beyond the door of my mother. Scott's door I'd seen behind, once. I remembered his fury during our fight, as if I'd opened a trapdoor to a horrible cellar of fury and pain. This was the pit inside people's souls, pits of secret boiling rage. It was vital to keep that door shut and locked. I didn't know the balm for that kind of rage. Did everyone really have that dungeon inside them? That we could wake and be the Minotaur?

I pictured my mother as a child and the accident that killed her brother, so swift and horrible, the blink of an eye, when he fell out of the car. My heart suddenly pounded with a thought. Did she push him? Did she unlock the door and in a swift thrust, push the boy out of the car? It all seemed so logical, the explanation for everything.

I felt I had been born to forgive my mother for this deed. I went into the kitchen and dialed the number. *Heaven and hell are what you experience on your deathbed, just before dying. Going over your life, you either feel okay about your actions, or you're in a hell of remorse. That hell of remorse is intense, a hell like no other.* I felt that if I forgave her, then on her deathbed my mother would feel the secret was known to someone, that she was forgiven, and that all was okay.

I got her voicemail. "I just wanted to say you are forgiven. You are forgiven. Your brother forgives you. I know everything." My voice sounded deep and full and far-away, like an angel from heaven. "You can talk to someone. You'll know if she's a good counselor if she's comfortable with silences. It's all right. You are forgiven, you are forgiven."

I hung up and went back to bed. In the cold light it all seemed strange and I felt doubt. I dialed her again. This time my voice sounded sharp and strange. "Hi. It's Wendy again. I just don't know. I just don't know," and I hung up.

I held the phone and pressed my lips together. Then I dialed my brother, getting his voicemail. "We need to talk. About Mom. I know now she's disturbed and that she's crazy and tried to kill us growing up. I want to talk to you. I don't want to fight anymore. It's all over. I'm cured now."

When I hung up, the phone rang immediately, and I jumped. "Hello?"

"Hey Wendy, it's Deputy Polozzi."

"Thanks for calling."

"No problem. The receipt was rung up at three forty-five pm." She would have been coming home about four o'clock, possibly rounding that bend, exactly when I hit the deer. I scribbled down a schedule of Diana's last day. First, she saw Dr. Hellmann, then Cynthia Andrews at 2:00. Then the health center. The drugstore. The party. She *must* have been at the party.

I closed my eyes. Bits of memories jerked through my mind like flip-book animation: of near-accidents, of unsupervised play, of cigarettes on the tip of gesturing fingers, one that brushed near my eye, little moments of danger or near-danger. It was not a normal childhood.

The phone rang and I jumped up again. It was Scott.

"Hi, I came back too late last night. But I got everything done. How are you? I've missed you."

"I'm okay I think," I said hoarsely.

"What's the matter?" His voice changed from light to worried.

"I think maybe I'm starting to remember things. Repressed things, bad things."

I heard the intake of his breath.

"God."

"I don't know. It might explain a lot. There has to be an explanation."

"Do you want me to come over? I can be there in twenty minutes."

"Okay."

I waited in the dark, until Scott strode into the kitchen and pulled me into his arms. His face was cold, and I pressed my cheek against his. "I'm okay," I said.

He led me by the hand into the living room, turning on the lights. "You don't have to talk about it," he said.

"It's hard. I realized that my mother is crazy. And I'm cured! I'm cured of a dissociative disorder I've always had!"

Scott sat back away from me and stared. "Your mother?"

"Yes."

He tilted his head to the side. "I've met your mother. She—" he stopped. "You mean, figuratively."

"She has a personality disorder."

Scott looked at me carefully. "You say you have a dissociative disorder?"

"Had," I corrected.

"Aren't you bipolar?"

"I don't know anymore. I don't know if I can be both. This is a big breakthrough. I'm cured of it now."

"Did you talk with Ann about how things have been for you lately? In the here and now?"

"What do you mean?"

"Are you sleeping? Are you eating?"

I started pacing. "I thought you'd be excited for me. Everything has been leading up to this, that's all. I've been on the edge of this big realization. When my mother was a child, her little brother fell out of a moving car and he was killed. It's the source of all the madness."

He stared. There was a long pause. "Doesn't your mother have older siblings who were there, too? To check this out?"

"Her older brother died a long time ago." I perched on the edge of a chair, jiggling my foot.

"You have to be reasonable."

"That's the thing. I'm reasoning everything out. It all makes logical sense. One thing leads to another."

"I see." Scott sank onto the couch. I didn't understand his loss for words.

I went on. "It's all connected. My mother's brother was killed that way, and now Diana. I see this long thread over the years, and it's all connected. Ann has been asking me a lot about mom, and the accident. Ann is guiding me into seeing this connection so I can solve the mystery. Both mysteries. Everything in life is a mystery, but you can penetrate it by following the logic. Then it's so clear, it's obvious."

"What does this have to do with Diana?"

"I don't know. She was killed. All I know is that it was for a reason, and I was born to figure it out. She was hunted. It's a question of who the hunter is. Who has all the dogs in the basement? Someone has a pack of dogs in the cellar, and he let them out. If I keep thinking about it, I'll figure it out. I need to meditate. Meditation is like entering the death state. And you lift the veil. I need to go to Chicago, to Diana's grave, and sit there and meditate. It will all come to me. Or maybe this: let's start practicing meditation together." Scott didn't speak. I wrung my hands. "It's over now. I'm cured." I laughed in relief.

"What are all the crumpled papers on the kitchen table?" he asked.

I jumped up. "It was just something I had to explain. It's nothing! You're not being fair. You're not listening!"

He rose and pulled me into his arms. "It's okay. Never mind," he said. "But I want you to get some sleep. You've got to sleep. Come here." He led me into the bedroom and lay me down on the bed. I got under the covers and he sat next to me. "Relax. Breathe deep. Close your eyes. I'll wait here with you."

"I'm tired. I'm not in trouble. Ann once told me if you have lack of sleep with no loss of energy, you're in trouble. But that's not it, because I'm completely exhausted."

"Okay. Let's rest."

CHAPTER THIRTY-ONE

I fell asleep. Scott sat next to me and watched my eyebrows fur-
row, and he knew this was an anxious sleep, but sleep nonetheless.
When he was sure I was asleep, he got up as quietly as he could. He
took his cell phone and went outside, dialing the number of the
school health center.

"Hi, I have a friend I'm worried about. She's in trouble."

"What do you mean?" asked a tired-sounding woman's voice.

"She's mentally ill, and I know she's seeing a counselor there
named Ann."

"I can't tell you anything. It's confidential," the woman replied.

"But she's falling into some kind of episode."

"Is she a danger to herself or others?"

"I don't think so."

"She's probably noncompliant," the woman said. "It's common."

"Noncompliant?"

"Off her medication."

Scott spoke quickly. "No, she's taking it. That's why I'm worried.
I'd like to talk to Ann about this."

"I can't let you do that. If she's in danger, you have to take her to
the hospital. There's nothing I can do."

"Thanks. You're a big help." He hung up.

He went inside to the kitchen cupboard and took out my prescription bottle. He checked the date and counted the pills. I was
taking them, he never doubted it. He wondered how bad I would
have to get before he should take me to the hospital.

He went to the living room to think, noticing my story about the collapse of civilization lying on the table. He read it with a sad feeling. It wasn't the old Wendy who wrote about Dostoyevsky's beard grooming. Then he saw my little schedule of Diana's last day.

He went back outside with his cell phone again and dialed the health center, hoping a different receptionist would answer. It was the same woman, but she seemed to have already forgotten him. "I'd like to get some counseling," he said. "I've heard good things about a woman there named Ann. Does she have anything available this week?"

"I'll see. . . ." A gust of wind blew snow off the trees by the road. The hill was deserted, and the world was silent, a winter desert. He felt the isolation in the piercing wind, thought about the Clutter family from *In Cold Blood*, how easily a murderer could pull up here and never be seen.

"Yes, she has an opening tomorrow at 12:30."

He shook his head and tried to ignore his morbid thoughts. "Thanks I'll take it. My name is Scott Garrison." He answered a few questions and hung up. Then he had to decide whether to miss work at the computer lab to stay with me. His cell phone rang. It was a co-worker, saying he couldn't come in. Now Scott had to go. He went back inside, wrote me a note, and left. He had homework to do, and decided he should try to keep up with his own life as normally as possible. I would want him to.

Through the evening, Scott worked on his assignments, calling my number every hour, never getting an answer. At 10:00, he got into his car and started driving the country roads around the school and the hills behind my house. It had stopped snowing and the moon was bright. He found me walking about a mile away. I was singing, my black down coat open. He pulled over.

"Hey!" he called, getting out of the car.

I ran up to him. "Hello! I'm glad to see you!" I threw my arms around him.

"Where have you been?"

"I wanted to walk."

"For four hours?"

"I also went to the library."

We got into the car. "You must be freezing," he said.

"I felt so hot, walking."

We drove to my house and went inside. "Have you eaten?" he asked.

"No. I feel so healthy right now. I'm not going to overeat anymore. That's all behind me."

"Have you eaten anything all day?"

"I think I had an apple. The fruit of knowledge. That's fitting."

He sighed and got out some eggs. He made an omelet and with a light, jovial gesture, sat me down and coaxed me to eat.

"The water tastes poisoned to me, because I'm so clear now. I'm so clear."

He nodded. "Would you like juice?"

"Okay."

We cleaned up the kitchen together while I sang at the top of my voice. "My love is like a red, red rose, that's newly sprung in June. Oh my love is like a melody that's sweetly played in tune. . . ." My voice soared.

When we were sitting in the living room he asked, "Are you ready for class tomorrow?"

It must have shown in my face.

"What's the matter?" He put his arm around me.

"I'm ashamed of this. It's Professor Hellmann. He thinks I did something, something terrible, but I didn't. I don't know what to do."

"I don't want you to go anywhere tomorrow. No four-hour walks through the snow. Just sit tight, okay? I'll try to sort things out."

"Okay."

He slept beside me. He was half-aware, in his sleep, that I was not asleep, but he was tired and didn't try to stay awake with me.

The next morning my eyes glowed beatifically. To speak to me at all, he had to pull me out of a trance. I was like a balloon on a string that he was tugging at, that kept floating away. He watched me take my lithium as he made some oatmeal for breakfast.

"Will you just stay here today?" he asked as he was leaving, holding me by the shoulders.

"Yes. I need to rest."

"That's right."

"There's a part in the Gospel where Jesus is drawing circles in the sand, just sitting, and I can feel that he must have been this exhausted. It's exhausting to know so much, to keep thinking and thinking and having the truth coming to you in these waves." As I looked at him, with my drawn, ashen face utterly relaxed, my eyes were huge. I looked like a young, helpless child, almost as if nature herself were trying to make me look as harmless and vulnerable as possible, as a form of protection.

He kissed my forehead and left. Scott went to the library and looked up books about bipolar disorder. As he read, the symptoms didn't seem to match everything he'd seen in me. I wasn't talking manically, instead I was withdrawn, and my thoughts seemed more delusional and disconnected than just mania. A chapter on schizophrenia fell open. Some things leapt out to him—coughing, extra-sensitive hearing, hallucinations of taste such as the food tasting poisoned. The lithium was having no effect, or at least it didn't seem to be curbing this episode. He wondered if I was a misdiagnosed schizophrenic. But further research would have to wait; it was time to go see Ann.

Scott sat in her office and looked around. There were a lot of books, mostly on dysfunctional families and adult children of alcoholics. The chair felt squeezed farther in the corner than it had to be. His head brushed the picture on the wall behind him. He reached down and pulled the chair slightly forward.

He was prepared to dislike her but tried to resist his judgment. She wore a completely black outfit, her hair stuck up over small, red-rimmed glasses. He felt it all pretention.

"I'm really here because of a friend. I guess that's a corny way to start."

"Someone you're concerned about."

"Yeah. Um, by the way, I'm just wondering. Would you mind telling me your qualifications? I don't see anything on the wall."

"I'm a resident finishing my master's in social work. In a few months I'll be a licensed psychotherapist."

He wondered how old she was. "Is there a psychiatrist on staff here?"

"Yes, the director is a psychiatrist."

"It's just that my friend—my girlfriend is on medication, and that's what I'm concerned about." Though he thought it would give him more authority, he instantly regretted adding "my girlfriend." It would probably make him seem like a possessive boyfriend.

"You feel this medication has changed her?" Ann asked.

He knew what she was thinking. Saying "girlfriend" was definitely a mistake. "No, just the opposite," he said quickly, sitting forward in the chair. "It's not helping her. Her symptoms seem to be getting worse."

"What was her original diagnosis? What is she taking?"

"She's taking lithium for bipolar disorder. But some of what she's expressed to me, well, it seems like somehow there's a little schizophrenia in there."

"A little schizophrenia?" she said with a grim smile. "That's usually hard to miss."

"Well, she's been very, *very* withdrawn, not all manic. She's had some mild hallucination at times. For example, she said food tasted poisoned to her. Her thoughts seem disjointed. . . ." He tried to remember more of what he'd just read. "I'm just worried because every day I can see her drifting off a little further."

"You say she's taking lithium. She must be under someone's treatment."

"Yes." He drew in his breath. "Her name is Wendy Zemansky."

She didn't react, and then she sat back and folded her arms. "I see. You say she's your girlfriend."

"We're old friends."

It seemed to dawn on her then, I had talked about him. "Oh. Scott. Yes, that's right." She paused. He wondered for the first time how I had described him to her.

"We're really very close," he continued. "I'm very worried about her. I think she's headed for the hospital."

"I haven't seen the signs you're talking about. She's always very insightful."

"Insight is a trait of schizophrenia," he found himself replying automatically. He had read this in the book. Then he knew this sank him.

Her face narrowed. "Insight is a trait of schizophrenia? I should think it's a trait of many things, like maturity and sensitivity, and being at a turning point in one's life."

His mind raced to recover. "Her insights tend toward the delusional."

"Delusional? I haven't seen it."

He leaned forward, trying not to feel crowded in the corner. "She's obsessed with her roommate's death. It seems to be causing her to have a breakdown."

For the first time, Ann looked surprised. "She's hardly talked about Diana's death to me. If anything, I feel I need to get her to talk more about it. She seems to have repressed all her feelings about it."

"And couldn't that repression be causing a breakdown? Look, I just thought you should be aware of these issues. I'm pretty concerned. It's possible she isn't being totally honest with you. I find her writing and writing these little notes, and she hides them the minute I see. Who knows what she's thinking, or who she's writing to."

That one seemed to get through to her. "I see. Well, I'll do my best to take care of her."

Scott rose to go. At the door, she said, "You know, I don't deal with having to hospitalize people and that sort of thing, usually, in my practice." She said this matter-of-factly, no apology in her tone.

So you're a psychologist, you just don't deal with mental illness, he thought, but he didn't say it. Instead he paused in the doorway, standing very close to her, and looked her in the eyes. "I met Wendy twelve years ago, and we were very close for many years. The Wendy I'm seeing now is a completely different person. She was intelligent, articulate, rational, and her future was bright." He lowered his voice, but the anger sharpened his tone. "You might think she's making progress with all her 'insights,' but I can tell you she has gone nowhere but downhill." Then he left.

CHAPTER THIRTY-TWO

The dark house loomed ahead. I floated over the street, yet the salt under my boots crunched loud. A foggy moon was setting behind the Victorian mansion, a Halloween picture. When I rang the bell, four notes echoed.

Dr. Kind opened the door and cocked his head. He was wearing sweatpants and a T-shirt, which shocked me. I realized I didn't know what time it was.

"Wendy, are you okay?"

He cared. Someone cared. "Is it late? I'm sorry. I'm so angry. I'm so angry that Dr. Hellmann would steal Diana's poem. Her writing is her legacy."

A dog barked from somewhere inside. He held the door half-closed. "You should go to him, then. Talk to him about it. Go right now, get it off your chest."

His face was weirdly happy. My thoughts flickered. My mind splintered into factions, and part of my mind was well, watching all this, and trying to tell me this was wrong. He was trying to make a fool of me for some reason. He looked too happy. Why was everyone being weird? I should go home and forget it. But another part of my mind knew I couldn't trust myself, that I needed advice, and he was giving me advice.

That's the thing. That's the thing. Sometimes when you know you're crazy, you have to trust someone. And sometimes that person lets you down in the worst way.

The barking dog grew louder. He turned his head, speaking sharply. "Quiet, Dolly. Quiet!" He looked back at me, smiling.

"Okay, Wendy? Run along to Dr. Hellmann. He'll be able to explain, I'm sure. Good night." He closed the door.

I ambled back down to the hill, avoiding the muddy shoulder and walking in the road. Suddenly the white stucco house, dirty and grayish, was beneath my hand reaching for the bell. A long pause. The creak of floors and doors. Lights coming on. What time was it?

Dr. Hellmann stood in the open doorway. At least he was dressed, as if he hadn't been home long, in cords and that fisherman's sweater that made him look like the model in a photo frame. "Wendy? Is this important?"

"May I come in?" Formal, the way drunk people were formal.

He opened the door and I stepped into the living room, so softly carpeted, so richly upholstered.

"Have you been drinking?" he asked.

I laughed, which I knew would seem to prove him right. "No. Really, I haven't. But I haven't slept. I've been upset."

"So have I." He stayed by the door, with forced civility. He was tall and strong looking. I had the sensation he wasn't above hitting me.

I looked around wondering what chair to sit on. It seemed I should stand to make my accusation, but I was so tired. I leaned against the mantel over the black, cold fireplace. "I saw your poem in *The New Yorker*. It was Diana's. That line, about jealousy. You took it from her."

He raised his hands and I flinched. He pushed his hands through his wavy hair and kept them over his head. "Don't be stupid. I don't have to steal poetry. You should go home."

"It was her legacy!"

In a few strides he was in my face. "I've had enough from you. You have been gunning for me for weeks. I don't know why. Your letters, now this."

"I didn't write that letter." My voice was high and weak. I'd momentarily forgotten about that. Now I knew I only enraged him. It was a mistake. Why had Dr. Kind told me to come here?

"Please leave my house." He put his hands on my shoulders.

"Can I use your bathroom first?"

With a strangled sigh he let me go, and I hurried down the hall. And this, with everything that happened and was yet to happen, was my lowest moment. My period had started. I had been the girl who had a tampon. Now I had nothing. I looked desperately in the cabinet under the sink. There were some thin panty shields. It wouldn't be enough, but it was better than nothing.

When I came out of the bathroom, Jean was in the living room, taking off her coat. She didn't look surprised. "Hello Wendy. Please, make yourself comfortable. Perhaps you saw Diana in the bathroom? Perhaps she's been hiding there, all along?" She folded her arms and smiled.

I stared, my eyes wide. *They should know I'm losing my mind. Why are they being so weird?* Jean's smile was especially unnerving. That's the thing—the other thing. Sometimes when you're crazy, the people around you act even crazier, and you may never know why.

And there's something else. You don't forget. It's not like you black out through this. You're crazy, you act crazy, and you remember it all afterward when you're well again, and the shame is there, always, and all you can do is try to forget.

"I'd better go."

"Oh, don't go. We can have another party."

I ran for the door, thrusting myself between the Hellmanns, and pitched out into the night. I jogged down the hill, my breath visible in the damp, cold air, and up Grange Hill, running on the deserted road, the moon running with me.

When I got to my driveway, the scar glowing on my windshield was harsher than ever. I'd had enough. I grabbed a sledgehammer from the porch and bashed in the windshield, pounding with all my might until it was just a pile of shattered glass.

CHAPTER THIRTY-THREE

It was a deer, I thought over and over, turning in bed. Then I heard the front door open, and the quiet tap of his steps. A warm calm came over me for a few moments. Scott entered the room.

"Hey, how are you?" he asked softly as he sat down next to me.

His concern touched me, and tears sprang to my eyes. "I'm sorry," I said.

He held me. "It's all right."

"I'm afraid. I'm afraid I'm the Messiah."

He kissed my forehead. "You're a very nice person, but you're not the Messiah."

"We all are. You are the Messiah every time you say the words, 'I forgive you.' That's what Jesus was trying to teach."

"You're an angel. Why don't you take a shower, and I'll make lunch."

Am I the angel of death? In the shower my shampoo bottle was empty. I used Diana's rosemary shampoo, and felt I was taking on a mantle, covered over with Diana's scent. I dressed in a white sweater, white for the angel of death.

In the kitchen Scott put a bowl of salad on the table. "I found a lasagna in the freezer to microwave, is that okay?"

Now I would eat Diana's food, the bad omen I'd avoided all along. I sat silently and ate. It tasted intensely bitter. *He's poisoning me. Because I did it.*

Now he stood at the counter with a knife in his hand. Everything was in slow motion. Slowly he turned to face me, the knife glinting in the cold light. Slowly a smile spread across his face. It was insane for him to be acting so normal. Nothing was normal. The knife cast a slash of light across the wall. I jumped up and grabbed the knife. *IkilledDianaandImustbesacrificedandIwillputmyeyesoutIwillputmyeyesout-nowandbepunishedandmakeitalluptoeveryonenownow.*

He held out his hand, his face calm. He didn't say anything. *I must let him decide.* I gave him back the knife. We stood a moment. He seemed to be breathing hard.

Still barefoot, I ran out the door as fast as I could, outside and up the road. *I did it. I killed Diana. I hit her. I must have.* My legs bounded over the snow like a deer. Great gasps of air flowed through my heaving lungs, I was drowning in it. I ran until I fell in the snow. *He's going to kill me, he's going to kill me now because I killed Diana.*

It seemed to take a long time for him to catch up with me. He bent over and pulled me up by the shoulders.

"All right, kill me," I sobbed. "Just don't hurt me. Please don't hurt me. Make it quick."

He pulled me into his arms forcefully, and with his right arm tight around my waist started walking me back.

"We're going to the hospital now," he said.

My stomach lurched. "Because of the poison?"

CHAPTER THIRTY-FOUR

Scott spoke quickly to the nurse at emergency. We were ushered into a small admitting room tightly furnished with a desk, chair, and couch. The man who did the intake sat at the desk and seemed to write up notes for a long time. Then a psychiatric nurse came down and took me up the elevator to the psych ward. The mild and angelic looking nurse looked a bit like my mother, with her long face and high cheekbones.

We sat down with a psychiatrist, whom I never saw again after this intake. I accused myself of killing Diana, claimed I'd been abused as a child and that I was just remembering it, and said I had driven my mother to commit suicide. I spoke in a slow, dreamlike voice that sounded far away.

"We are the Messiah every time we forgive," I finished.

"So do you think you should have some Klonopin?" the psychiatrist asked.

For a moment everything was in slow motion. The nurse glanced at him in a surprised and disapproving way, which I've wondered about ever since.

"I don't know what that is," I said. "I'm *sure* I've been taking my lithium. I'm *sure* of it. Did I hallucinate taking it?"

We went back out to the living area by the nurse's station where Scott was waiting. The psychiatric ward was arranged like a dorm, with small private bedrooms, a common living room, and a kitchen with a dining area. It was a small ward with room for about ten patients. The whole thing was nicer and plusher than I would have expected, like I was in heaven's waiting room, that I was on the point of death.

"I don't know how much sleep she's gotten," Scott said.

We sat at one of the dining tables. The nurse put a small capsule and a cup of water on the table and told me it was Ativan, and it would help me sleep. The nurse cocked her head in a bird-like way. She kept saying, "I would take it. It will help you sleep. I would take it."

I was confused because the nurse had brought the pill to me without its being in a labeled prescription bottle. I didn't know it was legal to dispense prescription drugs that way, not in a labeled bottle. I assumed it had to be properly labeled.

I became terrified I would be tricked into killing myself—not because I was afraid to die. What I was afraid of was that I'd be tricked into taking the easy way out, and die before I ever had the chance to make up for all the things I felt I had done wrong. I wanted to start over and live my life in a morally upright way. If I died, I would never have that chance.

Scott tried to convince me to take the capsule. Finally I took it and they walked me to a bedroom.

"You're just going to sleep," Scott said.

This suddenly terrified me, and I ran to a bathroom and threw up the pill. The nurse looked exasperated, at her wit's end. We sat on my bed and the nurse brought in a hypodermic needle. She looked nervous as she punched the needle into my arm with some force.

I wouldn't have tried to grab the needle from you, I thought. Then I passed out.

CHAPTER THIRTY-FIVE

When I awoke, it was evening. My first thought was of the message I had left for my mother. I was afraid maybe it was true, my mother had killed her brother, and that now I had driven my mother to commit suicide. I walked to the living area and stared out the window at the purple sunset. I felt I was watching my mother's soul rise up into that sunset. One of the nurses was watching me, and I knew I was being observed, and was annoyed that this nurse would think I wasn't aware she was staring at me.

In the adjoining dining area, five or six patients were eating dinner. Moving like a zombie, I took a dinner tray out of the rack and sat down and ate the macaroni and cheese and Jell-O. There was a distant murmur of people at the nurse's station, but all was mostly quiet. I finished and slid the tray back on the rack.

I went back to my room and found that while I had slept, Scott had brought over my purse and a small duffel bag with some clothes. I took out my wallet and went out to a pay phone in the corner of the living room. Using a calling card, I dialed Dayton information and got connected to the police there, and reported that I was afraid that my mother had committed suicide. No one stopped me.

"We'll look into it," the wary operator said before the call was disconnected.

I walked jaggedly back to my room, fell into bed, and slept again. The next morning when I awoke, the good night's sleep had done much to restore my sanity, almost amazingly. I wondered why they had let me call the police. *They don't know I have a calling card, that it was possible for me to make the call. What they think is that I fantasized the conversation.*

I immediately went out and found a man in a dark little office off the entrance hall to the ward, typing at a glowing screen. I had the sensation he was typing up transcripts of our phone calls. I lightly tapped on his door. The man turned from what he was typing and gave me a kindly smile. "Yes?"

"Hi. I'm Wendy. I wanted you to know something. I made this phone call."

"Yes?" he asked, pleasant. I was sure he thought I fantasized it.

"I have a calling card—"

His smile dropped. "A calling card?"

"Yes." Then I turned away.

I went to the dining area and ate breakfast: cereal and a cold English muffin. The food didn't taste poisoned now. A tall young nurse came up to me.

"Hi Wendy, I'm Jane. Can you tell me about this phone call you made?" She gave me an inviting smile, her cropped blond hair framing a large looming face.

"I called the Dayton police."

"And what did you say?"

"I thought my mother had committed suicide. It was probably a delusion. I really called them, with my calling card."

"I see." The nurse sighed, her smile fading.

I waited to be praised for my presence of mind, for telling them this important thing they didn't know. I'm still disappointed they didn't acknowledge it.

"Has anyone shown you around?" she asked instead, dropping the subject.

I finished eating and the nurse pointed out the arts and crafts room and the DVD cabinet, though no one was interested in the TV. Three patients were setting up jigsaw puzzles on the dining tables. A teenaged boy at one table drew my attention. He had a slight build, brown hair falling almost to his shoulders, and round frameless glasses. I felt I knew him.

"Do you have any questions?" the nurse asked.

I wanted to ask who the boy was but didn't know if I should. "No thanks."

"The doctor will see you soon. We have some medication for you." At the nurse's station they gave me two pills and I went ahead and took them.

I casually walked near the boy's table and looked down at his jigsaw puzzle, a landscape of hot air balloons. "That's pretty," I said.

He looked up. "Oh, hi Miss Z." He took me in with no surprise. The hot air balloons danced in the reflection of his glasses.

"Hi Geoffrey," I responded, his name on my lips before I consciously knew it.

Then the door to the ward opened and Scott strode over to me, putting his arm around me. His jacket was cold to the touch in the warm room, slightly damp from snow, but I pressed my cheek into the cool nylon.

"How are you? I assumed you wouldn't wake up last night."

"I did, but only for a few minutes. Enough to make trouble."

We went to my room and sat on the edge of the bed while I told him of my phone call to the police. "I should call my mom, but I'm afraid to. Will you sit next to me while I call? Would you dial?"

"Let's make sure it's private and use my cell." I recited the number to him, and he greeted my mother. I knew she was greeting him happily. "I'm afraid Wendy isn't well. She's right here. She'd like to talk with you."

I took the phone. "Hi Mom. I'm in a psych ward. I'm sorry."

"Are you all right? The police were here but I didn't know where you called them from."

"Now that I've slept, I'm a little better."

I could hear her puff a cigarette. "I was a little concerned, but then you left the next message and I thought you were okay. Are you okay there? What are they doing to you?"

"Just trying to get me to rest."

"I didn't realize how Diana's accident must have affected you. I'm sorry I didn't pick up on it. But if you're just there to rest . . . ?"

"Yes." I wondered how she pictured the ward. But everyone has that image: a ward full of cots with no private rooms, people in hospital gowns, barefoot, Nurse Ratchett. Images that have nothing to do with an actual psych ward. I felt tired and didn't try to correct her imagination.

"Do you want me to come up there and visit you? Please say yes." There was a plea in her voice that stabbed at my heart. I didn't know until later how worried she really was.

"No. I'm sorry. I'll be okay. I'd rather not see you right now."

"I'll call you more often. I know I've been so busy. Work has been crazy. Please call me any time. If you need anything. Any time of the day or night."

I wiped a tear from my eye. "Sure, Mom. I will. I guess I haven't been in touch very much, either."

"Your brother is worried, too."

I took a deep breath. It was weird to think people were talking about me. "Please tell him I'm okay. We had kind of a fight last year. He acted like choosing to live up here was my fault and caused my whole illness."

"Don't get your undies in a twist about Peter. Don't worry about it, honey. Don't worry about it at all. Just take care of yourself, and don't let anyone stress you out. Don't let anyone do that to you."

I wiped away a last tear and swallowed back the lump in my throat. "Okay Mom, thanks."

"I love you, honey," she said quickly, nervously.

It wasn't the kind of thing we said to each other. I felt embarrassed. "Love you too, Mom. Thanks. I'd better go."

"Goodbye, honey. Sleep well."

"Goodbye."

I handed the phone back to Scott. "Thanks for bringing my stuff. Thanks for everything. Are you fed up with me?"

He pulled me into his arms. "No, I'm not fed up with you. Maybe I'm fed up with the mental health system. This shouldn't have happened."

"I was taking my lithium. I trusted it to help me."

"I know."

We sat in each other's arms a while, and I breathed in his familiar, clean scent. "Let's see, spring break is in two weeks. Maybe I'll be able to come back to school after break."

"Talk it over with your doctor."

"Okay." I pressed my face into his jacket again, now warm. He was like a big brother again, and I tried to ignore my sense of inadequacy. "I'm a child, aren't I?" I asked in a hoarse whisper.

He leaned back and looked at me, his brow raised in surprise. We stared at each other a moment as he put his hands around my face. Tears wet my eyes. Desperately I wanted to grow up. What could I be to him but a burden?

"You're an adult struggling with something hard. It doesn't make you a child." His voice had never sounded so soft. "I want you to stop saying those things, thinking those things."

It hit me how alone I'd been through it all. It wasn't normal to be so alone, not to have friends. "I don't really know what I am."

"Then start defining yourself today."

"I'll try."

We stood up. "You're going to be okay. Let them help you. Someday you're going to write about this, and it will be some kooky comedy."

I shook my head with a smile. "I don't think so. My whole life feels like a dream."

We walked to the door of the ward, and he kissed my cheek. After he left, I looked over at Geoffrey doing his jigsaw puzzle, and wondered what to say.

CHAPTER THIRTY-SIX

It was a surprise to see people come into the ward wearing snow-dusted coats and wet boots. Here, the weather, like the outside world, was distant, irrelevant. It was gently warm, softly carpeted, the inside of the inside, a room at the center of the maze of the world, locking out chaos. I padded around the ward in my socks, feeling light, free of the burden of my big down coat. Out the windows, the sky was a blur.

After lunch, I sat across from Geoffrey at the jigsaw puzzle.

"I didn't expect to see you here," I said. "I'm here for manic depression."

He kept his gaze on the puzzle. He still looked so young. "I've been depressed, too." We sat in silence for a minute. "I'm not that surprised," he said.

"No?"

"You were sort of strange in class. So afraid of us. Why were you afraid of a bunch of seventh graders? We weren't going to hurt you." He pushed up his round glasses, looking at me matter-of-factly.

I gave him a wan smile. "I guess I was scared of everything."

"So what happens when there really is something to be scared of?"

Nurse Jane approached us. "Dr. Carson is ready for you, Wendy."

Geoff grabbed another handful of puzzle pieces from the box. "See you later," he said.

In the bare office, there was not a stray paper on the desk, nor were there books. On the desk were only a pen holder and a box of tissues. The room was simply furnished with a clean-lined desk, a tall filing cabinet, and two chrome chairs closer to the door. We sat in the two chairs. On the wall behind the doctor were two water-color paintings, childlike, done by either a patient or his own child. I decided they were by his child.

Dr. Carson was about forty, wearing a brown wool suit. His hair-cut looked expensive, so did his watch. He looked like he was from a large city, not from this rural area. He held my chart in front of his chest.

"Hello, Wendy. I'd like to ask you some questions. What is the date today?"

"March 3, 2007." It's funny to me now, that somehow with every-thing, I had never lost track of the date.

"Who is the president?"

"George Bush. The second one."

"How many fingers am I holding up?"

"Three."

He nodded, making checkmarks in the chart.

"You're in school? What happened?"

I started shaking. "I think I killed my roommate. I hit her with my car and thought it was a deer."

He set down the clipboard and reached over to hand me the box of tissues. "Why would you think that?"

"Because I have a dissociative disorder." I wiped my tears.

"According to who?"

"My therapist, Ann. She's at the school health clinic. She cured me."

He took that in for a moment, looking thoughtful, then stood up and took a form from the file cabinet. "This is a questionnaire about dissociation. I'd like you to fill it out. We'll talk again after."

I took the form. "Are you allowed to talk about the other pa-tients?"

He smiled. "No."

"It's just that I know that boy, Geoff. He was a student of mine when I was a teacher."

Dr. Carson raised his eyebrows. "You're allowed to talk with him, if you like." I watched his fingers rubbing together, turning his wedding band. "I can say, he had a traumatic experience. I can't say more. If you can open him up a little, that might be good for him. But then again," he extended a hand toward me, "don't try to play doctor either."

"No, I won't."

"I have you on Haldol for now. It's an oldie but a goodie. You'll be a little stiff, especially your facial expression, the affect. Nothing to worry about. The other pill is to mitigate the side effects." He rose and walked me to the door. "So please fill out this form and we'll talk again."

I took the form to my room. The questions began with, "Have you ever found you'd bought things you don't remember buying? Have you ever found yourself in a location and didn't remember how you got there?" I answered "No" for every question.

The nurse knocked on my door. "Visitor."

I came out to find Scott in the lounge with his laptop. "We still have to lay out that poetry journal, remember? I picked up some old copies of it for inspiration that were gathering dust around the department." He spread them out. "Some of these go back to the eighties." He pointed out a group photo of girls with permed 80's hairstyles and we laughed. I opened one to a poem called "Landscape and Longing," by Tommy Kind. "This desert, hot as the eye that stares in icy rage . . ."

"I think this is by Dr. Kind. He must have been a student here twenty years ago," I said. I handed Scott the book.

He looked at the poem, starting to read aloud. "There are no people here, dancing at the harvest, but only shadows, bending and tossing bales like mad manic mechanical dolls. . . .'" He read on silently, his brow furrowed. Then he shrugged and put it aside.

"We need a title for this volume of the journal."

I considered it. "I like 'Landscape and Longing.' Do you think Dr. Kind would remember his title? Diana has this one winter landscape painting. I was thinking of seeing if we could use it for the cover."

"I'll call the gallery and ask if we can use it. The art show is still going to happen, right?"

"As far as I know. I need to get the paintings to the gallery."

He nodded. "By the way, I'm getting your windshield fixed tomorrow. I didn't notice it until I went back to get your things. It was . . . pretty scary."

"Oh—I wanted to help. There's all the glass to clean up."

He waved aside my concern. "I'm just really glad you're here."

"I owe you a big favor. What can I do?"

He brushed the hair out of my eyes. "Just get well."

As I looked into his face, it seemed possible.

A voice talking on the pay phone drifted to us. "I know, it's important, but I have better things to do than this." It was Geoff, arguing with someone.

I slid the laptop closer and typed Geoff's name in a search engine. The article in the local paper came up instantly: "Local Teen Killed in Drunk Driving Accident." I recognized the name of the boy who was killed, another of my former students. Geoff was hurt in the accident, which happened six months earlier. The article was fuzzy on details.

"What's that about?" Scott asked.

"Former students of mine."

He put his hand over mine. "I'm sorry."

I closed the article. What could I say? I was in no shape to be of help to anyone. "We'd better get back to work."

We spent another two hours on it, evaluating submissions and brainstorming layouts, until I was exhausted, and it was time for dinner. I checked my email. There was a message from Daniel. "Wendy, I hear you are in the hospital or something. Are you okay? Can you still teach my class after break? I'm counting on you. Please let me know."

"I'll be there. I won't let you down," I wrote back, and turned to Scott. "Can you bring me some books on William Butler Yeats? I have to teach a lesson on him as soon as I'm out of here. Daniel asked me to as a favor."

"You're sure you can do that?"

I wasn't sure. "I promised."

He smiled. "So you have plans already. Maybe that's a good thing." He closed down the computer. "You know, the other day . . . I thought you were schizophrenic. But you're so much better already, except for looking like a zombie. It's a real mystery."

"Today they gave me an evaluation about dissociation. I never had a dissociative disorder."

He gave a frustrated sigh. "It's about time you got a sensible evaluation. Was it the medication? You had a bad reaction to the lithium?"

"I don't think so. I think it simply wasn't having any effect. I look like a zombie because I'm on Haldol now. It's called a flattened affect. I can't emote."

"Well, I'll be glad when you can smile again."

I tried to smile, but my mouth only twitched.

"Oh, I almost forgot, before I go." He took some envelopes out of his backpack, my mail from the house.

"Thanks."

He kissed my forehead and left.

There were ads for car insurance, charity pleas, a catalogue, and a letter. I stared at the envelope in surprise. It was from Mr. Fellowes. I'd forgotten I'd written to him in my manic state, the apology for the other crazy letter written years before. I would have to accept whatever he had to say, and I expected the worst. I went to my room and opened it.

"Dear Wendy,

It was nice to hear from you. I'm sorry, I don't remember the other letter you refer to. I have to read so much as a teacher, and I feel badly that I don't remember, also sad to hear you were having mental difficulty. You're very bright, and I'm sure you will get through it. I hope you stick with literature. 'History is a trick we play on the dead,' Voltaire said! Be well, Henry Fellowes."

So that was it. He didn't even remember the crazy letter. Another opportunity to start over. That was wonderful. I set the mail on the dresser and went to dinner.

I ate alone at the small table at first. There were four other people: an elderly woman, two younger women, and a big man with a black beard. The two younger women sat together, whispering. The elderly lady compulsively scratched her nose. I was almost through eating when Geoff set his tray opposite me.

"Hi," I said.

He shrugged and ate the chicken breast and peas. "Do you want my roll?" he asked.

One of the young women suddenly called over to us, "We're not allowed to share food."

He raised his shoulders and muttered, "Jeez." Saying nothing more, he ate quickly, his face flushed. He got up and slammed the tray back in the rack and went out to the lounge.

I finished my meal and followed him, with no plan of what to talk about. He was sitting on the edge of the sofa, flipping through a magazine. I sat on the nearby chair.

"It's too hot in here," he said, not looking up.

"Yeah." I glanced at the magazine. "Anything interesting?"

"Travel to Paris on a hundred dollars a day." He held it up for a moment to show me.

"Would you like to travel?"

"Sure. I've never been on an airplane."

"Really? They say it's safer than a—" I stopped myself. *Stupid!*

He picked up the magazine and slapped it against the table. "Safer than a what?"

"Nothing."

"That's worse. That you're afraid." He glared at me, sudden violence in his eyes.

"I'm sorry."

Geoff rolled up the magazine and squeezed it absently. "Do you remember Hank?"

"Barely."

"You don't remember him stapling Jenny's hair to the bulletin board?"

"Oh yeah. I remember that."

He laughed.

"He played the drums, didn't he?" I asked, suddenly remembering.

"Yeah. We had a band. The Pain Killers."

"Good name."

"I played bass." He held the rolled-up magazine like a guitar and plucked the air with his thumb. He closed his eyes, hearing the music. Slowly, he stopped, still clutching the magazine. "You know, right?"

"I didn't know until today."

He gave me a penetrating look, the magazine dropping to the table.

"I'm sorry," I said.

He made a sound of disgust in his throat. "Sorry." He got up and stalked back to the dining area. He plucked the uneaten dinner roll off his tray and threw it at the young women. It bounced off one of their heads.

"Hey—" She jumped up, grabbed it off the floor and threw it back at him.

A nurse hurried over. "Lisa, what do you think you're doing?"

Geoff laughed.

"He threw it at me first," Lisa pouted.

He turned and headed for his room, the nurse following closely behind him. My body hurt, stiff with tension. I went to my room, wanting to hide, and lay on the bed with the light on, staring at the ceiling.

CHAPTER THIRTY-SEVEN

As Scott drove back to the university, the town felt unreal. The white peeling houses, scraggly yards, trees bent from the wind, everything silent; the houses seemed empty. *This is such a ghost town.* A ball bounced into the road and he hit the brake, looking for a child to come running after it. The thought of Diana flashed through his mind. No one was around and he kept going. *It's like some post-nuclear holocaust.* He pulled over, for the first time feeling it all, trembling. He had to take me away from this desolation. He just needed to make sure I could finish school.

He went to see Professor Kind. When Scott entered, the professor was packing beanie babies into a box, carefully wrapping each one in tissue.

"My sister gave me one, I'm not sure why," he said to Scott by way of greeting. "And then people thought I collected them. I tried to sell them on Ebay, but it wasn't worth it. So I'm donating them to a daycare. But, I'm rambling. Please sit down."

"I wanted to let you know Wendy's been admitted to a psych ward," Scott said.

Kind smiled, giving one of the animals a little squeeze. "Well, I think it's about time. She's been writing me a long string of crazy letters."

"Oh, you're the one."

"And I think Dr. Hellmann has a problem with her. I really don't know if she should continue here at all. I've put that on the agenda of the next graduate faculty meeting. Obviously she's going to miss the rest of the semester now."

"I don't think that's obvious." Scott sat forward in his chair. "She could be back after spring break. She's so close to being through with the program."

"Most people who fail to earn their master's do so within a semester of finishing. That's typical."

"Well, whose decision is it?"

Professor Kind frowned impatiently. "The department will have to discuss it. Maybe you'd better plead your case with Dr. Hellmann. But he has been in a sour mood. I don't think you'll find sympathy there."

"This seems so hasty. Can't we wait and see, see how she is when she gets out?"

Dr. Kind snorted. "Her work has been declining all semester. But of course we don't want to be unfair. I just wonder about her motivation, if her heart is in this. First not teaching, and now going off her meds and going crazy. It's a question of reliability."

"She didn't go off her meds," Scott said tightly.

Dr. Kind shrugged. "Whatever. All right, this seems important to you. If you can motivate her to keep herself together, we'll see what her fate is. I don't think it's here. But we'll see. Perhaps you should run along to Dr. Hellmann."

Though irritated, Scott forced himself to be polite. "Okay, thanks."

He looked for Dr. Hellmann, but he wasn't in his office, so Scott went home. He got out the laptop and opened his email. After dealing with his messages, he pondered the screen. Then he opened the drafts folder. There was one message: the one he had composed to Diana and never sent. He deleted it.

CHAPTER THIRTY-EIGHT

As I rolled over in bed in the morning, my glance fell on a framed print on the wall by the bathroom door. It was meant to be a bucolic picture of a landscape with bunnies dancing. I didn't like it. Like the deer painting at Stanimer's, the faces on the bunnies frowned at me, creepy and judgmental. I rose and went to the picture, my skin pricking with discomfort. I tried to take the picture down, but it was fastened tight to the wall. I stood in front of it, angry that I had to live with this disturbing picture. It wasn't fair. I took a towel from the bathroom and draped it over the picture, squeezing the edges around the frame, feeling like a problem solver.

Geoff didn't come out for breakfast. As I slid my tray in the rack after eating, another picture caught my eye. It was a Cubist print of a subway station. But the slashes and bodies made me think of someone caught and mashed in a revolving door. I thought I liked Dr. Carson, but he really wasn't good at picking out art for a psych ward.

After breakfast I met with him and handed him the form on dissociation. "I guess I don't have a dissociative disorder?"

He read it and shook his head.

I hadn't slept much the night before. A sinking sensation came over me, that sense that my head was being held under water. I reached for his hand and he took it.

"Wendy?"

I couldn't talk. The room felt dark, as if a pinpoint of light was shining on us. I wondered why he wasn't speaking. I wondered if I was having a stroke.

"I think I need to lie down. Can I have some Ativan?"

I went to my room and slept until the afternoon. When I got up, a nurse told me Scott had been there and left to let me sleep. There was a bouquet of white lilies sent from my mother. I let the nurses keep it on the counter of their station.

Dr. Carson walked up to me. "How are you now?" His voice was tender.

"It's weird. Sometimes it's like I'm all better. But I'm not."

He nodded.

"Today's Friday, isn't it?"

"Yes."

"You have sixteen days to get me well, because two weeks from Monday I have to teach. I promised a friend I'd take over his class."

"Let's talk." He led me into his office.

As soon as I sat across from him, I burst into tears.

"What's the matter?" He handed me the box of tissues.

"My life. My life is a ruin. I don't know what I'm going to do. My resume is already horrible. I can't imagine I'll ever be able to support myself or live a normal life."

"You will. You'll finish."

"After I lost my last job I was on disability, three years of unemployment before I came back to school."

"Did you have any job at all?"

"A rural newspaper route. A freaking newspaper route."

He snapped his fingers. "Self-employed delivery and distribution. You have a teaching certificate, don't you?"

"Yes."

"Did you take the National Teachers' Exam?"

"Yeah."

"What were your scores?" he asked briskly, rubbing his hands together.

"Ninety-eighth percentile on general knowledge, ninety-fifth on professional knowledge, and ninety-second on English usage. I knew they wouldn't like my essay on the English part. I hate to write conclusions."

"That's still good. Are those scores on your resume?"

"No."

"Put them on. There's a lot you can do to improve it. All is not lost."

I swallowed and looked up at him. He looked so professional and unlike the locals. He was powerful, not only my psychiatrist, but director of the ward. I envied his status, wondering if I would ever be successful. But he was helping; he was holding his hand out to me to lift me up.

"This is weird, but I want to be you," I said.

"That would be great. Give me a day off," he said with a smile.

"Will I really make it? In life?"

"Yes," he said firmly.

"Diana's brother said that she came to North Carthage see if she could survive, where there's nothing."

He looked thoughtful, considering his reply, watching me intently.

I continued. "All these connections. Cerf and deer."

"Coincidence is a very cruel thing. Meanwhile, you must get good sleep at night, and eat, and take your meds, and you *will* be all right. I'm going to keep you on Haldol a while longer. I've been in touch with your psychiatrist at the health center. And I don't think you should be seeing an inexperienced resident for therapy." He held out a card. "This is the number of a woman who is an expert on bipolar disorder. It's her specialty."

I took the card, but my stomach felt cold with fear. "Ann is great. She was wrong about my dissociating, but she's right about all kinds of things. I . . . I'm not going to just drop her. That would be weird."

He sighed, clasping his hands, looking slightly frustrated. "There is help for you, Wendy. You fell between the cracks for a little while, but we'll get you on your feet. You have a future."

The words "you have a future" brought tears to my eyes again. I rubbed the tissue over my face and composed myself.

"You have things to do. Don't you have lessons to plan?"

It seemed so normal. I did have lessons to plan. "Thanks. I guess I'd better get that started."

I took a deep breath and we looked at each other, his face relaxed and confident. I tried to draw his confidence into myself. He didn't seem in a rush to finish the appointment. As I thought again about the future, I wondered about the other patients and their varying degrees of desperation. Did they have futures too?

"I've been talking to Geoff a little. . . . He was driving the car?"

Dr. Carson frowned, but nodded. "It's a matter of public record, so I can say yes."

"I don't know how anyone could cope with that guilt. What do you say to him?" I looked into his eyes.

He raised his hand in a gesture of futility. "The important thing is for him to talk to us. Before he becomes addicted to pain killers or alcohol, or God forbid both."

We walked to the door and he opened it, waiting for me to exit ahead of him. For a moment I had a sense of equality, a strange feeling. Something about his manner made me feel like we were equals, gave me the sense of adulthood I had craved for so long.

When Scott came that afternoon, he brought the guitar. "You promised you would practice."

We sat in my room and I tried to play diligently. After half an hour I was tired.

"Half an hour is good enough," he said when I apologized. "I wish I could stay, but I have to go see my mom on the farm. I promised I'd spend spring break helping my brother with some repairs. I'll be back when I can, though. You have this in the meantime." He strummed a few chords.

"It sounds so much better when you play."

"Well, you know how to get to Carnegie Hall."

"Practice?"

I walked him out. When I was back in my room there was a tap on the door.

"I thought I heard a guitar," Geoff said. He pushed his long hair behind his ears and leaned in a little to see.

"I've been trying to learn. I suck, though."

His lips stretched in a down-turned smile. "Let's see."

I realized I didn't know if he was allowed in my room. So I left the door open, and he sat on a small chair in the corner while I sat on the foot of the bed. I handed him the guitar.

"This is kind of a piece of crap," he said. "Nylon strings? Are you kidding me?"

He played the opening of "Stairway to Heaven," his eyes closed. "Do you think Hank is in heaven?"

"Maybe."

"And when you're in heaven you see everything. You can follow people around."

"Sure."

He started to play "Dust in the Wind," humming softly.

"You play very well."

"Thanks. So is that guy your boyfriend?"

"I'm not sure."

He chuckled. "Whatever."

I considered things I could say. I could say, *I know what you want. To be forgiven. You want to apologize. But the person you need to apologize to isn't here, so you can't. You can talk to his parents. You can apologize to them. If you can't talk to them, then maybe you can try writing a letter.* But deep down, I felt inadequate to help him. My potential advice seemed lame in the face of the enormity of what he was dealing with.

He finished the song and handed the guitar back. "Can you play anything?"

I started to stumble through "Scarborough Fair," singing to it. To my surprise he joined in by singing the canticle from Simon and Garfunkel.

"I'm impressed," I said when we finished.

He shrugged. "I have eclectic tastes. Why is there a towel over that picture?"

I blushed. "I didn't like the faces on the bunnies. They frightened me."

He snorted. "You are a trip. Hey, do you remember the time the bee got in the classroom? And you rescued it?"

I smiled. "Yeah. It's my only good memory of that year."

He laughed. "It was hilarious. Hank was so impressed that you saved the bee. I made fun of him for it. That was when we became friends."

"I'm glad you knew him," I said.

His laughter stopped short. He abruptly rose and left.

For the next few days he didn't talk to me. I busied myself preparing for the class I was determined to teach. Daniel had emailed the syllabus. Over the week, well-medicated, some of the fog lifted.

After another session with Dr. Carson, we went out to the entrance hall by the nurse's station, where Geoff was waiting with a duffel bag.

"What's going on?" Dr. Carson asked.

Geoff looked away from him. "I gotta go. I called my mom. She's picking me up."

I could see the frustration on the doctor's face. "Don't you want to come to my office and talk about it?"

"No. I just need you to sign the form. She's on her way."

"The three of us could talk about it when she gets here."

Geoff stared at the counter. "I gotta get ready for my trial. Just sign the form." His face was implacable.

Dr. Carson hung his head. "Just a minute." He went to the other side of the counter and typed on the computer, printing up the form. "Jane has to do an exit interview." When Geoff started to protest, the doctor said, "We need you to sign off on the fact that you're leaving with everything you came with, for example. It's required."

Jane took Geoff back to his room. Dr. Carson walked heavily back to his office. I sat in the lounge, and in a few minutes a slight woman about forty entered from outside. She wore no makeup, her camo coat too big around her.

"Hi, I'm here for Geoff," she said, her voice strained and tired.

"He's almost ready," the nurse said, gesturing her to the lounge. Geoff's mother sat on the sofa, looking at me hesitantly.

"Geoff is a good kid," I said.

Her lips were tight. "He's always been a puzzle. Goes along with the crowd too much. Who'll bring the beer? Who'll drive the truck through the corn field at midnight to party? Geoff will do it." There was a catch in her voice.

I nodded.

"Do you think he'll be okay?" she asked.

I reached for her hand. "Yes, he will be."

She grasped my hand in return. "You people are good to talk to," she said. I didn't know if she'd mistaken me for a nurse.

Geoff came back from his room, crumpling the discharge form in his fist, and they left. It was strange for him to suddenly be gone. I went to my room. There was a note on the dresser, the writing a small square script.

"Hey Miss Z. Don't forget to practice the guitar. Take your meds. Be cool. See you around. Geoff. PS Don't be afraid of pictures. Take a look."

I lifted the towel. He had taped happy faces all over the faces of the bunnies. I took the note and lay on the bed. I thought of all the wise advice I'd like to have given him, but there really wasn't any. I couldn't help him. I closed my eyes and let the tears fall.

CHAPTER THIRTY-NINE

"You don't have a problem." Tommy's smile was generous, confiding. His pale eyes glinted with a flash of yellow in the dark. Stanimer's was almost empty at four o'clock in the afternoon, and the two teenaged servers were loudly arguing in the kitchen. "It's only wine, Jean. On the other hand, maybe we'll never be able to place our order, anyway."

"Maybe we should just order at the bar." Jean hid her trembling hands in her lap.

"No. I like to be waited on. Otherwise I may as well be home."

The sullen teen finally strolled over to them. Tommy ordered two Chardonnays. "You could get a bottle for twelve dollars," the girl said. Jean felt the server's glance go right through her.

"All right, the bottle," Tommy said. "At least we'll know it hasn't been sitting open all week." The girl ambled away. "She probably figures if we have a bottle she won't have to come back for a while."

The server came back with the glasses and wine.

"These are red wine glasses," Tommy said. "We need white."

Jean's stomach tightened at having to wait longer.

The girl looked baffled. "These are the only glasses we have."

Tommy chortled. "Very well." He waved his hand for her to go, then inspected the glasses. "I suppose they're clean." He filled Jean's glass and gave himself a smaller pour.

Jean sipped the wine. It was good that it was a new bottle, as Tommy had pointed out. The cool liquid softened her tensed throat. For a moment the bar receded from her view. She was at an outdoor café in Santa Barbara. Dan was reciting a poem. She had never been with a man who memorized poetry, and had lovely words for every occasion, a man whose idea of culture wasn't limited to action movies. A real man, an adult.

Tommy whistled a snatch of a tune, and she opened her eyes. He was gazing at her serenely. "I can tell you're thinking about him," he said.

She felt herself blush. "I thought I wanted to know. That's why I wanted to see you."

"Know about . . . ? Others? All of them?"

Her chest felt heavy. "So many?"

His face was sympathetic. "No, not so many. Not at all." Her shoulders relaxed until he continued, "that I know of." His smile broadened. She drained her glass, and he poured her another. "But trust me, I would know. He tells me everything. There were just the two. And Jean, it meant nothing. It was nothing to him."

His glass was still untouched as she took another sip. "Really?" She hated the pleading sound of her voice.

"Is he even capable of loving a woman?" Tommy asked. He looked so cool, so reasonable to make such a statement, that it hit her like a slap.

"He's a romantic."

Tommy chuckled his little barking laugh. "That's exactly my point. That's how these romantics are. They disguise their true feelings under this mask of romance."

She wanted to leave and take the half-empty bottle with her. She was surprised to see her glass was empty and he was pouring her another.

"I don't think that's true," she said, hesitating before taking the glass in her hand. "He loved me. Maybe he doesn't now. But he did."

Tommy shrugged, his face doubtful. "Of course. You would know."

Jean realized that it all played with her very sense of reality. Who was Dan? What did she ever mean to him? Maybe that was why she had wanted to talk to Tommy. Not to find out about the affairs, the secrets. Not to know if Dan loved her. But just to know what was real. And she knew this drinking was only slipping her farther away from reality. But as she tried to think what to ask that would get at all of it, she sipped more wine.

The bartender turned up the music as more people started to come into the bar, and the noise pulled at her, pulled her under a whirlpool.

"Jean?" Tommy was waiting with his gentle, sympathetic smile.

"I'm afraid."

He nodded. "Of course. But in one department, you have nothing to fear."

She furrowed her brow. "What's that?"

He finally took a sip of his wine. "The girl, Wendy. She won't talk. Or at least, no one will care."

"What do you mean?"

"She finally cracked. She's in the psych ward. The bug house."

"Oh." Jean wasn't sure it really mattered.

"Aren't you relieved?"

"I suppose."

The server came by and filled their glasses, finishing the bottle. "Another?" she asked.

"No," Jean said quickly. "We'll take the check."

Tommy patted her hand. "Good girl. But you don't have a problem. You've just been under a lot of stress."

CHAPTER FORTY

So far I had been in the hospital for ten days. It might seem like I was suddenly all better. Certainly I could carry on a conversation, and Scott and I continued to work on "Landscape and Longing." My Yeats lesson was pretty much set. But I was not entirely without delusions.

Sitting across from Dr. Carson for our session, I asked him something that had been bothering me for a few days—if I'd said something that prompted Geoff to leave.

"No, it wasn't you." Dr. Carson smiled sadly. "He didn't want to give us time to help. Treatment must be consented to."

"I'm glad it wasn't me. I've been thinking. . . ." I looked at him brightly. "I think what I said to my Mom was what this was all about."

"What do you mean?"

"I told her she was forgiven. Someday, maybe late in life when she's dying, she'll remember and know it's okay. That she's forgiven."

"For what?"

I told him my theory that my mother had pushed her brother out of the car as a child. I went on to say I thought most of the people around me had personality disorders of some kind, like Dr. Hellmann and his wife.

Dr. Carson gazed at the carpet, his hands clasped in his lap. Then he straightened and gave me a determined look. "I don't normally do this, but I think I'd like you to call your therapist, Ann. We'll try to get in touch with her this afternoon."

I was happy to agree. As we came out of his office, a familiar voice rose in anger, over at the nurse's station. "Of course I know she's here!"

When she saw us, Jane gestured helplessly at Dr. Carson.

My brother turned around. "Here she is. Why are they lying to me? I'm her brother, for Christ's sake!"

Dr. Carson raised his hand. "I'm sorry. We have confidentiality."

Jane turned to me. "Would you like him to visit?"

"I'm family!" Peter said.

Shocked, I felt something like that old underwater feeling, my breath painfully held in my chest. "It's okay." I managed. Everyone was looking at me. "Dr. Carson, this is my brother Peter."

"How is she?" Peter asked him.

I felt a flare of anger that he asked the doctor—not me.

Dr. Carson shook his hand and Peter took in a deep breath. "I'll let you decide," Dr. Carson said. I was disappointed he didn't say how great I was doing, especially considering how well I was reacting to this shocking visit.

Peter and I sat in the living area. I hadn't seen him since the previous summer. He was three years older than I, a thin, serious man whose mouth always seemed to turn down. He was always moving, his crossed leg jiggling or his fingers tapping. We settled down and he paused to take me in.

"What do they have you on?" he asked.

I wasn't offended. "Haldol, and something to mitigate the side effects, Cogentin."

"You don't look well."

"I feel pretty well."

"Seriously?" His face was dark. "Is this what you wanted? Stay in the middle of nowhere, go back to school? So, this is *good*?"

It sucked my breath away. "I didn't choose to be bipolar." I wanted to tell him to be quieter, but I was afraid to.

He cleared his throat and glanced around the ward. He'd never been in a psych ward before. I looked over at the nurse's station. Jane was glaring at us.

Peter saw it and sank down, lowering his voice. "Your problem is, you aren't doing well at all, and you don't know it."

"I know I'm in a psych ward."

"Do you?"

It was true, that the psych ward wasn't the disturbing place to me that it must have seemed to him. This division between ward and "real world," between sanity and insanity, between order and disorder, was porous, was not as sharp to me. Maybe I needed to appreciate that difference more, but I wasn't so encouraged by what passed for sanity.

"What do you want from me?" I finally asked.

He sat up, jamming his index finger on the table with each point. "Going backwards is not the solution. There are no opportunities here. You need to come out to Indiana, where Dad and I can be nearby. There's a call center hiring all the time. You can get a job, and there are cute little apartments where you can start over." Having gotten this out, he relaxed a little and tried to soften his approach. "Meeka just had puppies. I can give you a puppy." He gave me a wan smile.

I was stumped how to answer this. I couldn't fathom why he would think I'd ever want to work at a call center. I didn't want a little apartment and a dog. He seemed to think that staying out in this admittedly desolate place was the root cause of all my problems, and I didn't think I could convince him otherwise. At the time, it didn't occur to me how much he was trying to just take control.

He continued to try being softer. "Maybe I'm being harsh. I was up all night, the flight was at five a.m."

"Sorry," I said. I didn't want to apologize, though. I hadn't asked him to come.

"I didn't know what I would find. I thought you might be strapped to a table getting electric shocks." He glanced around again; perhaps he was seeing it now as more normal than he'd expected. "That's what Mom thinks," he added.

So that was why my mother wanted to visit so badly, imagining something out of an old horror movie.

"They don't just throw you on a table and shock you," I said. "First of all, that's a treatment for depression. Second, you have to give permission, it's not against your will. It isn't the 1950s."

He smiled. "Maybe we were getting dramatic."

I returned his smile. At least he had calmed down. "In terms of my future, my plan is to go on for a PhD and teach college. Do you approve of that?"

"Where would you go? Do they offer that here?"

I shook my head. "I think I agree with you, about going somewhere more . . . alive. A city. I don't know. Maybe NYU. Or Chicago."

His face brightened. "That sounds intriguing. I could see that."

I was surprised. Somehow I'd gotten him on my side. We finally started to talk normally. I told him about the literary journal and my classes. He told me the latest about his son Jason, who was five, and took out his picture from his wallet. His wife was planning to go back to work soon.

He laid the picture of his son on the table. "So . . . your roommate was killed in some accident?"

I told him about it.

"And that set you off?" he asked when I was finished.

"I don't know."

He seemed to be considering something. "Do you think . . . this kind of thing is inherited, isn't it?"

I paused. I had never thought of this: he was worried about his son. "Maybe sometimes," I said.

He nodded, looking down at the picture. I couldn't offer to reassure him.

"Diana's death makes me think of that accident from when Mom was a kid," I said. He looked at me quizzically. "When her brother fell out of the car."

"You mentioned that to me, when I was a teenager."

I was surprised. "You don't remember Grandma always telling us to pray for Uncle Johnny?"

He shook his head. "No, I only heard it from you. I wasn't sure it was even a true story."

This shocked me. How could he forget Grandma going on about it?

"I thought . . . I was afraid that . . ." I didn't know whether to tell him my delusion.

But he put the picture away and rose. "I'm sorry this has to be so short. I'm flying right back. I have a meeting at four o'clock."

It might have been offensive, the way he had barged in and tried to control my life, after months of not being in touch, but I was struck by his generosity to fly out just for an hour to make sure I was okay. I knew he would never come out and apologize for our argument, but actions speak louder than words.

"Thanks for coming. It was really nice of you. Please don't worry about me."

"I do worry. Don't be overconfident. Don't think you're doing so well."

I bristled but I didn't respond. He gave me an awkward hug. As he passed the nurse's station, he meekly apologized for being angry earlier. Then he left.

I did a load of laundry—yes, they have laundry rooms in psych wards—then after lunch, Dr. Carson brought me into a small meeting room for me to touch base with Ann on the phone. The doctor left me alone and I dialed the number, trembling. I was excited to be able to talk with her, but I also had a feeling of foreboding.

It was a joy to hear her voice. She asked how I was, and I exclaimed I was doing great. She asked about my medication and how long I would probably stay. I told her I had to leave by the end of spring break to teach Daniel's class.

"Wendy, you can't possibly do that." Her voice was firm, authoritative.

The breath was sharp in my throat. "Why not? I've been preparing."

"You aren't well. We decided you shouldn't teach yet. That was why you got the grant. Right? Wendy?"

"I promised Daniel. I can do it. I'm sure I can."

Her exasperated sigh pricked at me. "Tell me what you've been doing recently."

I told her about doing the literary journal with Scott.

"With Scott . . ." she said his name with annoyance, but I didn't know the cause.

"And I just did that very adult thing. I told you about how I drove to Chicago to bring Diana's car home. I saw my Mom. I think you were right. Actually, I've been thinking. Aside from my mom having a personality disorder, I think a lot of people I know do. My professor, Dr. Hellmann. And his wife. It's like everyone I know could fill up the *DSM*." I laughed.

Her response sucked the laugh out of my throat. "So you think everyone has a disorder. Your mom. Your professors. It's rather unlikely, isn't it?"

I was shocked by this, anger flaring up through my chest. It was true it was deluded to think everyone was crazy. But this idea that my mom had a personality disorder was *Ann's* idea. She had made the diagnosis. She was jubilant when I accepted it. And what? Now she was denying it? I couldn't speak.

Everything drained away then. Like a hysterical person doused with a bucket of cold water, my theories and delusions drained away. I held those delusions because there had been a manic pleasure in them. Now the pleasure burned up like an old letter in the fire and turned to cold gray smoke. It was all gone. I wrapped up the call with the few words I could muster, nearly speechless with anger, and she wished me well. The hard click of the receiver was like a gunshot. I never wanted to see her again.

*   *   *

I had a few more days in the ward after that. I didn't tell Dr. Carson what had happened in the call. I felt he knew on some level. Partly, I was ashamed for my delusions. Beyond that, I was angry at the whole profession, and I figured he would defend Ann, as one professional would another, and I didn't want to hear it.

I knew he was doubtful about how much better I was, even as he and I signed the forms that permitted me to leave. I left with an appointment made to see a new therapist in two weeks, the expert he'd recommended.

When Scott brought me home, he had a cupcake waiting for me on the table and a balloon that said, "Welcome Home." I cried for a long time, but I didn't tell him why. It all seemed like too much to say just yet. Instead, we sat quietly in the dark. Scott wanted to stay the night, but I asked him to leave; I wanted to spend some time alone. He left reluctantly, suggesting I take a bath, maybe light some candles.

So I soaked in the tub, candles flickering, until the water grew cold. The cold revived me a little.

Then I got out of the tub and wrapped myself in a towel, remembering how Diana's fancy toiletries had once filled the now empty shelf. I switched on the harsh overhead light and looked in the mirror.

I looked like hell. But I felt I had survived—felt it and knew it.

CHAPTER FORTY-ONE

The undergrads trickled in, young men hunched under book bags, young women shrieking with laughter. The fluorescent lights shimmered on the white desks that squeaked as the students squeezed into them. I perched on the teacher's desk, a newly purchased briefcase open next to me. Geoff's note was on top, a cheery encouragement. To my left was a stack of biographies about William Butler Yeats. I took attendance, wondering how soon I could memorize their names. They all looked so much older than my former seventh graders. These were adults. Immediately I felt they were probably more adult than I was. I tried to shake it off.

"I'm filling in for your class for at least a few weeks. I'm Ms. Zemansky. You can call me Miss Z. Ms. Z is a little weird to say. Mizzy." I gave a nervous laugh, but no one joined in.

One of the young men raised his hand. "How about if we call you The Man?"

Everyone laughed while I blushed. To my surprise, the door opened, and Dr. Hellmann entered. He gave a small wave, in a gesture of "Don't mind me," and slipped behind a desk in back. I understood immediately: the department wanted me observed. They didn't trust me. I froze for a moment and cleared my throat. His eyes seemed to X-ray me from the back of the room.

I started the class. "So for today you had to read the poem 'Easter, 1916.' What did you think of the poem?" There was silence. I waited. "Did you like it?"

There were a few shrugs. Finally the same man, Miguel, said, "It was kind of boring."

"Yeah." A woman named Shawna nodded.

"What was boring about it?" I felt my face get hot, as silence hung over the room. No one answered. "Let's look at the opening:

"I have met them at close of day
Coming with vivid faces
From counter or desk among grey
Eighteenth-century houses.
I have passed with a nod of the head
Or polite meaningless words,
Or have lingered awhile and said
Polite meaningless words,
And thought before I had done
Of a mocking tale or a gibe
To please a companion
Around the fire at the club,
Being certain that they and I
But lived where motley is worn:
All changed, changed utterly:
A terrible beauty is born."

The room was silent again. Finally Miguel raised his hand. "Okay, so what is 'motley'?"

"It's what a clown might wear. The idea is that he thought everything was kind of lighthearted. He would have joking conversations, not knowing how serious it would become."

"How serious what would become?"

"The war."

"World War I?"

"No, the uprising of Ireland against England."

Another man sat up and said, "So, like, Ireland and England were at war or something?"

I was shocked. *They don't know anything. They are kids.* My eyes met Hellmann's. He had a little smile on his face and nodded.

"Yes. Ireland was once a colony of England. They'd been promised independence and England put it off because of World War I.
So, on Easter weekend of 1916 they tried to have a rebellion, and
they lost. Sixteen men were executed. Shot by a firing squad. They
were hardly given a trial." I looked out at their glazed eyes. They
weren't interested. In the back, Hellmann folded his arms, nodding
his head to encourage me. "These were men Yeats knew, friends of
his, whom he describes in the poem." Still no reaction. They were
waiting for me to say something interesting. I wiped my sweaty
palms on my pants. "They shot the husband of the woman Yeats
was in love with."

A few heads snapped to attention. "What woman? Wait, who?
His rival was shot? Did they get married after?" Shawna asked.

"Read those lines, here—" I turned on the projector and displayed
the poem. "His name was MacBride. Yeats calls him 'a drunken,
vainglorious lout.'"

"Harsh. Kind of mean, considering he's dead," said Miguel. "And,
like a hero."

"Here's her picture." I called up the image of Maud Gonne. "She
was the most beautiful woman in Ireland, six feet tall. She was always being compared to Joan of Arc or Helen of Troy."

"I don't see Yeats winning over someone like her," a girl named
Laura said.

"No, he didn't. She refused to marry him all her life. She was only
married to this man John MacBride about a year before she tried
to divorce him. Then he was executed, shot by a firing squad. He
refused a blindfold."

"Cool," Miguel said. A few other students looked interested, too.

"After Maud refused to marry Yeats again for the hundredth time,
he asked her young daughter to marry him."

"Ew! Like Woody Allen?" said Shawna. The class laughed. I could
see Miguel and Shawna were going to be the main speakers for the
class.

"Well, in those days it wasn't quite so weird. Besides, he didn't
raise her. She was Maud's illegitimate daughter from another rela-

tionship. She kept her daughter a secret and pretended she was her niece."

"That's twisted," said Laura. Conversations started to break out among the students. "Can we see more pictures of these people?"

We spent the rest of the class talking about Yeats and Maud, his secretary Ezra Pound, looking at their pictures, and finding other poems of his, looking up Pounds' poetry as well. The hour was gone before I knew it. I loaned out the biographies from the desk.

As the students filed out, I heard Shawna remark, "She doesn't seem crazy at all. Maybe a little zombie-ish."

Miguel whispered, "Zombie Zemansky. She's okay though."

Everyone knew. I wondered if Hellmann had heard that comment. He walked up to me when the students had left.

"Not bad," he said with an encouraging look.

I wanted to collapse. "We didn't analyze the poem."

"But you got them interested. That's the place to start." He seemed so calm now, as if nothing had happened between us.

"I'm sorry about that night," I began.

He waved his hand. "I should understand that you're battling something. Maybe I didn't understand before. And I was wrong about that letter, so I'm sorry for that. It wasn't your handwriting. Let's forget all about it."

I exhaled. The words were such a relief. It did still bother me, though, how strangely people had acted toward me when I was ill: Dr. Kind telling me to confront Hellmann, and Jean being so strange and rude that night. I wondered if I could say anything or ask about it; it didn't seem like I could.

"Yes, forgetting sounds good. And, um, I'm also sorry I upset your wife."

He smiled grimly. "That's okay. She'll have another glass of wine and be done with it."

I started. *That* was it. Jean had been drinking that night I was at their house. I was crazy, but she was drunk. Of course. Dr. Kind had said she'd gotten a DUI the night of the party.

I nodded and tried to give him a look of sympathy.

Scott entered with a bouquet of daffodils. "Hi. How was it?"

I took the daffodils and inhaled the fresh green scent. "I think it was okay."

"She was fine," Hellmann said. "She'll be observed once more, but then I think the semester will go fine. Only a few weeks left, anyway, and this will all be behind us."

I closed the briefcase. "It was actually kind of fun after a while. I think I can do this."

"They aren't going to bite you," Scott said.

Hellmann gave my shoulder a pat, and left. His step was slow and heavy, yet as always, it seemed self-conscious, like he wanted me to notice he was burdened. I shook off the feeling. Maybe I was the one being dramatic.

I sat on the edge of the desk, my shoulders slumped. "They all know I was just released from a psych ward."

Scott put his arm around me. "But you did it. You can do it. And you know what? They're just a bunch of kids."

"Yeah." I held the daffodils up to my face and took a deep breath.

CHAPTER FORTY-TWO

The next day at home, I curled up on the couch. I suddenly hated being alone, feeling tired but also restless. Scott couldn't be there all the time. As I lay there, depression settled over me. I thought of my hospitalization and failures. Despite the class going well, I couldn't see my future; everything was dark. The depression quickly deepened. *My future has been erased.* It didn't occur to me to call anyone, such as the new therapist I hadn't seen yet. I wasn't used to thinking there could be help.

Scott had told me about his talk with Dr Kind. I felt angry that Kind had gone to the Dean behind my back to complain about my letters. It seemed like he was being hypersensitive. I had *confided* my thoughts to him. And he had told me to, hadn't he? In so many words, he'd told me to go ahead and write to him. It was that sort of hypocrisy that angered me. Suddenly I remembered that I had given him Diana's poetry book. *He shouldn't have it,* I thought. I wanted it back.

I quickly dressed and walked to campus. All I had to do was ask for it back. He already knew I was crazy; this wouldn't be any crazier than anything else. As I walked, the pounding of my steps reminded me of the madness before.

So I slowed down. The sky was clear and the air moist with melting snow. I resolved I would not be crazy, could not be crazy anymore. I'd been through a hard time, anyone could agree, but it was over.

Professor Kind's office door was closed. When I knocked it opened slightly and I peeked in. It was empty, to my relief. Glanc-

ing about, I saw the slim black volume on his shelf. I grabbed it and
started to leave. But then, I thought I should explain.

I took up his mahogany Mont Blanc pen and wrote on his memo
pad,

"I took back Diana's poetry book, which I gave you before. I
thought I could confide in you, and I'm sorry I was wrong. We
need to talk. Wendy."

I went home and collapsed on the couch again. Scott would be
busy all day. I made myself eat something, got some work done,
then took up the book. In the mad dash of being hospitalized, then
teaching, Diana had been pushed to the back of my mind. Now she
came back to my thoughts centerstage.

I can just honor your memory. That's all I can do for you, Diana, I thought
as I opened the book. But there was something strange. On the
inside of the cover there was writing:

"Dearest Dan, Are you my man or my Hell, Professor Hellmann? If this is hell, Heaven has no place for our passion. I
hope this book will bring you sweet memories of me after we
have gone our separate ways, no matter our Fate. Diana."

My heart pounded. Was I losing my mind again? Was I imagining
it? I flipped through the pages. Notes from Diana appended some
of the poems, along with little drawings. This wasn't the copy I'd
given to Dr. Kind.

My heart raced as everything came to me at once. *He* was the Dan
on the program who wrote "Keep writing!"—Dr. Hellmann. I saw
again the portrait, the face of gray and yellow smears surrounded
by wavy gray hair, which had seemed so hauntingly familiar. It was
him. And the line in Diana's poem—he really hadn't stolen it. She
must have taken it from him, sharing his early drafts.

I was shaking, afraid of going crazy again. I knew I should talk
to someone, but my new psychologist had been booked up for two

weeks. And I was afraid that if I started making wild accusations, I'd be put right back in the hospital.

I'd left a note. It was all wrong. The book was in Kind's office. He knew, and was protecting Hellmann? They did always seem weirdly close. Exhausted, I pulled my boots back on. I got in the car for the first time in weeks. The driving didn't scare me now, my only thought was to take the note back.

The building was emptying-out and growing dark. Dr. Kind's door was locked. It was too late. Sighing, I leaned against the wall. A janitor came by, jangling his keys.

"Oh, sir, excuse me!"

The old man stopped, a knowing look on his face. I felt he already had an explanation for me, and I went with it.

"I left a paper for Dr. Kind, but I left off the bibliography. Could you possibly let me in so I can take it back?" I tried to sound like a young, ditzy freshman.

He chuckled. "You kids." He opened the door and let me in, remaining near the door but not watching me. The note was still exactly where I had left it. Nothing seemed changed. I snatched it up and locked the door behind me.

"Got it okay?"

"Yes, thanks."

I hurried out, hoping not to see anyone. Sitting in the car, I wondered where to go. I needed to talk to someone about this. Dr. Carson was someone I could trust.

It had been only a few days since I checked out, but it seemed strange and even unfamiliar to be there as I walked down the blue and white hallway to the ward. As soon as I stepped in, a woman stopped me by the nurse's station. I didn't recognize her.

"I was just released, but I wanted to ask Dr. Carson about something."

The nurse spoke with a firm but gentle air. "You have to talk to your current doctor at this point. I'm sorry. He can't see you."

My heart sank. I only nodded and left. My footsteps echoed in the hall and I felt alone, like there was no one else I could trust to talk to about it.

Back on campus, at the union, my coffee turned cold while I silently stared at the young woman typing on her laptop. She was angled slightly away, her red-framed glasses reflecting blue light. She was casually dressed in flannel pajama pants and a denim jacket. She looked like a kid, a teenager. She was typing quickly, wearing ear buds, in a world of her own. I watched her a long while before I got up and threw away my coffee.

I took a seat opposite the laptop, and Ann didn't notice me for a moment. Then she gave me a blank smile, a face that revealed nothing. She took out her ear buds.

"Hello, Wendy, how are you?"

"I'm better."

"Good." She nodded. "Sorry you had to be hospitalized." Her remark was perfunctory.

"It's okay."

Ann started to put her ear buds back in, as if the conversation was over. When I didn't move, Ann set them down again. "You don't want a session, here? You could make a new appointment."

"I don't want a session. Just a conversation. I've found sometimes a decent conversation is worth years of therapy."

Ann closed her laptop with a look of impatience and took a sip of her coffee. "You look medicated."

"Haldol. I look like a zombie, but I don't feel like one. Just, no affect."

"Yes, it does do that."

I rubbed my face. "I know you saw Diana on the last day of her life. You never told me."

Ann took off her glasses, her gray eyes intent. "Why should I have told you that?"

"I guess I wanted a picture of her last day."

"She wanted to quit smoking. That's all there was to it. It was the first and last time I ever saw her. What is this about, Wendy?"

I raised my eyebrows in surprise. "Don't be defensive. It's natural to be curious."

Now Ann looked surprised. She opened her mouth and closed it again.

I gave a little laugh. "But can't you tell me? You know everything. You know my grandfather who died almost three decades ago was a secret alcoholic. You know my mother whom you've never met is crazy. You know how wrong I am about everything. You know so much."

Ann's look grew to one of concern. "Wendy, maybe you shouldn't have been released so soon. Maybe I should contact Dr. Carson."

"I'm sure he'll be impressed. I just want to ask you. Why? Why did we spend all that time, waste all that time, talking about the past, the ancient past, even my mother's freaking childhood stuff, when what I wanted help with was coping with the present?"

Ann took a deep breath and spread her hands over the cover of her laptop. "Tell me, Wendy, what was the one problem you always brought up that you wanted to deal with?"

I hesitated, trying to think.

"You know," Ann said in an exasperated tone.

"That I didn't feel like an adult, like a grown-up."

Ann nodded. "And what do you think is the major block to growing up? I'll lay my cards on the table for you. It's separating from your parents. You were totally codependent with your mother, probably still are. You're probably back to defending her. But we have to deal with the childhood stuff and even your mother's 'freaking' childhood stuff, to get you separated from her. Otherwise you'll never control your fate." Her face was irritated, and she spoke with such confidence, as if it were all that simple.

"Okay. I can never win with you. I think all I can do is say good-bye. You believe in Fate, but you're not writing my life. And you know what? I was codependent with you, too. I think you wanted to take her place, in a way." I got up to leave, and turned back. "And you should put on some real clothes. You look twelve years old." I left. I never saw her again.

CHAPTER FORTY-THREE

Mark called as soon as I got back home. "It was such a great idea you had, to do Diana's art show. It's all set. I'll be coming over for the paintings, and I'm wondering if . . ." He sighed, struggling. "If Diana left behind the titles. They'll want to post them next to the paintings." His voice faded at the end, and I felt his pain.

"I'll look around and see if I can find anything."

"Thanks."

I went into Diana's room, examining the paintings on the walls. Because I had always been distracted by the smeared portrait, I hadn't looked as closely at the others. There was the yellow, sunny one of flowers Mark had remembered. Another was jagged splashes of red and black, with subtle sprays of other colors, purples and ochre, flame-like, which grew in intensity as I stared at it. Suddenly I saw all the faces, subtly worked in black brushstrokes, screaming. The other two paintings were more monochromatic, one a twilight vision of dove gray, like glowing clouds lit by the moon. The last one was curving shades of white.

I had packed away Diana's things to return to her family, except the paintings and her datebook. I opened it to the month of the show. In her sharp writing it was there: "Spring Street Gallery: *Sunflowers, Foggy Moon, Winterscape, Hellscape, Leave Him Alone.*"

It seemed clear which was which. *Hellscape* was dark purple and ochre flames and screams, and the gray pearlescent one was *Foggy Moon*. The scary portrait was called *Leave Him Alone*. I stared again at the white one called *Winterscape*, the one I thought would make a good cover for the literary journal, seeing for the first time subtle shots of blue, indigo, and charcoal gray: bounding snow-covered hills, obscured roads, distant tangled trees. I took a picture of it. Then I jotted down the titles on post-it notes and stuck them to the backs of the canvasses.

A little while later, Mark was outside. This time he wasn't wearing those murderous-looking gloves. "Hi. Here for the paintings."

I led him to Diana's bedroom. We stood in the middle and looked from painting to painting. Mark didn't seem to be in a hurry. He went to the one on the easel, the blurred portrait with threatening teeth.

"Looks familiar somehow," he said.

I pulled my thin cardigan tighter. "I don't like to look at it." I wondered if he could guess, if anyone would, now that it was so obvious to me who it was. I had decided not to tell him what I had found, until I at least talked to someone I could trust, like Scott or the new therapist.

He took the portrait off the easel and took another painting off the wall. I took down another and followed him out. He slid the paintings into the back of the car, and we went back inside.

He stood before *Sunflowers*, bright with sunny yellows and greens. "I'm so glad I was there when she did this one. Glad it exists, glad I knew her. I don't even know what happened. I mean, why we broke up. Just the stupidest, most trivial shit . . . Maybe I'll buy it from the gallery." He took the painting off the wall. "I liked her painting better than her poetry. Words are always inadequate."

Commit nothing to writing. "Would you like to stay and have some coffee?"

He shook his head. "I promised the gallery I'd bring these today. Thanks. Maybe some other time."

"Are you sure?"

Mark looked down at the worn wooden floor, then his watch. "I guess I do have time."

I put the coffee on while he loaded the last painting in the car. "I'm wondering if I could use the winter painting as the cover for our literary journal," I said when he came back in.

"You can call the gallery and ask." We sat in silence a while, and I didn't want to intrude upon his thoughts. Finally, he spoke. "I spent a lot of mornings sitting here while Diana made the coffee."

I had forgotten again that he had lived there. I tried to give him a warm, open look, to invite him to talk.

"I wanted to go to Chicago for the funeral. But her brother thinks I'm somehow at fault for what happened. It didn't seem like the right time. But I know where she's buried, in that old cemetery full of monuments. Big, Victorian sculptures, Doric pillars. The old guard is there, Marshall Field, and Pullman. These old Victorian men, and now this young goddess has joined them, Diana the huntress. I bet she's shaking things up. And she's like a beautiful Greek statue. . . ." He stirred sugar into his coffee, then seemed to forget about it.

"You know the ancient story of the sculptors. There's a contest to create a beautiful statue of a goddess to put on top of the temple. One sculptor creates a lovely, delicate thing. The other makes this blocky, rough, angled statue, hardly looks like a woman. They lift the pretty statue up, and the features disappear. It doesn't look like anything. So they try the other one, the rough blocky one. As it goes up, the distance changes everything. All the features come out, softened and beautiful, and the distance smooths out everything. Diana is like that. She was rough and edgy. But in our memory, with the distance, it will all be smoothed out like a pearl.

"But I'm going to try to remember the rough one. The one that smoked, the one that tore the air with her words, the one that screamed at me." He finally took a few sips of coffee, looking tired. "Do you mind if I smoke?"

I shook my head. "You said Diana screamed at you? But she wasn't like that. At least, I don't think so. We did have one argument, but normally she didn't get angry."

He shrugged. "All I did was refer to one of her friends as the fat chick."

"Did you know her mother is anorexic?"

A stream of smoke poured out of his nose. "No. She never told me. Why wouldn't she tell me that?"

"She was secretive." It hit me then. It wasn't just that she was a private person. It wasn't my fault she didn't talk to me. She was secretive.

I hadn't heard the car, and was startled when Scott suddenly entered. "Hello?" he asked. He looked puzzled and strained.

"Mark just came for the paintings, for the art show."

"They're all loaded up, so I'll go now," Mark said. He put out his cigarette. "Thanks again. I'm really grateful for this." He surprised me with a quick hug as he left.

"So he's your new best friend?" Scott asked, taking off his coat.

I felt Scott, like Greg, had never trusted Mark. "You're jealous?"

He shrugged. "Should I be?"

"We're all in a bond now, aren't we?" I poured Scott some coffee.

"I don't know about that," he replied. "It's over, isn't it?" He yawned and took a sip, clearly tired.

I was eager to show him Diana's poetry book, but felt torn because I could see the strain he'd been under. But the impulse won out.

"I have something to show you. It's kind of serious." I handed him the book.

He turned the pages, looking confused. "What is this?"

"I went back to Dr. Kind's office to get her book. Because I'd given him the copy I found in the trash. I decided to take it back. I grabbed this, but it's not the same copy. Diana gave this one to Dr. Hellmann."

Scott shook his head, confused, thumbing through it in silence.

"What do you think?"

"So . . . let me get this straight. This is Diana's writing in here? And you got this where?"

"From Dr. Kind's office."

"He gave it to you?"

"No, I . . . took it." I didn't like where this was going. "But that's not the point."

He drew in his breath. "Well. I can see it isn't your handwriting."

I was stricken. I was officially crazy now, capable of anything. "Of course not! I'm not crazy. You think I'm *that* crazy?"

"Let's just take it easy." He started to reach for me.

"If you think I'm crazy enough to pretend Diana wrote all these things, that I wrote them myself, maybe you should leave now."

He raised his hand. "I said it wasn't your writing."

"But you thought it could be!"

"No! Honestly, but some people might—"

"No one would think that!" *Would* they?

I sank down opposite him, feeling like I felt when I spoke with Ann, deflated but angry.

"Okay, let's say no one would think it. The point is, how did you come by this?"

I couldn't look at him. "I *gave* this to Dr. Kind in the first place. All I did was take it back."

"When he wasn't there? How did you get into his office?"

"The janitor let me in. That doesn't matter."

Scott cleared his throat dramatically. Disapprovingly. He looked at me as if I were a child. "But this isn't the copy you gave him?"

"Right. I gave him a copy. And this one is different. This one has love notes written from Diana to Dr. Hellmann."

"You don't know that."

"It's right there!"

"Fine." He set the book down on the table with a sharp slap. "The point is—what is the point? Diana wrote some kind of love notes to Dr. Hellmann. Maybe. That's all we know. What does it matter now?"

The more he argued, the more certain I felt it did matter. "If he was the father—"

"Wendy!" his loud voice startled me. But he only looked at me, intensely, struggling with how to respond. Then he said very quietly, too quietly, "Listen to yourself. First, you break into someone's office. Then you make all kinds of connections, accusations—"

I jumped up. "What accusations?"

"You're becoming obsessed all over again. My God, relax. Just relax. I thought everything was better. I don't know if I can take this."

I felt like jumping out of my skin. "Then leave, if I'm so awful. Just leave!"

"Please calm down. I'm not leaving."

Was he going to force me to shout, to become hysterical? "Then I'll leave myself."

"Don't."

I jumped up and ran, not bothering with my coat. I was in the car before he could stop me. I sped away, not knowing where to go at first, but I found myself headed to the sheriff's office. The outpost by the pine trees was a lonely light in the darkness.

Inside, I asked for Deputy Polozzi. As I was being told he was out, he came in behind me.

"I see you fixed your windshield," he greeted me.

"Scott did it for me, while I was . . . away."

He nodded, a knowing look on his face. "What can I do for you?"

"I don't know." We sat together on the bench in the hallway, as we had that first morning. "It was all just an accident? Diana. No meaning to it. Just a random accident?"

He looked at me with his big brown eyes, seeming younger than ever. "Is there something you want to tell me?" he asked in a low voice.

I stared at him, uncomprehending, trying not to comprehend. "What do you mean?"

He tilted his head down, almost murmuring in my ear. "I doubt it was an accident. Or, it was an accident, but the driver wasn't blind that night. The driver knew she was hit. Do you want to talk about it?"

We were alone in the bright hallway, our voices a hush. In the background was a quiet static of scanners. I felt I was in another world, like when I first entered the psych ward. "What do you mean?"

"I think the body was moved. She was wearing one pearl earring. And I looked all down the street. I found the match down the hill with some broken glass. She should have been headed that way to come home, right? But someone brought her back up the hill, to the bend in the road where it's more treacherous, looks more like an accident. Do you want to talk about it?"

My hands sweated. "I hit a deer. There were witnesses. There were witnesses." It was bizarre. My suspicion it was really me had been a psychotic delusion. Yet here he was, suspecting me. It was madness, but now there was no way to make people sure of me. I could only say, "I'm not that crazy."

"I hope not."

I was already up and walking away as he spoke. I left, feeling there was nowhere to go. I drove around for a bit. I hadn't taken my cell phone, so at home Scott had left a note on the fridge, saying, "Sorry. Please understand. Give me a call." Why should *I* be the one to understand?

I wished I could drive to Chicago that night and start my life over.

CHAPTER FORTY-FOUR

Like his office at the school, his office at home irritated Jean as she searched for some tax forms. The files were a mess, old papers that should be in storage if kept at all. Anything current seemed to be in various stacks on top of the desk. She flipped through them, careful not to knock them to the floor. Near the top of the second stack, a letter drew her attention, from McGill University. Dan had applied to teach there, promising Jean a new life in Montreal.

"Per your request, we've forwarded the accusation. We regret this unpleasantness. . . ." A newspaper clipping about Diana's death, stapled to a small cream-colored piece of stationery. "You might want to know that Dr. Dan Hellmann knew her very well."

Jean sank into the chair. She already knew about this, Dan had told her. It was the round, flowery writing that struck her. Writing she had seen in a Christmas card. She shook her head. It couldn't be the same—there was no cause for such a betrayal.

As she set it back, her shaking hand knocked over the stack. She swore and started to gather it up. A poem rose to the top.

"For My Wife

Some things are beyond words
Beyond reach
A moment flickers like a match
When the moon is a whisper in the sky
Just before darkness
That was my favorite time for us

Knowing the rest of the world
Was sitting down to dinner,
This communion
Not the secret of midnight
But the time when all is shared,
The gathering evening
When I gather you
Gather all your
Lovely lovely"

The poem stopped there as if he didn't know how to finish it. Jean stared at it a long while. Slowly, her breath came back. She put it gently back on the desk. Maybe. Maybe it was possible, it wasn't over. He cared. As she remade the stack, another poem came to the top. She stiffened.

"For D.

I could not protect you.
What could I do?
And what if I could choose
Between the security of age
And the flight of youth?
You flew.
And I knew your rage,
Too. And the truth
Stares at me like a sick dog.
I am a thief, I stole two lives.
Unable to save either
Neither survives.
I should have been a knight;
I was a thief,
A jester, not the king,
And in this spring my grief
Drifts in shame

To a dull relief
Of going back
To the dull unworthy same
Of what I was."

She pushed the poem back into the pile, trembling. Then she crumpled the poem he'd started for her, threw it away, went to the kitchen, and poured herself a big glass of wine.

CHAPTER FORTY-FIVE

Spring Street Gallery was in an old, converted church, a Romanesque style heavy and dark. Between the Ionic pillars lining the nave were low moveable walls displaying the art. Over the front door was a stained glass window of Abraham sacrificing the ram, Isaac bound nearby, and golden clouds above—the voice of God. In Diana's memory, I'd deliberated on what to wear, choosing my one navy blue suit, with the green gloves from Chicago. As far as my wardrobe, I felt as adult as anyone else there.

In the semicircular apse at the far end, two guitarists accompanied a flamenco dancer whose stamping feet echoed like machine gun fire. The crowd slowly moved in circles around the art. The paintings looked bigger on the gallery walls, their colors bolder. Diana's show was shared with another, a Victorian landscape artist who had died in a TB ward at the age of thirty. He'd done a series of the Seasons of Man: the last, Death, was unfinished, a river emptying into the sea, an angel steering a small boat with its white-haired passenger, sails glowing red in the sunset. The name of the show was "Gone Too Soon."

Mark spoke with the gallery owner, a bald man with a fringe of black hair who looked like a funeral director but for his pink and purple tie. Mark caught my eye and waved me over, introducing us. "Not canceling was Wendy's idea," he said.

The owner grasped my hand warmly, thanking me. I smiled as best I could, for now a regular person.

We stood before Diana's one sunny painting. "It's fate, isn't it?" he said. "The fate of art to outlive the artist."

Daniel joined us. "Here's a nice one. What can I say? I like art to be pretty."

Mark gave a bitter chuckle.

"I didn't expect to see you," I said to Daniel. "How's your father?" He looked grateful I had asked. "His surgery is the day after tomorrow. How are you doing with the class?"

"I think it's going okay." I felt stronger, being able to say that. "You have nothing to worry about."

"Thanks. That's a relief." He looked awkward for a moment. "Not that I doubted it," he added with an anxious smile.

So, he *had* doubted it. But it was okay; I was getting through it.

A woman's voice rose above the din for a moment. Jean was stumbling, a glass of wine in her hand.

Daniel nudged me and whispered, "I always thought she was a bit of a bitch."

My eyes widened. "You said that about Diana, too."

He shrugged. "Maybe I feel that way about any woman he seems to favor." He put his finger to his lips. "That's between you and me."

As the crowd surrounded me, everyone seemed suspect. I went up to the eerie portrait, looming large on the wall. Dan Hellmann was beside me. I glanced nervously between him and the image, wondering if anyone would notice, side by side, that it was of him. He didn't seem to recognize himself.

"It was just her fate, wasn't it?" His eyes searched mine, full of grief. "It was her fate to go. She couldn't go on. Life couldn't allow it, somehow."

Jean was weaving toward us and I slipped away. The flamenco dancer's heels pounded in a barrage. As I melted into the crowd my cell phone vibrated. I squeezed through the crowd to take it outside. I rarely got any calls and didn't know who it could be if it wasn't Scott.

"Hi Wendy, this is Len."

"Len?"

"I met you at Stanimer's. You were asking if we knew who stopped the night you hit the deer. I checked around for you. It was Clint and Bob Hanson. They remembered you real well. Said you cracked your head pretty hard. They'd like to know if you came out okay. Said they're about through that deer meat."

I almost laughed. "Thanks, yes, I'm fine. Thank you." After I hung up, I realized something so ridiculous, I laughed out loud. I had found the receipt *in her car.* Of course she hadn't been on her bicycle when she went to the drugstore. What a dolt I was.

Mark came out to smoke a cigarette, his smoke swirling in the moist air. "You look like you got some good news."

I nodded. "Yes. By the way. There's something I wanted to tell you. I should have told you before. About that time I called you. I . . . wasn't well."

He shrugged. "I'd forgotten about it. But I did wonder. When you told me about that line from her poem, the one Hellmann used. Did he confess to you?"

"Confess . . . ? You knew . . . ?"

He took my elbow and we walked further from the door. "I didn't know anything until you told me that. But when you told me they used the same line, I knew they must have been involved. That he was the father."

"You wanted me to confront him."

"I thought he might talk to a woman, someone soft and understanding." He dragged down the cigarette quickly. "Sorry. I guess I was using you."

I wanted to be angry, but I was too relieved after everything. "It's okay. Never mind about it."

He tossed his cigarette on the snowy pavement. "It was nice meeting you. Diana said you were the bravest coward she ever met. Be careful out there. Be careful on the road." He went to his car and left, and I went back inside.

Now it was Dr. Kind standing near the portrait, holding a glass of wine. I screwed up my nerve and went up to him. "I was wondering why you encouraged me to confront Dr. Hellmann that night. It seems like you helped make a fool of me."

He took a sip, his eyes twinkling over the glass. "No, my dear. I never meant that. It seemed like you needed to get the right story, and I thought you could get it straightened out. And I thought maybe if he told you straight, it would be a bit like cold water being splashed on you, and maybe you would snap out of it. I was trying to help you, honestly. Why, you're one of our star students, and it seemed like the pressure had been getting to you. I could see you were cracking. I thought talking with him would help glue you back together again. No one wants to hurt you. We all want what's best." He gave my shoulder an awkward pat. He seemed sincere, but I still flinched at his touch. "After all, how can you judge, in the state you were in?"

It all came out so smoothly, as if he'd been prepared for my anger all along. I didn't know how to say it hadn't felt like he was trying to help me that night.

Dr. Kind seemed satisfied. He sipped his wine and turned to the painting behind us, the portrait with gray smears and long yellow teeth. "This is lovely. I might buy it."

CHAPTER FORTY-SIX

I hiked up the hill to the spot I couldn't let go of. The fringe of trees was dark before the setting sun, the snowy field turning violet. It was warming, and the snow in the drainage ditch had melted into a stream. There was still some broken glass on the shoulder, and my red earring. I picked it up and put it in my pocket. That should have been everything, but it still didn't feel over.

A car with a broken headlight drove slowly by and stopped. Dr. Kind opened the window. "Are you all right?"

I turned and nodded.

"You don't look it. Are you still on heavy medication?" His tone was sympathetic, exaggerated.

"Thanks," I said stiffly. "I'm okay."

He turned off the ignition and got out to stand beside me. We looked over the fields and darkening sky in silence, while he lit up a cigarette. The blue flash made me think of that night, when I thought Diana was lighting a cigarette. It suddenly hit me she hadn't been lighting one for herself, but for someone else.

"You shouldn't have taken that book," he said.

I caught my breath. I'd hoped he hadn't seen the note before I came back for it. He had.

"You always have to sabotage yourself," he continued. "What are we doing? Here we all are, returning to the womb of the intellect, in school again. Always in school again. And sometimes we just need a little escape. Like an asylum. How was your escape? They didn't keep you long."

"They don't keep people long these days. Even without medication, mania wears off."

"Mania? Is that it? Good old-fashioned madness isn't good enough? But tell me, how do you trust yourself now? Now that you've gone over the edge. How do you trust what you know is real? I suppose you think you know everything now. But it's all a fantasy. Everything is in your head. Mania. Yes, it's all mania."

He puffed his cigarette, and my eyes watered from the smoke.

"Even love. Love is just mania." He stamped his cigarette out on the ground. "Would you like a ride?"

Never get in the car. "No, thanks."

He shrugged and got back in the car. Through his open window he asked, "How's teaching. Little twerps treating you okay?"

I personally don't mind if she kills the little twerp. "Sure."

He nodded and drove off. I thought back to the night of the party. Out on the patio, I'd thought I heard a man's voice say, "You're not alone." It came back to me. That wasn't what he said. I could hear it now. It was, "Leave him alone."

I walked back down the hill and when I got home, I drove to the library. I looked up Dr. Kind's novel. It was there: *Mother's Milk*. I retrieved it from the shelf and took it to a carrel.

Two boys, brothers with a strong bond, are threatened by a female vampire. The main character has to protect his older brother from her evil. It was a horror story and a coming of age novel, about the boy defeating the vampire to save his brother. The vampire could only be defeated by a virgin. In the end he has control of a pack of wolves that attacks and kills her in a violent orgy of blood.

The subtext was dark and mysterious, malicious. Perhaps it was all in the boy's mind. Perhaps the vampire was his mother. He killed her to defend his brother, but since he had to be a virgin to kill her, perhaps he did it to free himself of the pledge of chastity.

I sat and read it all evening. The gloom darkened over the echoing library. It was not a fully realized book. There were unanswered questions. But it was masterful in its disturbing tone and imagery, as teeth glistened and snapped, and the engine of the story drove

forward to its relentless and violent conclusion. I was sweating
when I was done.

When I looked up from the book, the library was a haze of shadows, and I felt a nightmare could come true even here. I returned
it to the shelf, a little afraid of what might be around the corner
of the dark stacks, wanting to sneak out and hurry home to safety.

CHAPTER FORTY-SEVEN

Jean Hellmann told me a little about this, long afterward. It was part of her Alcoholics Anonymous step of apologizing. She was still rattled by it all, and grateful I had kept so much secret. She spun the wedding ring around on her finger, saying, "When you're used to embarrassing yourself, sometimes it's a shock to find someone else is . . . beyond . . ." Her shoulders twitched in a shudder. Our coffee grew cold as she told me about it, and when she was through, she said, "Let's stay in touch," but she never did.

It was eleven o'clock in the morning, and Jean had a quick glass of wine in the kitchen while she made the coffee. Dan answered the bell and voices came from the living room, a friendly, affable voice and Dan's, stiff and formal. It was time.

Jean sipped some coffee to disguise her breath, and fixed a smile on her face as she poked her head out of the kitchen. "Coffee?"

"Sure, Jean," Tommy said.

Dan shook his head, his face stern and tired. When Jean came back with the mug, Tommy was at the piano, noodling chopsticks. Jean didn't know where to set down his coffee. She waited, holding the mug that grew heavy in her hand. She waited for Dan to say something. They were supposed to do this as a team.

Tommy finished with a pounding chord and jumped up. "Ah, thanks." He took the mug and sat in the chair by the sofa, where Jean sat next to Dan. The manila envelope seemed to glow on the table in front of them.

"Thanks for having me over. We should do this kind of thing more. You know, we should do, I don't know, something. A show.

Like a poetry night. For the faculty." Tommy perched on the edge of the chair, his knee touching Dan's.

A pause that felt like forever. Tommy's face bright and happy, not at all uncomfortable. Dan staring at the envelope. Jean staring at Dan.

Finally Dan spoke. "There's something I need to ask you about."

"Sure. What's up? Is it about Wendy?"

"Why would it be about her?" Dan asked.

"Since I have to observe the little basket case this afternoon. One o'clock, right?" He rubbed his hands together.

"Yes. Yes and no, about this being about her."

"We'll be rid of her soon enough."

Dan cleared his throat. "Tommy, there's something I need to show you." Jean's heart began to race as he slid the note and the Christmas card out of the envelope. "There was a letter sent to McGill, about Diana."

Tommy nodded over his coffee. "Yes, exactly. Like we've been saying. The basket case. You should have had her dismissed the second it came up."

"This is her writing." Dan slid over the sentence I'd written in his office. "And this is the note to McGill."

One was a jagged scrawl. The McGill note was round and flowery.

"Uh huh?" Tommy asked, puzzled.

"And this is your Christmas card. I'd forgotten about it, but Jean saw it, and . . ."

Jean steeled herself from trembling.

Tommy cocked his head. "I don't get it. What does this have to do with the price of tea in China?"

"Did you write this note?" Dan's voice was low, quietly angry. It was the same voice he used when he asked Jean if she'd been drinking.

Tommy laughed. "What? What are you saying? We know it was Wendy."

"We don't think so."

His laughter abruptly stopped. "We?" He looked from Dan to Jean. The look he gave Jean made her skin cold.

"We just want the truth," Dan continued.

"We?" Tommy repeated more loudly. "We, as in you and Jean? What in holy hell do you mean by we? You're suddenly on the same team? The marriage from hell?"

Tommy raised his hand as if calling for silence, his tongue darting to his mustache. "This is rich. This is a riot. You pour your heart out to me about your lousy life, your lousy *wife*," his voice rose erratically. "You use me. *Use* me for your disgusting little *romps*, your messy rotting *flesh* games. Oh, it's okay, if anyone asks, I was with *you*. The loyal friend. What am I? What *am* I? While you soil the sheets with these corpses. These rotting *corpses*." He spat on the s's. "That's what it means, what bodies are. A body is nothing but a corpse waiting for the grave. And what am I? Am I your puppy? Your devoted pet? And what is she now?" Then he spat at Jean for real.

"Where was *she* when you needed to talk? When you needed real friendship, real love? Where in this godforsaken hell can you find someone to look up to, someone to care about, someone to whisper to in the dark? *Her*?"

He was sitting stiffly, shaking like a slender tree in the wind. Drops of sweat beaded on his face like an icicle, his eyes cold as the glittering winter sky. He stopped, and folding his arms, hugged himself and grew calm.

He sighed and relaxed suddenly, and smiled. "Okay. I can see when I'm not wanted. But don't you dare blame me for any of it. Now that you're the happy couple, all warm and snuggly. It wasn't me. It was Wendy, the basket case. We all know she's a loon. I'll see it for myself today. It was all her. I don't give a damn for your amateur handwriting analysis." He rose and smoothed out his suit, straightened his bow tie, and walked quickly to the door. He turned with his hand on the knob. "But let me tell you what you are. You're a vampire. A bloodsucking vampire."

He left. And he was in my classroom two hours later.

CHAPTER FORTY-EIGHT

This time when the students entered, I greeted them by name, and they smiled back. I was relaxed, ready to continue the lesson on Yeats. I was about to close the door when Dr. Kind appeared.

"The department just wants you observed once more. Then I'm sure everything will be hunky-dory."

My hands trembled as he took a seat in the back, his cold gaze on me. "Would someone like to read 'The Dolls' aloud?" I asked the class.

Shawna volunteered:

"A doll in the doll-maker's house
Looks at the cradle and bawls:
'That is an insult to us.'
But the oldest of all the dolls,
Who had seen, being kept for show,
Generations of his sort,
Out-screams the whole shelf: 'Although
There's not a man can report
Evil of this place,
The man and the woman bring
Hither, to our disgrace,
A noisy and filthy thing.'
Hearing him groan and stretch
The doll-maker's wife is aware
Her husband has heard the wretch,
And crouched by the arm of his chair,

She murmurs into his ear,
Head upon shoulder leant,
'My dear, my dear, O dear,
It was an accident.'"

Shawna smiled at the end. "I had no idea that rhymed. The whole thing rhymes. It's so subtle."

Dr. Kind snorted from the back of the room. A few students turned with a glance.

"Yes, I think part of the genius of Yeats was how subtle his rhymes are," I replied.

Miguel raised his hand. "So was this a real life thing too? In terms of his life?"

Kind chuckled softly.

I cleared my throat. "I don't know if we should always rely on biography. But there was something. Yeats was having an affair with a woman named Mabel Dickenson, who had a pregnancy scare. Yeats was angry about it."

"This does seem like a really angry poem," Laura said. "Bitter and angry."

"Come now," Kind said.

I looked at him. "Excuse me?"

He shook his head. "Nothing, sorry."

"If you'd like to add anything, you're welcome to."

He smiled, his pale eyes gleaming like marbles. "This is your class, Miss Zemansky. I wouldn't presume. Unless you're too frightened? Or too medicated?"

Laura gasped as the class looked at me in surprise.

"No, I'm fine. Thanks. So do the rest of you feel the poem is angry and bitter?"

Most of the class nodded. "So we're talking about mood. The mood grabs you. Let's talk about the ideas. What is happening in the poem? What has taken place?"

Shawna answered. "Okay, a human baby has been placed in a room full of dolls made by a doll-maker. And the dolls hate it."

"And the doll-maker hates it, too, and the mother apologizes for it," Miguel said.

Dr. Kind started laughing quietly, a hissing laugh.

"Great," I said, determined to ignore him. "And what is the difference between a doll and a baby?"

"The doll is made by someone," someone said. I was losing focus.

"Hey, people make babies," Miguel said to general laughter.

Another student joined in. "A doll is this perfect thing. And it's artificial. A baby is messy like human beings are messy."

"Ruinous," Kind said. "Messy and ruinous."

The students glanced back at him and shifted in their seats. I met the eyes of several students, trying to draw them back in. "That's right. Babies are messy, squalling. Imperfect. And dolls are made on purpose, but here we have this accident."

Kind laughed more loudly, making a show of smothering his mouth. "Sorry, sorry, do go on."

The students didn't turn their heads this time. Sitting up straight, they looked up at me with supportive faces. I sensed they were with me.

Shawna spoke. "It's interesting how it's the wife taking all the responsibility. Like it's all her fault, hers alone. That adds to the bitterness, a very male bitterness to the poem." The rest of the class nodded.

Kind gave a loud, startling hiccup. He rose and walked out of the room, his hand over his mouth. His laughter echoed from the hallway. I was frozen for a few moments as the laughter pealed. After he was gone, the room relaxed. But I had a bad feeling. After we compared "The Dolls" to another poem, "The Mask," I dismissed the students a few minutes early.

I went to Kind's office, but it was locked. There was a note on the door, round and flowery, which said, "See you later." I knew I would.

CHAPTER FORTY-NINE

After my blowup with Scott the previous week, he'd left me a voice-mail, but his apology was not sufficiently apologetic; he was still excusing himself, talking about what—"Some people might think . . ." I sent him an email saying I wanted to be alone for a while, to please stay back until I said it was okay. I lied and said I'd pushed up my appointment with the new therapist, just to reassure him and keep him away. It worked and I hadn't heard back.

Now I was alone. I sat in the living room considering my options, trying to weigh them like an adult. Objectively, Dr. Kind had disrupted my classroom. What kind of power did I have as a graduate student? As a recent mental case? Under normal circumstances, I could complain to the Dean about his behavior, but my position was more delicate. Besides . . . I knew. I knew. . . .

But perhaps that *was* madness. I recalled how much more understanding Dr. Hellmann had been now that he knew I hadn't written the letter to McGill. And he had a bond with Kind—it was only that, wasn't it? I decided to try to talk to Hellmann, and I picked up my keys and headed out the kitchen door.

I hadn't heard the car in the silence. He came like a wolf on silent paws. But as I stepped out, he was pulling in, blocking my car.

There was no one to call. No one would rescue me. Nowhere to escape to. I knew he would come. This was the predator I'd somehow been expecting all along: not the winter or my illness, or Ann or Scott, or my fears of being a child. It was this. The day was still and windless. Damp rose from the last of the melting snow, and the wet black trees were tinged with red buds, red bark—red, the first color of spring.

I stepped back, back into the house. He was swift as an animal, his foot on the door, pushing it open. I backed into the living room. Dr. Kind leaned in through the archway, one hand in the pocket of his trim tweed suit. "This place is ghastly."

"It's Salvation Army Gothic," I said.

He circled me. "It all looks so heavy. How did you ever move it in here?"

I wondered. "It was already here. Diana must have, somehow."

His eyes narrowed at the mention of her name. "She must have cast a witch's spell." He looked far away. He circled me again, restless, almost sniffing the air. Then his pale eyes locked on me. "Did you tell? About the book? Perhaps you wrote a letter?"

"I tried to tell someone, but they didn't believe me."

He smiled. "No. As I had hoped. No one will believe you, because you're crazy, you know. Mad as a hatter. Everyone knows that, I made sure."

My stomach tightened in fury, but I had to control myself.

"But now there are doubts," he continued. "You're teaching. You're bouncing back. Dan praised you to the Dean. People might think it was only a setback." He pulled a small gun out of his pocket. "You know why Virginia Woolf killed herself? The voices. Do you hear voices?"

"No." Anger overcame my fear. "Do you want the book? Just take the book."

His mustache twitched with beads of sweat, and he wiped his mouth with his free hand. "Yes, of course."

I rose and went to my room. I put the book in my backpack, picked up my cell phone, and dialed 911, then slipped the phone into my bag.

"What's taking so long?" he said, approaching the doorway.

"I was looking for it. I forgot it was in my bag." I turned around to face him. "So, did you kill Cassandra too?"

A voice came from the bag. "Nine-one-one. Is this an emergency?"

He looked puzzled, then laughed, training the gun on my head. "Nine-one-one. What is your address?"

He motioned and I handed him the bag. He took out the phone. "Just a mistake, sorry," he said, ending the call. He tilted his head back and laughed his barking laugh. "Do you think this is television? You think you're clever?" He pulled book out of the bag, and suddenly struck me on the head with it.

My head stung. I jumped back, but he took a step forward and hit me again, clipping my ear.

"She parked her bike in the back just as I came out for a smoke. I said you shouldn't be here. I said leave him alone. I saw Diana's face, and I knew. Somehow, I knew. I said, are you pregnant? And she only smiled a wicked, knowing smile while she struck the match. I'll never forget her evil smile. Then it suddenly started snowing, and I said you should go before it gets bad. I said you can tell him tomorrow. I said, I'll follow you home. She trusted me. People trust me."

I backed up to the desk, furiously trying to think if I had anything like a weapon.

"And now, the thing is, even without the book, you know. We can't have that."

There was an X-Acto knife in the top drawer. I pried the drawer open behind me. "So you're going to kill me?"

"You're going to kill yourself," he said almost tenderly. "Because you can't live with the pain anymore. The pain of your mental illness. The pain of being utterly mad."

I squeezed my fingers into the drawer, teasing out the knife.

"First you'll write a note. One of your pesky notes. The last one."

I lunged and slashed the knife across the back of his hand. The gun fired with a bang that momentarily stunned me. I leapt for the door, but the seconds had cost me. He grabbed me, twisting my arm behind my back, shaking it so that I feared it would break. The knife fell from my fingers. His sticky blood oozed onto my hand.

"That's the last time you're going to try to be clever." His voice was hoarse as he breathed in my ear. "Now you're going to write a note."

"Don't kill me here. I'll do what you want, but I don't want Scott to be the one who finds me. It would hurt him too much."

He pushed me against the desk. "Whatever. Just write the note."

Shaking, I tore a piece of paper out of a notebook. "What do I say?"

He laughed. "You're a writer. You can think of something."

Code. What could I write that would let Scott know the truth? My hand was damp with sweat as I wrote.

"Scott—I'm sorry. I know an apology is all you'd want right now. Because I feel too guilty for what I've put you through. I have to end it. I can't start over again. And the jealous seed inside me won't let me. It's screaming for help. I'm sorry. I love you."

It didn't make much sense, but I tried to say things he would question. He would never want an apology, and he knew I knew that. Maybe the line about jealousy would make him think of Kind. I was grasping at straws.

Kind grabbed the note and gave it a glance. It didn't seem to disturb him, and he tossed it on the desk. "Okay, now."

I held his gaze. "But not here. Take me somewhere. To the woods or something. Not here. Please." Anything to buy time.

He blinked, and shrugged calmly. "All right. Quick."

We went out to his car. The sight of his broken headlight made me queasy.

"And it's your fate," he said. "You belong to your fate. We have no choice."

Sour sweat mingled with the scent of his cologne. He sat behind the wheel and started the car with a roar, tearing backward into the road without looking. He drove down the hill away from campus, and up the next hill away from town.

"What about Cassandra?" I asked. The car glided quickly around the bend, and I was squeezed against the door.

"She was going to tell. Actually lodge a complaint. That he took advantage of her."

He corrected the wheel with a jerk, and I fell against him, feeling disgust at his touch. "The bullet that killed her was still inside her skull. Forensics will match it."

The landscape rushed past, the poplars streaking by. Road salt rattled over the fender.

"I don't have much faith in our officers of the law," he replied.

A large white ball bounced into the road from the right. It sailed up and down, silent and slow. The child was a boy of three. I could see every blond hair on his head as we bore down.

"Let's all go together," Dr. Kind said.

"Maybe I deserve to die," I said. "But you are not my fate. You are not my fate!" I leaned against the force of our speed and grabbed the wheel, pulling hard as we skidded to the left.

I was thrown back against the door, and I yanked on the lock, flying out. I landed hard in the muddy ditch, the squishy wet grass slightly softening the blow, but my ribs cracked as the wind was sucked out of me, almost knocking me unconscious. A boom jolted me back. Gasping, I rose to my knees in the mud.

The boy stood wailing at the side of the road, his arms outstretched. His mother burst from the house and ran to scoop him up. The car was crushed against a tree. I didn't have to look hard to know Kind was dead.

CHAPTER FIFTY

Today in class, a student wrote a short story about a bipolar woman. Another student commented, "You never know with bipolar, if they're about to have a psychotic break." I kept my mouth shut. That was the "today" I mentioned at the beginning of this story, when I said I didn't want to take any more BS.

I used to be more open about it, but now I'm guarded. In the six years since I finished the Haldol and switched to Risperdal, I've barely had any relapse. Ultimately my diagnosis was bipolar disorder with psychotic features. I know I shouldn't be overconfident. A couple of years ago when I went for another long drive, I had a problem, but it was mild, something to treat with an increased dosage; I didn't need the hospital again. No one has to know. What I feel is that psychiatry is the science of overcoming fate. Mental illness gives you a fate. And that fate can be overcome.

The young Wendy was my ghost. My sad ghost. She was a fragment, a fractured part of me. And I don't know the moment when I arrived at now, at being an adult. It has been gradual, year by year, that I see a therapist less and less, that co-workers started referring to me as "the voice of reason."

But at that moment, when the student made her comment about how "You never know, with bipolar," that was the moment I felt the crack in time, the cleavage between then and now. I've been holding her hand, the young Wendy, holding the hand of a shadow, a child's shadow, our arms stretched over a little ravine, and in that moment she leapt across to me, and the shadow, the ghost, melted into and through me and dissolved. The sun is bright and there is no shadow.

During the afternoon that Kind was breaking down in my class, Scott ran into Jean in the science building. He was leaving the computer lab near her office, and she was trying to unlock her door. Tipsy by then, she was rattling the jammed key in a staccato of grinding metal, muttering swear words a little too loudly under her breath. She called Scott over to help, a tense smile not quite covering her anger at the unmoving door. After determining she was using the wrong key, he slid the right one in and the door glided open.

"Ah, thanks. How are you? Is Wendy okay?" She waved him into her office.

"I wish I knew. I haven't seen her in over a week." He'd last seen me the night I'd shown him Diana's poetry book. Now he awkwardly wondered what, if anything, Jean knew about the possible love notes to her husband, which by then he felt sure were genuine.

"She needs you," Jean said. A sudden look of raw fear on her face startled Scott. She continued. "Tommy—Dr. Kind—hates her. I mean." Then she laughed, her shifting moods making Scott's palms sweat. "I'm sure he isn't dangerous. Right? People aren't . . . dangerous. It's fine." Then she looked up at Scott as if surprised to see him.

He went straight to my house. The note I'd left was disturbing, but confusing. He didn't know if I was breaking down again. Then he saw the large streak of Dr. Kind's blood from the slash on his hand congealing on the door of my bedroom.

At the scene of the crash, Deputy Polozzi arrived with the once again useless ambulance. The paramedics went ahead and checked me out as state troopers also arrived to take over. Polozzi drove me to the sheriff's office to make a statement.

And there was Scott, sitting on that hard bench, utterly overwhelmed by the strain of the past month. He was crying. I sat beside him, once again brought back to that first-grade scene with the school psychologist, but now I was the one offering comfort. As it should be. I held him. Everything slowed down in the dark hallway, everything still as the eye of a hurricane, my arms around him as he shivered. I knew I would count that day as the first of my adult life.

*   *   *

I never did go for the PhD. I don't know if I would have had the mental stamina. I guess I didn't want to find out. Dr. Kind's replacement was a chirpy young woman who'd made a big splash with her MFA. She coached me on my thesis, and helped get it published. I ended up developing my idea about mental illness in Gothic literature as a whole book, and it was well-received. And it was lucky I got it published because the advance covered the balance of my hospital bill. It was from then that I started to feel my life has been lucky, overall.

We traveled, Scott working as an adviser to international charities. We had a blog about his work, and for a while my only home was my home page. But I still had my sights set on Chicago. When we finally made it, I managed to get a job teaching at a quirky arts college, where they don't require a PhD; my book was enough.

Every two years we vote for the Water Reclamation Board. No one ever knows what they do or who they're voting for. Scott now works for that board. Want to know what they do? Buy me a drink and I'll tell you. It's more interesting than you might think.

We don't own a car. We go for long walks. I see a great blue heron almost every time I walk in the park or over the river. I rarely saw one in all that nature of upstate New York.

I took his name. I've never been fond of my given name. Wendy Garrison. It has a nice ring. He was flattered, but the truth is I wanted to make it slightly harder for people from my past to find me. I just wanted a clean break.

At first, I wanted to keep what I knew a secret. Diana could have just stayed a hit and run. But when they extracted Kind from his car, of course they found the gun and tied it to Cassandra. Checking out his car, they found traces of Diana's blood. So that much came out. I talked to the Hellmanns. I believed him that he'd known nothing of what Kind had done because such obliviousness seemed in keeping with his obtuse vanity. The police believed him, too, eventually. Hellmann might not have believed me about Kind's motive at all, if it hadn't been for that scene when Kind exploded at him and Jean. Hellmann quietly took an early retirement, never heading the MFA program everyone was so excited about. He did come out with a book of poetry, and the Amazon reviews were not kind. There were phrases like "a Ted Hughes has-been."

Jean eventually left him to move to LA. Did she befriend Kind's ex-wife? One night I turned on one of those crime shows, and the plot was strangely similar to what had happened.

When Scott and I made up, I asked him for the truth about how well he knew Diana. He said he had met her at the reading and was attracted to her, asked her for a copy of her book, but she wasn't interested. He didn't know why he couldn't tell me, but once he'd lied he felt too embarrassed to turn back.

It's strange now to be in the place that Diana left, or it would be if I gave it a lot of thought, but I try not to. I don't see her family much. I do see Greg in plays from time to time. I don't try to see the city through her eyes, don't know what neighborhoods she used to frequent, what shops or cafes she haunted. She left, but I love it here. This is my city now, my place, my new start. So I don't connect it to her, even though it seems like an easy tie to make, or some kind of metaphor. I've never been good at metaphors.

My mother died last year, of a smoking-related cancer. She refused any attention for it and she died alone, before my brother or I could get there. I asked her once if her father was a secret alcoholic. She looked baffled. "You grandfather got two master's degrees at night and was vice president of the Knights of Columbus. There was no time to drink. And if I'd known about alcoholism, I would have run from your father as fast as I could."

Feeling brave, I asked her about Uncle Johnny's accident. She shrugged and said, "I don't remember Johnny's existence." And the subject was closed.

It's winter now, a fierce wind shakes the tendril of my ivy plant on the windowsill. I don't usually think of it, but I realized this morning with a start that it's the anniversary of the day I found Diana

in the snow. For some reason, the date happened to leap out at me
from my Outlook calendar.

I went over to the bookcase and opened her book. Inside the
back cover, she'd written:

"Dan, I couldn't finish this. . . .
I hear the rose opening
The petals parting
A sound like silk sliding
Over skin.
A name in the dark,
Answered with another breath.
Perhaps we made a life tonight.
Life is brief as an echo,
The echo crying Yes.
And I'll remember,
Because you did not say No.

Though much will be forgotten
I will not forget your love
Even if we end
In arguing and tears.
In twilight as I turn
From day to dark,
For a moment I'll remember
And be glad, so glad
I knew you, gladness so clear,
With no regret, not a pinprick of regret,
Filled with love again
Because we loved, because"

It ended there. I picked up a pen and wrote:

"There is no end
To love that teaches yet,

An endless lesson,
Blossoms yet,"

—then the phone rang, and my day went on with a lunch meeting and some research, picking up the dry cleaning, a trip to the Apple store. After dinner Scott was interested in some Netflix series I didn't care about.

In the bathroom, I took my pill. I recalled that image in the mirror, when my face was distorted, and I'd lost my mother's bones. Now my face was my own.

The unfinished poem came back to me. Scott was watching his show, and I curled up on the end of the sofa and opened the book again. I finished the poem:

"Beyond fate, beyond all fear."

As I wrap this up, it's January of 2013. Barack Obama was just inaugurated for his second term. It's snowing in big, fluffy clumps—a clean, freshening snow. I feel well, and optimistic. I'm hopeful, and not just for myself. Maybe things are getting better. Yes—I think the world is becoming a saner place.

The End